WISH UPON A STARFISH

A TOUCH OF MAGIC
BOOK 2

DAPHNE JAMES HUFF

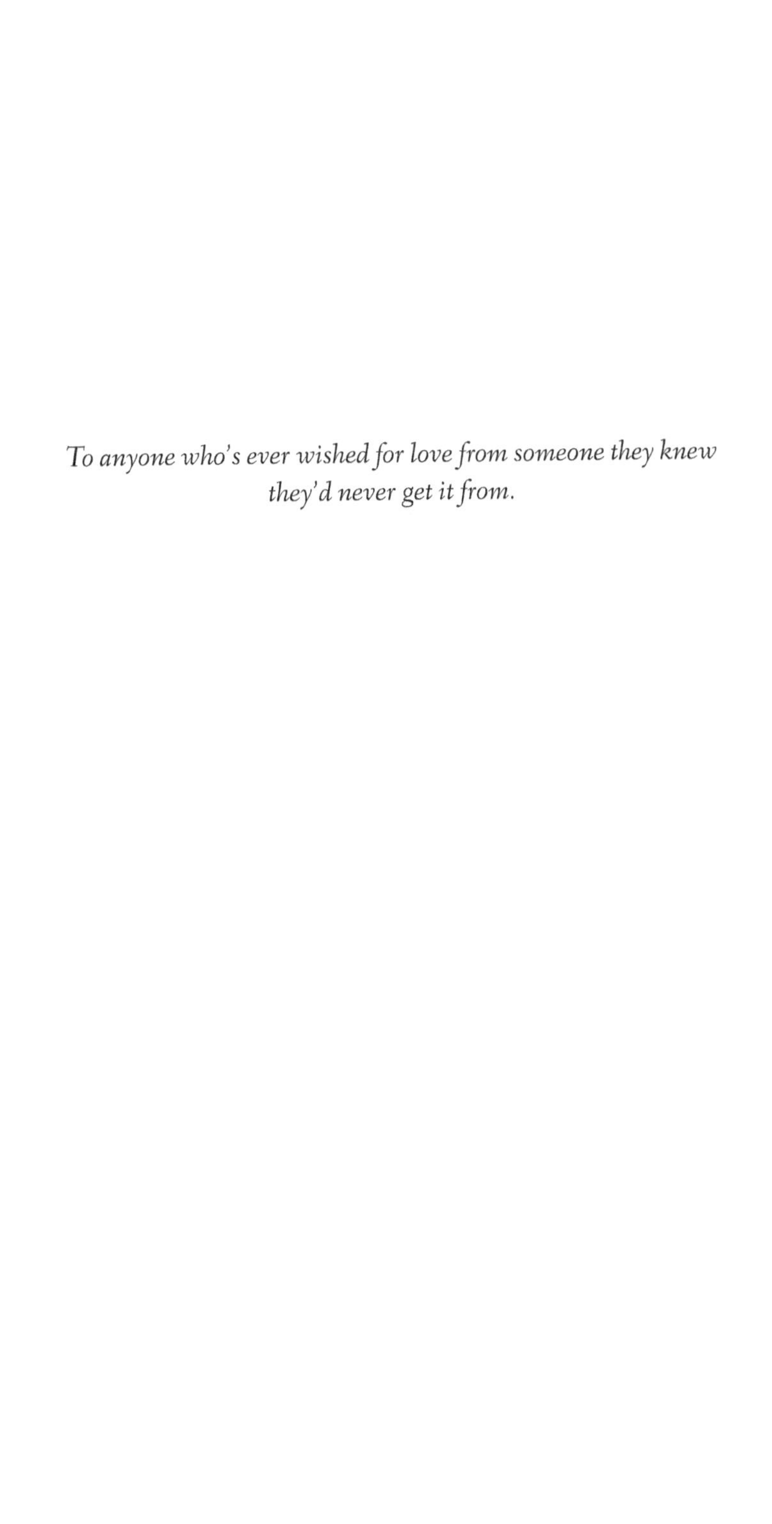

*To anyone who's ever wished for love from someone they knew
they'd never get it from.*

PROLOGUE

The starfish pushed water through her ampulla and moved a few centimeters to the left, drawing the response she was looking for.

"Ooh, Mommy, look!"

From the tank several feet above the child's head, the starfish preened. Well, she waved around some of her tube feet. The child squealed and started singing.

"Twinkly, twinkly little star—"

The starfish let out a sigh of water through her papulae. Was this the only song humans knew? She shook her head. Or rather, she would have if she had one.

"Ah, I see you've met Stella." A smiling, dark-haired woman with metal fish hanging from her ears squatted down next to the child. "Do you know what kind of animal she is?"

"A star! Make a wish."

The woman laughed, the sound bouncing off the tank. Stella liked this woman. She worked at the aquarium and took pictures and videos of all the fish, but spent most of her time filming Stella. She was Stella's favorite human.

"I don't know if it works the same with starfish the way it does with real stars."

Not a real star? Stella had an eye at the end of each arm and rolled every single one of them at this comment.

"But she looks just like a twinkly star, because of all her arms."

"That's because she's a sunflower sea star. They're endangered. Do you know what that means?"

The child shook its head.

"That means there aren't that many of her. The scientists here are working on a way to help."

What?

A few of Stella's dozen arms trembled in the warm water. Was that why all those humans with glasses kept poking and prodding her? It wasn't helping anything, just making her irritated. She much preferred having her picture taken.

"They should just make a wish."

The woman laughed again. "Why don't you make one?"

"Okay, but you have to do it too."

"Charlie, that's enough." The child's mother tugged at his hand. "This woman is trying to work. Let's just go look at the turtles again."

"It's fine." The woman stood up, still smiling. "This is my job. To help educate people about the animals here and help raise money so that the scientists who work here can save them."

Someone else walked by, and her head turned. "Like Dr. Rhodes."

It was one of the humans with glasses. He liked to bother Stella more than the others. She started to slide away, hoping to hide in the tangle of leaves in the corner of her tank until the next day.

Charlie blinked up at the man with glasses, looking just as distrustful as Stella was of him. "You're helping save the stars?"

"Yes, we're working on a program to cryogenically freeze the—"

The dark-haired woman cleared her throat and muttered under her breath. "It's a kid, Dr. Rhodes."

He frowned and pushed the glasses back higher onto his nose. "We're trying to make lots of baby starfish."

Charlie nodded as if this made perfect sense. In her tank, Stella's escape attempt stalled. This was the first time Stella had heard anything about this. Maybe the prodding wasn't so bad if it meant more babies.

"I'm going to wish for a million dollars so you can make all the baby starfish." Charlie scrunched up his nose and closed his eyes. "That's what I'm going to do right now."

The man with the glasses looked between the child, his mother, and the woman, then let out a sigh. "I don't really have time for this, Aisha."

"It'll be quick." Aisha smiled again, but it wasn't quite as big as it had been before, and her teeth weren't showing. Stella spent a lot of time watching humans and considered herself somewhat of an expert. If any of the other animals in her tank had asked her—not that they would, because none of them could talk—she would have told them with complete confidence that Aisha's smile looked sad.

Pursing his lips and turning slightly away from Aisha, Dr. Rhodes leaned forward to peer at Stella through the glass.

Charlie opened his eyes. "Did you make a wish too?"

"What?" Aisha looked down. She'd been gazing at the back of Dr. Rhode's head with the same longing in her eyes that Stella had for the ocean.

"Who's making wishes?" Another man appeared, one Stella had only seen a few times before, and always on this side of her tank.

No glasses. Good. He probably wasn't going to poke at Stella.

Aisha's face lit up. "Bram, I have the best idea. All thanks to little Charlie here." She smiled down at the boy. "Why don't we all make a wish on a starfish? I'll wish for a ton of new visitors."

Charlie clapped his hands, but Dr. Rhodes frowned again. "Are visitors really the priority?"

"More visitors means more money." The other man, Bram, put a hand on Dr. Rhodes' shoulder, and Dr. Rhodes shuddered. If Stella could laugh, she would have.

Not so fun having someone invade your personal space, is it?

Aisha pulled out the little rectangle she used to take pictures of Stella. "Could we do a quick video for social media? It'll only take a minute, Dr. Rhodes, I promise."

"Come on, Cody, it's for the fish." Bram flashed a set of teeth whiter than seashells.

It took a moment for Aisha to position the two men the way she wanted to, and Stella did her best to wriggle herself in between their heads, so she'd be clearly visible.

They made their wishes out loud, though only Aisha's had anything to do with starfish. Dr. Rhodes wished for something to do with the weather, and Bram said something about a printer, whatever that was. Only a starfish of Stella's exceptional abilities would be able to detect what they were really thinking. It was written on their faces, plain as day, for anyone with twelve eyes to see.

I wish someone would love me for who I really am.
I wish I could find a way to tell her the truth.
I wish she felt about me the way I feel about her.

ONE
BRAM

The compostable paper cup in Bram's hand was uncomfortably hot. He switched it between his left and right, a delicate balance that he knew looked ridiculous, but at least there was no one in the office to notice. As he approached Aisha's door, he kept it firmly in his right hand, the heat of it nearly bringing tears to his eyes.

"Good morning." He searched for a clear spot on the cluttered desk. The burning in his hand forced him to deposit it just a little too forcefully between two untidy stacks of paper, and the whipped cream on top sloshed over the side.

"Thank you?" Aisha turned her dark eyes up to him, a smile quivering at the edge of her lips. "I don't remember ordering a chocolate desk."

"It's hot."

"What's the occasion?" She grabbed a napkin from the stack of break-room brown paper towels that were crammed in between two books of ocean photography. This made a book fall over, knock into a cup of paperclips that tipped onto a stuffed penguin that then rolled across her keyboard and bumped the hot chocolate, sending more of the drink over the edge. The penguin's white chest was now spotted with brown.

"Your desk already has a layer of chocolate on it. When's the last time you cleaned it?"

"Excuse me, Mister 'I wear the same blue polo shirt every day.'" She moved the penguin away from the pool of chocolate. "I'm messy, not dirty."

Bram crossed his arms and leaned against the doorway as he watched her mop up the mess that was only partially his fault. The absolute chaos on her desk could in no way be blamed on him. Though he had bought her the penguin from the gift shop on a day she'd been uncharacteristically sad. Not that she knew it was him. He'd just placed it on her desk as a little surprise.

"I have five aquarium shirts, all different colors. I don't wear the same one every day."

"If you say so." Her own shirt was white today, with tiny green seahorses that could almost be mistaken for polka dots. More seahorses dangled from her ears, just visible beneath her masses of wavy black hair which she usually pulled back with clips. Today it flowed loose around her shoulders.

"We just hit a million dollars in the fundraising." He nudged the cup. "All thanks to your starfish marketing campaign."

Her face lit up, all efforts of cleaning up abandoned. "Really?"

Just before she jumped up, he grabbed the cup, anticipating just how excited she'd be about the news. She swung out her arms, jumping up and down, then threw them around him. This pushed him off balance, and he stumbled back into a human-sized penguin in the corner that fell onto them.

Which knocked the hot chocolate from his hand and onto the floor.

He let out a sound that was part-laugh, part-sigh, but regretted it as soon as it left him. Aisha removed her arms from around his neck and bent to pick up the empty cup and soak up the spill. A hint of coral colored her tawny brown cheeks when she realized what had happened.

It only lasted a moment though. Nothing ever kept Aisha's

energy down for long. It was one of the things he loved most about her.

No, what he *liked* most about her. Because he definitely wasn't in love with his funny, smart, gorgeous, tornado of a colleague. Absolutely not.

"This calls for some madeleines." Popping back up, Aisha tossed the cup into the trashcan. Then she grabbed Bram's hand and tugged him out into the turquoise carpeted hallway, his heart hammering in his ears at the contact. He breathed through his nose as she led him past walls full of marine wildlife photographs to the staff kitchen.

Absolutely, definitely, most assuredly *not* in love with her.

She dropped his hand as soon as they entered the small kitchen. Across from the world's tiniest sink and a fridge that could barely fit everyone's Tupperware lunches, six chairs were crammed around a round table in the corner. Thankfully, they were all empty this early in the morning.

"Are you sure there are any left?" Bram raised an eyebrow and leaned back against the doorframe as he watched her drag the one non-wobbly chair into position so she could hunt in the back of the highest cabinet for her favorite French snack.

"I put the bag up here last time."

Bram laughed and shook his head. "I brought those to share, not for you to hide them."

They were his favorites, and as soon as he'd found out she liked the little shell-shaped sponge cakes too, he'd asked his brother to pick some up on his recent visit to France. Even if Bram had stopped going on extravagant vacations, that didn't mean the rest of his family had. They seemed to have increased theirs, in fact, as if to make up for the intentional decline in his transatlantic trips. As if bringing him his favorite snacks made up for their massive carbon footprint.

To avoid arousing suspicion, Bram had left them on the table for all the staff at the aquarium. Aisha had eaten almost an entire bag herself the second she'd spotted them and hidden the second bag.

Now, perched on a chair with her head in a cabinet the same shade of turquoise as the carpet in the hallways, she turned around to look at him, scrunching up her nose in that adorable way that made her eyes sparkle at the same time.

"I am sharing. With you." Her smile almost stopped his heart. Then she shrugged and rummaged in the cabinet. "It's not my fault if no one thinks to look up here."

"Why would they? Only an evil genius like you would do this."

Her exaggerated "muahaha" laugh echoed in the small room as she stepped down from the chair, bag of treats in one hand. She offered him one first, which he declined, then popped a soft cake into her mouth.

Her eyes briefly closed as she chewed. "I haven't been there since I was eight, but there's just something so familiar about the taste of madeleines, you know?"

Bram chuckled, filing away this new bit of information about her. He knew she'd lived in France as a child, but no other details. "How very Proustian of you."

She winked, clearly getting the reference, and his heart shot into his mouth. He swallowed hard.

Ask her now.

It was the perfect moment. Every day since he'd joined the Lowcountry Research Aquarium three months ago as their head of development had been leading up to this. From Aisha's radiant smile on his first day to her brilliant marketing ideas to her adorable evil genius laugh, Bram's crush had slowly been growing from minuscule to massive. It was time to do something about it.

First, bring her hot chocolate.

Then, tell her the good news about the campaign.

Finally, ask her out to dinner to celebrate.

Aisha was humming to herself, something that sounded like

"La Vie en Rose" while she dug into the bag. He cleared his throat, and she looked up, her dark eyes fixed on his.

"Hey, so I was thinking—"

"Good morning."

Their heads swiveled in unison to greet the newcomer, and Bram's stomach dropped to the floor.

Dr. Cody Rhodes.

TWO

BRAM

Dressed in a beige outfit as dull as his personality, the aquarium's head researcher was oblivious to what he'd just interrupted.

He was also oblivious to the effect he had on Aisha. In an instant, her expression shut down. Bram watched the joyful brightness that had been there just moments before disappear, while her entire body seemed to shrink back into itself.

"Good morning, Doctor Rhodes," Aisha said in a trembling, barely audible voice.

In almost every other situation, the word Bram would use to describe Aisha would be boisterous. Whenever Cody was around, however, she was contained. Shoved into a tiny box.

It wasn't just because Cody's mother was the aquarium director. Everyone was a little extra polite to him because of that, even Bram, when he could manage it.

This went beyond politeness, however.

Aisha had a massive crush on Cody.

Not that she'd ever told Bram that. It was obvious in the way she completely changed her behavior around him, something Bram had figured out within days of working with her.

Something Bram had never been able to figure out was why

he'd been put in the friend zone while Cody, the most boring human on the planet, got her undying devotion.

Sure, the other man was attractive with his light, close-cropped hair and brown eyes that still managed to be annoyingly piercing behind his glasses, though his fashion sense was that of a middle-aged accountant.

Of course, he was beyond smart. You had to be to do what he did saving an entire species from extinction, a process he would go into great detail about with the slightest provocation.

And yes, Cody had won some big fancy science award that Bram made sure to include in all of the fundraising materials he sent out, even if he rolled his eyes each time he had to type the words.

Was that really all it took to impress Aisha?

Sometimes—every other day at the most—Bram worried it was because Aisha could tell that Cody didn't have the kind of baggage Bram did. The scientist was boring, but that also made him safe. No family drama or secrets. No hiding who he really was the way Bram had to in order to be taken seriously.

Despite how he felt about the other man and his own gigantic crush on Aisha, Bram found himself yet again trying to help her out.

"Morning, Cody," he said, calling him by his first name the way literally everyone else did except for Aisha. "Did you hear that we hit the fundraising goal? All thanks to Aisha's great campaign."

She turned scarlet, and her eyes threatened pain for Bram.

Cody nodded, his face as serious as if Bram had just announced a round of mass layoffs. "I did, yes. Good job."

At this, Aisha beamed. Was this smile brighter than when Bram had given her the same compliment? His throat tightened. He wished he'd eaten the offered madeleine, so he'd have something in his churning stomach other than coffee.

"Thank you for helping me with it." She tucked her hair behind her ear, the seahorse earring catching the light, then ran her hand along it to smooth down the unruly waves that hung thick around her shoulders like opera curtains. "Your video got twenty-three times the views as any of the others."

"You mean *our* video." Bram pushed off from the counter and looped an arm around Cody's shoulders, knowing exactly how much the other man would hate it. It had taken Bram less than a day to realize the attractive, smart, award-winning scientist was not a touchy-feely kind of guy. "We did that one together. Double the chiseled good looks means double the views."

Just as Bram expected, Cody stepped away from him. Luckily, not closer to Aisha.

"I believe she said it got twenty-three times the views." He pushed up his glasses in a way that could only be described as condescendingly. Bram had seen his father make the same move his entire life.

"So each of us is worth eleven and a half times the views."

Cody's brow crinkled as though he was double-checking the math.

"You were both great." Aisha shot Bram a salty look, and he almost jumped for joy at the little glimmer of the true nature of his feisty friend. "Maybe we could do another?"

"We could always use more funding." The glance Cody sent Bram's way was heavy with accusation. "Especially from our biggest donors."

It was only thanks to years of training at family events that Bram kept his face neutral. Beneath the smooth surface, his pulse hammered as he wondered exactly what Cody meant. The Lowther family was indeed one of the aquarium's biggest donors, but not because Bram had asked for anything from his parents. They certainly wouldn't have given anything at all if he hadn't worked there. Unlike everyone knowing about Cody being the director's son, this wasn't a connection Bram had ever mentioned at work. Though of course Cody would know about it, thanks to his mom.

"Don't worry about it." Bram shot an icy smile at Cody. "I know what I'm doing."

He raised an eyebrow. "Luckily, so does Aisha."

Her face lit up so brightly it was like the sun had burst through the walls.

"Dr. Rhodes, maybe we could do a video now? If you're not busy?"

"I actually have a meeting I need to get to." He made his way to the fridge. "I only came in here to grab something quick to eat."

Bram held his breath, wondering if Aisha would offer him a madeleine from the bag in her hand, but she didn't. Maybe it was because she forgot it was there, or like his idiotic heart wanted to believe, because it was something only she and Bram shared.

"Of course. You have important work." Aisha flushed again. "I'm sorry we kept you from it."

Cody seemed to ignore this as he pulled a yogurt from the fridge, but it was just as likely he hadn't heard her small, quiet voice.

"I'll do a video." Bram couldn't stop himself. It was petty and childish, but he'd never claimed not to be. Especially when it came to getting Aisha's attention. There were still marks in the kitchen wall from a particularly rowdy lunchtime game of charades the month before. "I bet I can get twenty-three times the views all on my own."

This got a very uncharacteristic eye roll from Cody. "Good luck with that." When he headed out of the kitchen, Bram felt the sweet rush of victory along the inside of his chest.

It wasn't the date he'd hoped for, but it was more time with Aisha, and that's all he could wish for today.

THREE

AISHA

"I can't believe you just did that." Before she could think better of it, Aisha threw a madeleine at Bram. Luckily, he caught it, so the precious treat wouldn't have to be thrown in the trash.

"Did what?" He popped the cake into his mouth, smiling as he chewed.

They really were the best treats. Like a mini cupcake but slightly denser, sweet but not too sweet with a hint of lemon, they were perfect for breakfast . . . or dessert . . . or a snack. Before he'd brought them in a few months ago, Aisha had forgotten they'd been her favorite as a kid. Her early life in France was a patchwork of memories she usually tried to bury deep inside, but the madeleines were the exception. Now she had a sweet reminder of her childhood, thanks to Bram, who always remembered her favorite snacks and drink order.

When he wasn't being annoying, like this morning, he was really quite thoughtful.

"You always goad him." Aisha put the bag of madeleines down on the table and pulled two hair clips out of her pocket. What a state her hair must be in after running her hands all over it the way she always did when she was nervous. It had to be near rat's-nest levels of messy at this point. "Why?"

"It's not like I do it on purpose." Bram's attempt at remorse consisted of a halfhearted shrug and a smirk that showed off his dimples. "It's just so easy. Everything ruffles his feathers."

Aisha knew that. Which was why she tried so hard to behave herself around him. The unruly, unhinged way she acted around everyone else wouldn't work with Cody.

She desperately wanted it to work. From the moment Cody had started working at the aquarium six months ago, Aisha had wanted him. From his dark-brown eyes to the straight, even creases in his pants, everything about him was orderly and serious. So that's exactly what she was around him.

At least when Bram wasn't there making things worse.

"Well, just try harder to not do it." Aisha's voice cracked on the last word, and she quickly stuffed a madeleine in her mouth to cover it up.

The last thing she wanted to do was cry in front of Bram. Though he was without a doubt her favorite work bestie she'd ever had, it hadn't been that long since he'd gotten there. He knew she liked tea better than coffee, and hot chocolate most of all. He knew where the emergency napkins were on her desk.

He did not need to know what she looked like when she cried. There were some things you had to work your way up to. "What he thinks of me matters."

"Why? Because his mom is the aquarium director?"

Aisha blinked. "Yes." That was a much better reason than her massive crush. Though it did factor into her good behavior, she hadn't known this fact about Cody until several weeks after he started working there. Despite being a little embarrassed everyone had realized it immediately—they did have the same last name and sharp gaze, after all—she liked that he'd kept it quiet, that he didn't try to wield any power because of it. He was just another researcher, nobody special.

Not everyone was like that when they came from important families, Aisha knew from harsh experience.

Bram rolled his eyes. "After this marketing campaign, Mrs. Rhodes probably loves you more than you love these madeleines."

Glittery excitement fluttered around her chest. "Really?"

"Aisha, you hit the goal in less than a month. I've been in development for over a decade, and I've never seen it happen so fast. You're incredible. She should be falling all over herself thanking you."

Heat rushed through her, and she brought her hands to her cheeks, stomach swirling. Bram always did this. Exaggerated to make her feel better, just like her best friends, Krista and Brooke. "It was only a few videos."

There was a pause while Bram took a deep breath, his blue eyes never leaving hers. A corner of his mouth ticked up. "So then let's go make another and raise a million more."

She rolled her eyes, fighting back her own smile at his unabashed cockiness. Not that it wasn't merited. He was just as gorgeous as Cody. Even more so when he smiled like he was now, his lips curved up on one side with his dimples winking at her.

Bram was that suave, polished, tan-in-December kind of handsome that you only got growing up a certain way. The way that involved fancy vacations and private schools and new cars for your birthday. Every other guy she'd met like Bram in the dozens of jobs she'd had over the years treated her like she was invisible, while the girls from that same fancy world would put on a friendly smile but make snide, syrupy-sweet comments about her clothes and hair. It still didn't seem real that Bram had actually befriended her.

What did they even have in common besides working at the aquarium? Sure, they both cared about the environment and were unreasonably competitive about inane things like who could get their colleagues to say the word "tank" the most during a staff meeting. But Bram was so clearly out of her league, Aisha didn't even let herself imagine him as a possibility. From the sleek waves of his dark hair to his worn leather shoes, there was no way he'd ever known what it was to miss a meal or be late on rent. This was a spectacular specimen of a man, and he'd end up with a spectacular woman standing next to him.

Cody, on the other hand, was more within her stratosphere. He was shy and serious and so passionate about his work it was all he seemed to talk about. When he'd take off those little wire-framed round glasses and rub his eyes with the palms of his hands, Aisha would just melt.

Meanwhile, all Bram had to do was smile at her, and she got heart palpitations. It couldn't technically be categorized as a crush when someone was that attractive. It was just an instinctive response. There had to be a scientific explanation for it.

By far, Cody was the safer choice. The more logical one. The one Aisha might actually have a chance with, if she could only learn to control her chaotic impulses when he was around and talk to him normally. Today she'd done really well, all things considered.

Until Bram had done that cocky, smiling, competitive guy thing he always did with Cody.

"Fine." She grabbed her phone off the table and tucked it into her back pocket. "Let's make a video."

FOUR

AISHA

Once Aisha had safely stored the remaining madeleines back in the topmost cabinet, Bram followed her out of the staff area and toward her office. "I'll have to ask my brother to get you more on his next trip."

She glanced back at him. If anyone else she'd known like him had said it, it would have been a humble brag, a way to flaunt the wealth Aisha so clearly lacked. With Bram, she knew it was a sincere offer. "I can also order them online."

"Ah, but it's not the same, is it?" His lips curved up in a mischievous smile that made her own mouth want to split wide in a grin. "To know it came from a store in France and flew all the way over the Atlantic just for you—doesn't that make it taste so much better?"

Something in her chest squeezed tightly at this. It wasn't the treats she wanted to fly over the ocean for her, but she did her best not to think of her mother while she was at work. Or ever, but like Proust and his madeleines, she was always surprised by what would trigger those painful thoughts. Bram's casual references to the wealth of his family, which he normally tried so hard to hide, didn't usually do it. Maybe it was the way he'd phrased it. Or maybe the mention of France.

"He doesn't bring them back for me. He brings them for you." Aisha wasn't that special, wasn't worth that kind of effort. Not from someone in Bram's world.

They stopped in her office quickly to pick up a tripod, then headed into the aquarium. "We can only film one. This account is supposed to be about the fish, not the staff."

"What if I put on a mermaid tail and swam in the tanks?"

They were in the main exhibit now, their feet tapping against the gray concrete floors that looked almost black in the semi-darkness. The overhead lights were still low since the aquarium wouldn't open to visitors for another hour. Aisha groped along a side wall for the hidden switches and turned on a few of the spotlights by Stella's tank.

"You know, I did that one summer during college." Aisha unfolded the tripod. "I didn't swim in the tanks, but I was a mermaid for meet and greets at Ripley's Aquarium."

Bram laughed and shook his head, leaning against the tank while Aisha finished setting up her phone on the tripod. His wavy brown hair was surrounded by a halo of water and light, his gaze intense, like some male version of Botticelli's Venus. Her fingers itched to draw him like this, but she'd have to settle for a video. "I didn't know that, but it makes total sense. What color was your tail?"

"Bright pink."

"Of course it was." His grin widened. "Were you the most popular one?"

"Maybe." But like almost every job she'd had, it had only been part-time and temporary. Her social media and marketing job for the Lowcountry Research Aquarium was the first one that felt like it could be a real career. The kind that Krista and Brooke had. At thirty-two, it was long past time for Aisha to have the same.

A few months ago, Cody had complimented her work in front

of his mom, and Aisha had finally been offered a full-time staff position. It felt like a sign that her new grown-up life was falling into place, with Cody at the center of it.

Then Bram had arrived.

Aisha hit the record button on her phone. "Now, what are you going to wish for today from our magical starfish?"

With a mischievous gleam in his ocean-blue eyes, Bram tapped a finger on the cleft in his chin that was only just visible beneath the three-day scruff he usually had. "My wish upon a starfish is . . . " He paused for dramatic effect, then his mouth split into a wide smile. "A secret."

Aisha huffed in frustration and stopped recording. "Bram, come on, I have work to do. I thought you were serious about this."

"I am serious." He gestured at the phone. "Keep recording. I think secret wishes are the way to go this time. Lure people in with mystery."

She pursed her lips. That wasn't a bad idea. "I guess you're right. Mystery works for Ripley."

"Pretty sure they were all coming to see you."

Ignoring how his offhand teasing made her body tingle all over, she focused on the camera. "Let's just get this finished."

While Bram squeezed his eyes shut, Aisha couldn't help but do the same. After all, it had been working so far for the aquarium. Why wouldn't it work for her?

I wish I could spend more time with him. Just the two of us.

When she opened her eyes again, Bram was grinning at her like he'd just won the lottery. His eyebrows waggled when he caught her eye.

"You made a wish, didn't you?"

"Maybe." She took her phone off the stand and tucked it back into her pocket. Before she could begin disassembling the tripod, Bram was at her side, breaking it down for her. "Thanks."

"You're welcome." He handed her the folded-up stand. "Will you tell me what you wished for?"

Her face burned. "Nope."

His eyebrows arched. "Not even if I tell you what I wished for?"

"You probably wished for something to do with the broken printer."

"You know me so well, do you?"

They made their way back through the tanks, the swimming fish casting flickering shadows along the walls. It was quiet and peaceful here, even when there were visitors. They didn't get many, not like the Ripley Aquarium, or the one in Charleston. This was a small, research-focused institution that didn't see more than a few hundred thousand visitors per year. Though that number had ticked up a little in the year since Aisha had started working. Even though he'd only been there a few months, Bram had already brought in a few really big donors.

"I do." Aisha arrived first at the door leading to the staff-only area, and Bram held it open for her. "I pay attention."

"So do I." Bram followed her through the door. "You wished for something to do with Cody."

Heart dropping to her knees, Aisha spun around, the tripod gripped tight in her hands. "What? I don't know what you're talking about."

"Aisha, come on." Bram lowered his voice and leaned toward her. The way he said her name sometimes, all blurred together almost into a single syllable, did funny things to her pulse. "It's pretty obvious."

"Is it?" After all of her efforts to always be calm and collected when Cody was around, was she still coming off as nuttier than a five-pound fruitcake?

"Not to him, don't worry."

She let out a sigh of relief and closed her eyes. They popped open again when she realized something.

"You're not going to tell him, are you?"

For the first time since she'd met him, Bram looked surprised.

There was no swagger about him, just hurt flickering in those fierce blue eyes. "Of course not. You're my friend."

At this, a smile spread across her face. "You are. Thank you."

They made their way down the hall to her office, her heart mostly coming down to a regular rhythm.

Then it kicked right back up when she saw Cody was waiting for her there.

"Can we talk?" His eyes cut to Bram standing behind her. "Just the two of us?"

FIVE

BRAM

Did Bram want to leave Aisha in her office with Cody? Of course not. He didn't have much choice, however, and didn't see her for the rest of the day. Somehow, he'd even missed her leaving that afternoon and walked through the empty hallways at five o'clock, alone and irritated.

The second Bram stepped into the parking lot, his phone rang. He looked down, and a wave of foreboding washed over him when he saw who it was.

"Hello, Mother." He lifted the corners of his mouth as he said the words, hoping she wouldn't hear the exhaustion in his voice.

"Don't you dare use that tone with me. You're the one working somewhere without any natural light. You chose to be this tired."

He rolled his eyes, let out the sigh he'd been holding in, and opened his car door.

As if the day couldn't get any worse.

Instead of walking Aisha to her car while listening to the usual flurry of excited chatter about her day, he got to talk to his mother.

This was definitely not what he'd wished for from Stella.

"Don't roll your eyes either."

"What can I do for you, Mother?" Bram turned on the car, and once his phone connected to the speakers, he dropped it onto the passenger seat.

"I wanted to discuss our contribution for next year."

Bram pulled out of his parking spot and onto the main road. "This couldn't wait until dinner this weekend?"

Once a week for the past ten years, he'd eaten dinner with his family. At least, he did on the weeks he couldn't find a good excuse. "Feeling sick" only worked in winter, and if he used "working" more than once a month he had to endure a lecture on how "non-profits expect you to dedicate your life while being paid next to nothing" followed by the ever-present job offer his parents liked to dangle in front of him on a regular basis.

Ever since he'd first refused that offer and moved out the day he graduated from college, Bram had been trying to put as many boundaries as he could between him and his family.

"Trying" being the key word. Sometimes it felt like he'd spent the entirety of his thirty-two years finding ways to live his life without their influence.

This would be a million times easier if they didn't keep donating money to whatever nonprofit he happened to be working at. His parents would always give a huge one as soon as he started, and whatever annual pledge amount kept them at the top of the donor list. His brother and two sisters weren't quite as consistent, but when they did give something, it always had a huge impact.

It wasn't like he could refuse their money when it was literally his job to fundraise. After working in nonprofit development for over a decade, Bram knew his family's connections were part of the reason he was so successful.

Which was why when applying for this job at the aquarium, he used his middle name, Howard, as his last name. It was time to see if he was actually good at his job or just relying on the Lowther name to open doors. Things were going well so far, but whatever he called himself, he knew he'd never be able to fully escape the fact he belonged to the Lowther family.

Family was everything to the Lowthers, after all.

On the phone, it was hard to tell if his mother's sigh was a weary one or a sad one. "No, it can't wait until this weekend. The sooner you know, the better."

His stomach dropped as he took a sharp turn that led back to his place. The house was paid for by his salary, unlike his siblings. If all went according to plan, Bram would be able to donate his entire trust fund to charity within the next twenty years. It had already been ten years since he'd touched it for any personal reasons, and his family didn't understand why.

"The sooner I know what?"

"Well, it seems your little aquarium is doing very well fundraising, so I don't think our contributions are necessary."

He took the next turn a little faster than usual, and his stomach lurched.

"Excuse me?"

"Whoever's in charge of your marketing is doing a very good job. You don't need big donors like us anymore."

"Of course we do." Bram slowed the car to a stop this time before making his turn. This did nothing to settle his stomach. "Mother, the impact of recurring donations on the financial stability of an institution are—"

"Yes, yes." He could picture her waving her hand, unconcerned about any logic or arguments that weren't supportive of what she'd already decided. "But surely you can make up for whatever you lose from us with some of these new people?"

"This was a one-time fundraising drive, so the focus was entirely different from long-term support of the—"

"I'm sure you'll figure out something, Bramwell. You're a very smart boy thanks to that degree your father and I paid for."

I would have paid for Harvard myself if you'd have let me, was what he wanted to say, but he held his tongue. Of course he'd fought as hard as he could at the time, but like everything with his mother, eventually it had just been easier to give in. At least going to the Ivy League school five generations of Lowthers had attended meant he made some decent connections on his own. They were all up north or out west, however. In South Carolina, the Lowthers had so much influence, it would be asinine to ignore it, as much as he wished he could.

Bram had never asked for this life, never sought out the wealth that had surrounded him since birth. It was like he was missing whatever programming the rest of his family had, or had a faulty chip in his brain that made him care more about others than the Lowther name the way his parents wished he would.

Biting back the dozens of replies he knew would make zero difference with his mom, Bram took a deep, long inhale through his nose. "Can I call you back in a moment? I'm almost home."

"There's nothing to discuss," his mother said. "We've made the decision."

Meaning she'd decided and his father had gone along with it without asking questions.

"Mother, please." There was only one thing he could do. At the next stop sign, instead of turning right to his small ranch house in a sleepy little suburb of Beaufort, he turned left toward the highway that would take him to the island with his hometown where the membership fee to the country club was more than his mortgage. "Why don't I come to dinner tonight, and we can talk about it?"

"Oh, how wonderful!" She sounded delighted, and not in the least bit surprised. This had been her plan from the beginning. He knew it, and she knew that he knew it, but in the end, she got what she wanted, so what difference did it really make? "Drinks are at seven."

"I know. See you soon." He disconnected the call, then rammed his palm into the steering wheel.

This was definitely not what he'd wished for from Stella.

SIX
BRAM

Why did driving up the familiar, winding, tree-lined road feel so much like driving to his own funeral? Bram pulled up in front of his parents' house with his stomach in knots and his chest wound tighter than a grandfather clock. The storm-cloud gray siding was new, part of a renovation the previous year, along with the brick path leading up to the column-flanked front doors. The inside was just as new, marble replacing the worn wood and carpet, the kitchen stocked with the latest gadgets. It didn't look a thing like his childhood home anymore, but walking inside still gave him the same pulsing anxiety it always had. Like he had to be on his best behavior or face serious consequences.

You're an adult. You can't get in trouble with your parents.

The internet meme sadly didn't apply to the Lowther family.

The first thing Bram did when the maid let him in was run upstairs to change. His jeans and polo shirt with the aquarium's logo were not going to be acceptable to Evelyn and Richard Lowther. Even now, after a decade of living on his own, of paying his own mortgage with the money he earned from a job he loved, Bram still felt like a failure to have a room full of clothes at this house. They were things he only wore here, he reasoned, but that didn't ease the tightness in his chest.

Making his way down the wide marble staircase, he tucked a crisp white linen shirt into tailor-made navy trousers, wishing he could have at least kept the polo shirt. It was much more comfortable, and felt much more like him.

"Well, don't you look handsome."

He tensed as he rounded the final curve of the stairway, expecting to see his mother or one of his sisters, but when he saw who it was, his shoulders instantly relaxed.

"Hey, Darcey." With a teasing wink, he grinned at her. "You look ravishing tonight."

His best friend rolled her eyes when he reached the foyer and planted a kiss on her cheek. "Don't let your mom hear you. You know she only invited me to see if somehow you'd fallen in love with me since the last time I had dinner with y'all?"

"How could I resist? Is that a new tattoo I see?" Bram scooted out of the way before she could smack his arm.

"Don't you dare." Her heels clicked on the marble as she speed-walked to catch up with him. The mid-thigh length, green silk dress she was wearing covered up a wide variety of tattoos but limited her range of motion.

"I'm not the one who snuck off to Mexico when I was seventeen." He slowed down and let her catch up with him.

She raised an eyebrow at him. "And who paid for my ticket?"

"Only so that you wouldn't tell my parents about what happened on the lake trip." They linked arms and continued through the rabbit warren of hallways to the smaller dining room on the other side of the house.

The Yates had been friends with the Lowthers since both families had come over on the Mayflower. Darcey and Bram had been born within months of each other, so of course they'd been expected to grow up, fall in love, get married, and take over their respective family businesses of yacht building and merge them into a single, unified company.

They'd only managed the first.

Instead of making them fall in love, growing up side by side as the eldest of their families had given them both the best friend they'd needed to escape the plans their parents had for them. Though Darcey was still winning in terms of parental disappointment. Bram's family may not understand his choice of career, but at least it provided useful contacts. Countless new yacht orders had started at the dozens of fundraising events Bram had planned over the years.

Darcey had become an environmental lawyer.

Their parents hadn't even blinked an eye when she'd taken a girl to her senior prom and come out as bi. All the elder Lowther and Yates generations had heard was that there was still a chance she might end up with Bram. Which wasn't ideal by any means, but all things considered it wasn't the worst way they could have reacted to the news.

When she'd announced her law school internship at the firm that had gone after every single luxury business in the tristate area, they'd stopped speaking to her for six months. But like everything in these kinds of families, they eventually swept it aside in the name of saving face, and simply avoided the topic of her work altogether.

"Be good tonight," Bram said as he re-tucked his shirt. "No work talk, please."

"Uh-oh, the serious voice." Darcey raised her eyebrows. "What's up?"

"Just trying to get my mother to agree to something she's already decided she doesn't want to do."

Darcey squeezed his arm and led him into the drawing room next to the dining room, their footsteps muffled on the thick rug covering the marble. The three white couches were empty, as was the rest of the room, except for his father, who was fussing over the drinks cart.

"I'll do my best," Darcey said quietly. "But the case against Lowther Yachts is heading to court in a few months. If they bring it up, you know I won't be able to stop myself."

"Case?"

Darcey frowned. "I can't really say more."

Foreboding crept along Bram's spine at Darcey's grim expression. Of course his mother would be looking for ways to economize if there was trouble on the horizon. Pulling out her support for the aquarium wasn't the way to do that. In fact, the opposite might be true.

"Interesting . . ." Bram considered how he might be able to use this new information, but before he could get very far, a highball glass was shoved into his hands by his father.

"Good evening, Bramwell." He peered at him over his glasses, then a tiny smile appeared when he saw Darcey's hand on his arm. "Darcey."

She smiled up at the older man, a grumpy and graying carbon copy of Bram. "Mr. Lowther. How lovely to see you."

The three of them chatted for a few minutes about nothing important, while Bram's heart rate slowly ticked up. His mother had yet to make an appearance, which he knew was just her way of throwing him off. Reminding him that she was the one with the power. His father may be the one with the Lowther name, but his mother was the one who knew how to wield it.

Finally, she strode into the drawing room in a familiar cloud of perfume and imperiousness.

"Apologies, I got a phone call from Betsy about the new logos, and I lost track of time. Shall we eat?" Without waiting for an answer, she turned and walked out.

Darcey shot him a glance as they followed her into the dining room, one they'd perfected over the years to tell each other, "Watch out."

It was time to find out what his mother had in store for him.

SEVEN

BRAM

Since it was just the four of them, they were spaced far apart at the long cedar table covered with crystal dishes. Bram sat across from Darcey at the long ends, and his parents were at the short ends.

"So, how was your day, Bram?" his mother said mildly, as if this was their regular weekly dinner. The cook placed a plate in front of her, then his father, then Darcey, and finally Bram.

Seafood stew? Really?

"You know how it was, Mother." Fighting to keep his tone polite, he picked up his spoon. "I'm in danger of losing my biggest donor."

"We can't really be the biggest, can we?" She smiled, knowing perfectly well that she was.

"You know how important your donation is."

"Yes, I got the personalized thank-you letter from the head of development." His mother arched her brow to let him know how insufficient she found this.

Darcey's eyes bounced between them as she ate, while Bram's father was completely absorbed in his meal.

Bram shifted in his chair. "It's making a huge difference in research."

"Research." She scrunched her nose, but thanks to all the fillers in her face, no lines appeared anywhere. "We like to give to places where we can see what we're supporting."

"You can come to the aquarium anytime you want." Bram smoothed out his napkin against his knee. "You can come after hours. All you have to do is call member services. Or me."

That last part was a little desperate, but he was feeling a little desperate. Losing his family's donation would leave a huge hole to fill that wouldn't be possible without months of work, and even then, it wouldn't be guaranteed. The corporate partnerships he'd been working on weren't nearly close to the finish line, and individual donors took time to source and develop. And once people heard that the Lowthers had stopped contributing, it would be that much harder to get other big donors to contribute. It was like a game to them, who could give more to the current trendy charity.

Still, he was head of development. This was his job. He was good at it, he reminded himself. The interview process for the role at the aquarium had been very thorough, and going by Bram Howard instead of Bramwell Lowther meant no one could claim he hadn't earned it. Well, as much as someone with his amount of privilege could ever be said to earn something.

"I don't want to go to the aquarium after hours when there's no one to see." His mother took a delicate, soundless sip from her spoon.

"You're more than welcome to host an event there. We've had several large parties." Birthday parties, but she didn't need to know that.

"Now why would I plan something when I could go to the art museum or symphony and they've organized a lovely evening where I can just enjoy myself?" She blinked her aesthetically enhanced eyelids at him and gave him a wrinkle-free smile.

"You know what she wants, Wellington," Darcey stage-whispered across the table, using the horrendous nickname she knew he hated. "The sooner you give it to her, the sooner we can all get to the next course."

Bram bit back a groan and returned his mother's smile. "You know, I was just thinking that a gala would be a nice change of pace for the aquarium's events this year."

His mother clapped her hands. "A gala? What a wonderful idea!" Her grin widened into something resembling a jack-o'-lantern's mouth. "The second weekend in September would be the perfect weekend. We have plans every weekend until then, and after that we'll be in Monaco for the yacht show."

The chair beneath him seemed to fall away, and his stomach dropped onto the floor. "That's less than two months from now."

"Honestly, Bramwell, I've seen people put together much bigger events in much less time." She gestured at Darcey sitting next to him. "Didn't your law firm have some sort of charity night just last month? Maybe Darcey can help you out."

The woman in question choked back a laugh, though Bram found nothing funny about this blatant attempt to set them up. "That wasn't me, Mrs. Lowther. We have an incredible office staff who—"

"Oh, don't be silly. You have a head for these things." With a single bejeweled hand, Bram's mother waved away any further discussion. "I'll expect an invitation within a week. My schedule does get very full, you know."

Somehow, Bram swallowed down the fire that had been steadily building in his throat.

All he'd wished for from Stella this morning was more time with Aisha. Instead, he'd gotten an unbelievable amount of extra work that might still end with his mother pulling out of her support for the aquarium. Then he'd be out of a job and would never see Aisha again.

If he actually believed in magical starfish, he'd be disappointed. Bram knew Stella was just a marketing ploy. That first silent wish that he'd made while filming the video that ended up going viral was that Aisha would feel the same about him as he did for her. Even then he'd known that was about as likely as his mother suddenly caring about anyone other than herself.

Though in her mind, she was just protecting the Lowther family and its interests.

It took every ounce of control in Bram's body to stay calm, though the white-knuckled grip he had on his spoon probably gave him away. "Of course, Mother."

The smile on his mother's lips was closer to a smirk. "Thank you, sweetie." She pushed away her half-empty bowl of seafood stew. "Now, I think it's time for dessert, don't you?"

EIGHT

AISHA

There were paw prints in the middle of Aisha's mural that hadn't been there the day before.

She frowned and took a step closer to inspect the damage. The project for the animal shelter was small, just one wall. The day before she'd sketched it all out quickly, then started on the painting rather than wait until the next evening. Painting was something Aisha did for fun, and she always got completely wrapped up in her projects. Had she been so wrapped up she'd missed putting away her paint the night before? Probably. That did sound like her.

"Brooke?" Aisha called for her best friend, who must not have heard the chime of the bell over the door when she came in. Turning around, she scanned the reception area. The long benches with worn cushions were empty, and no one appeared behind the bright reception desk.

From the hallway leading to the back where the kennels were, a tattooed, broad-chested man emerged and smiled at her, a tiny dachshund puppy cradled in his arms. "She ran out for a minute. What's up?"

"Ethan!" Overwhelmed by the unexpected joy at seeing Brooke's boyfriend, Aisha threw her arms around him. With her new full-time schedule, Aisha hadn't been able to volunteer at the shelter as much and missed seeing him. The puppy in his arms barked, either from happiness at being included in the affection, or because he could no longer see. "I didn't think you usually worked this late."

She released them both from her hug, then scratched the puppy's chin. Ethan nodded toward the window, where late summer sunlight was still streaming through the windows at six p.m. "Daylight savings."

Ethan had retinitis pigmentosa, a degenerative eye disease that made it difficult to drive at night. Eventually he'd lose a lot more of his vision, but it was a long, slow process that was as unpredictable as Aisha's art projects.

This paw print was a classic example. Aisha gestured at the mess of green paint in the middle of her mural of flowers and trees that she'd started—but apparently not finished—the day before.

"Do you have any idea who might have done this?" She bent to give the puppy a kiss on his tiny head. "It couldn't have been this cutie-pie."

Ethan chuckled. "Chip just got here today, along with his brother Dale. The owners moved overseas."

As usual, Aisha had the urge to adopt the adorable puppy, but if she gave in to that urge every time that happened, her apartment would be full to the brim of abandoned cats and dogs. She contented herself with lavishing the shelter animals with as much attention as she could manage these days.

"I didn't see any animals with blue or green paws today," Ethan said as he narrowed his eyes at the marks on the wall. It looked like a four-legged friend had been trying to climb into the half-finished tree. "Did you leave your paint out last night?"

Heat streaked up Aisha's neck and pooled in her cheeks. "Um, I don't think so?"

Ethan smirked. "So that's a yes."

His laugh and the playful bump of his shoulder on hers only

made Aisha more embarrassed. Ethan was the office manager for the animal shelter Brooke had opened the previous year. Where Brooke was all about order and predictability, Ethan was . . . well, more like Aisha. Sometimes. They might have both been more on the "let's try it and see what happens" side of the chaos spectrum, but Ethan was about eight thousand times more responsible than Aisha. Probably because of all the years he'd been a firefighter.

Would she be that sure of herself if she'd been in the same job for a decade? It seemed like the more she took on at work, the less she felt like she knew what she was doing and the more chances they'd realize she was a mess.

At least Cody thought she knew what she was doing. That's what he'd said that afternoon to Bram. And then there'd been his unexpected request for help that only she could give him, apparently.

"I honestly don't remember." She pulled her hair up into a bun on the top of her head. She'd stopped off at her apartment after work to change into her painting clothes, so she was ready to keep going. If she could settle her thoughts and solve this mystery first. "I was thinking about the next campaign for the aquarium and the newsletter for the shelter and taking a picture of the new animals and—"

"It's fine." The way Ethan said it didn't totally reassure her, however, no matter how sweet he was.

Aisha put her hands over her face and groaned. "I swear I thought I put everything away. I'd never want to put the animals in danger."

"You didn't." Kindness laced Ethan's words. "I'm sure last night's volunteer just put it away and cleaned up whoever did that. I'm more worried about who managed to break out of their cage without anyone noticing."

A new voice cut into their conversation. "That would be Sprinkles, who's even more of an escape artist than Cloudy was."

"Brooke!" Aisha turned and grinned at her best friend. The

raven-haired shelter owner planted a quick kiss on Ethan's cheek, then scratched behind the puppy's ears before coming to stand in front of the mural.

"I like the paw prints. Should we get the other animals to put some up there as well?"

Dropping her hands, Aisha tilted her head and considered, mind whirling with the possibilities. "No, but this is giving me a brain tingle . . ."

Silence descended as she tried to organize her thoughts into something resembling a logical sentence. Ethan and Brooke waited patiently, and Aisha was grateful for the quiet. Well, as quiet as an animal shelter with a dozen animals in the back could be. When the puppy in his arms started to squirm, Ethan headed across the bright-blue floor toward the back again, calling over his shoulder that he had to let the dog go outside for a bit.

A minute passed, then two, the cat clock above the reception desk ticking away the minutes as the tail swung back and forth.

A familiar pressure started to snake its way up Aisha's neck. This was why she didn't paint professionally. Doing this as a favor for Brooke meant it didn't matter if she messed up.

But that didn't mean she wanted to ruin the wall of her friend's animal shelter.

Is that what she'd managed to do?

The pressure in her throat spread down into her stomach. What if people saw the wall and thought the shelter was unprofessional or unsafe? What if this one moment of being typical Aisha made the shelter shut down and then the only thing to show that Brooke had ever saved a single animal were these footprints . . .

"I have an idea!" The excitement burst out of Aisha with such force, Brooke jumped. They looked at each other and giggled.

"Yeah?" Brooke wrapped an arm around her shoulder, and Aisha's heart lifted at the familiar warmth. "It's okay if it means starting over. There's no deadline on this."

Stepping to her left, Aisha moved out of Brooke's embrace and lifted a hand to adjust the clips in her hair. Brooke was just being nice, but the pressure along Aisha's neck was heavier now.

Brooke, Krista, and Aisha had known each other since elementary school. When Aisha arrived from France, Krista and Brooke welcomed her into their little duo to make it a trio. They'd been inseparable other than for a few years when they went to different colleges. Though Aisha and Krista had both been raised by amazing dads, and Brooke by her late grandmother, who they'd all called Gran, it sometimes felt like they grew up mothering each other.

Or at least, what they assumed mothering was like. None of their moms had been in the picture since they were little. So they watched out for each other a little more than was probably normal. Gave advice with the kind of care and attention that meant they saw each other's successes as their own.

Which was why this slight criticism, as gentle and reassuring as Aisha knew Brooke had meant it, still crushed her the way it would from her mother. At least it hadn't been Krista.

Aisha shook her head. In this case, the criticism was merited. Leaving paint out, messing up and needing to start over, that was the kind of person she didn't want to be anymore. "I'll finish the mural tonight. Then you can start putting paw prints on it on purpose."

"On purpose?" There was no judgment in Brooke's voice, only cautious curiosity. The pressure in Aisha's neck released a little.

"When they get adopted. This way, you have a visual reminder of how many animals you've helped. And when people walk in, they'll see it too."

"That's a great idea." Brooke wrapped her arms around her and squeezed. "I never would have thought of it. You're so creative."

Making a mess of a painting project and finding a way to fix it? Typical Aisha.

Not making the mess to begin with was who she wanted to be. Who she needed to be if she was going to catch Cody's attention.

"We did something similar at the aquarium for the 'Wish Upon a Starfish' fundraising campaign." Aisha shrugged out of Brooke's embrace. "We set up this ocean scene in the lobby and added fish every time we hit ten thousand dollars."

"That sounds adorable."

"It is." There was an undercurrent of worry in her voice that she hoped Brooke wouldn't pick up on.

Of course she did, though. Brooke turned to her, brow furrowed. "What happened?"

"Cody came into my office today to talk to me."

"That's great!"

"Well, sort of." It had been just like Aisha had wished from Stella—just the two of them. Except it hadn't been the intimate moment she'd expected. "He wanted me to get the fundraising poster taken down. Apparently, it's blocking some of the informational plaques he'd worked so hard to get installed."

"That sounds . . . like progress?" Confusion scrunched up Brooke's nose.

"I guess so." It wasn't her poster—it was Bram's. Cody was worried he'd take it the wrong way, and said that since she was friends with Bram, maybe he'd listen to her.

"Did you get all flustered when talking to him?" Brooke rubbed a consoling hand on Aisha's shoulder.

"Yes. Incredibly flustered." Aisha shook her head and let out a weak chuckle. That was a lot easier to understand than whatever complicated feelings Aisha had about his odd request. The politics of working somewhere longer than a few months was not something she'd ever had to deal with before. Any long-term graphic design gigs had been as a remote contractor, so she'd never been in an office. Maybe it was totally normal for people to ask favors like this from colleagues. She wouldn't embarrass herself by asking Brooke about it. "He said I was the nicest person there."

"That's a great compliment and one hundred percent true."

Brooke looked as pleased as a proud mother being told her children had good manners.

Not that Aisha had been particularly mannerly, or nice for that matter. Her heart had been pounding while she just nodded mutely, and Cody walked out without her having said more than a few dozen words to him, most of them "of course" and "I completely understand."

While it still felt like a win to have a conversation with him in her office at all, next time, she'd have to be a little more specific with her wish. The wording was clearly important in the wishes. All the other wishes had worked, but those had been very specific. The little boy had wished for a million dollars for Stella. Cody had wished for good weather for his research trip, and Bram had wished for a new printer for the office. All of that had come true.

On a whim one morning, she'd stopped by the tank and wished for more visitors for the aquarium, and they'd gotten twice as many as usual that month. Another time, after a longer than usual stretch of not painting, she'd wished for inspiration for a new art project, and a few days later, Brooke had called her about this mural. Now she'd gotten alone time with Cody, just not for a super interesting reason. Stella was clearly magical, and she just needed more guidance.

Which had to be why the starfish hadn't granted her first secret wish, an exceptionally big ask. Having someone love her for herself was asking a lot. Expecting Cody to fall in love with the chaotic, forgetful whirlwind that she really was would take a whole ocean's worth of magical starfish. His panicked glances at her messy desk during their short conversation had been like a giant neon arrow pointing to just how unsuitable she was for him. Tomorrow, after she asked Bram about the poster, she'd get it organized. Making herself into the kind of serious, responsible person that fit into his orderly, logical life wasn't something the starfish could help Aisha with.

"You'll figure out a way to stay calm around him." Brooke

squeezed her shoulder. "Just like you figured out how to make the mural even better. I love your idea."

Warmth flooded Aisha's chest. It was the reminder she needed, from one of the people who knew her best. Like what a mother's love should be, Aisha, Brooke, and Krista's for each other was unconditional.

"Thanks." She picked up a paintbrush and smiled at Brooke. "I'll be done tonight."

NINE

AISHA

Despite all her best intentions, Aisha did not, in fact, finish the mural that night.

First she got distracted by Chip, who managed to wriggle away from Ethan once they got back inside. Then Brooke wanted her opinion on something for the shelter's newsletter, which Aisha had been handling up until she'd gone full time at the aquarium.

By the time Ethan and Brooke were closing things up for the night, very little progress had been made on the mural. Brooke didn't seem at all bothered by this, but the lingering sense of failure followed Aisha all the way home.

She didn't want to be this flighty, forgetful person anymore, but she didn't even know where to start.

When she got to the aquarium the next morning, Aisha made a stop by Stella's tank. If there was one thing Aisha was more than a little willing to believe in, it was magic. Like the smoothies Brooke's grandmother had called magic potions that gave you a little boost of beauty for a date or focus for a test.

Or the fortune-telling abilities of those MASH games played as kids. Aisha had held every single one of the silly jobs they'd predicted for her: mermaid, cocktail waitress, body painter, golf ball diver . . . when she hadn't found a job right away after college that used her graphic design degree, she'd taken whatever job came along, as long as it sounded fun.

Now she was finally in a serious, steady job that no one would ever have predicted for her. She wanted that same, settled feeling in all areas of her life. It was well past time. For a career, for people to take her seriously, for a boyfriend who didn't drive a scooter and live with five roommates.

Aisha stood with her hand on the glass, looking for Stella. Wishing on an empty tank wouldn't do anything. It might even be bad luck. There was a little flurry of movement in a corner, and one long, multicolored arm was just barely visible.

"Hey there, beautiful." Smiling, Aisha kept her voice soft. "You must be tired after granting so many wishes."

Another arm poked out from behind the rock as if to agree with her, but the starfish remained mostly hidden.

"I'll come back when you're feeling better." Aisha brushed aside a strand of hair that had escaped her clips. "And when I've figured out what to wish for."

There were so many options, but which one would work the way she wanted it? Obviously, she couldn't wish for someone to love her, but wishing Cody would come talk to her had worked, so maybe she just had to do that a few more times. Or she could wish he'd come save her from some danger . . . but then she'd be in danger, which didn't sound like a lot of fun.

Or maybe she'd wish to be more organized and then—

"I like to walk through the tanks, too, in the morning."

Aisha let out a little yelp of surprise, then turned around and bumped into the tank.

"I'm sorry. I didn't mean to startle you." There was a frown pulling down Cody's features.

Heart racing, Aisha put a hand to her chest and tried to smile.

Could have used a little warning, Stella, but thanks for the second chance.

"It's fine." It came out as a squeak. She took a deep breath through her nose and tried again. "How are you today, Dr. Rhodes?"

"You can call me Cody, you know." There was the tiniest flicker of a smile on his lips that kicked up Aisha's pulse another few notches.

Despite his proclamation that she was the nicest person here, she'd never made him smile before, not once the entire time he'd been working here.

Stella was granting wishes Aisha didn't even know she'd made.

"How are you today"—she swallowed hard, her tongue thick— "Cody?"

"Fine thanks. And you?"

"I'm doing well."

It was the smallest of small talk, and yet, it still felt like progress. At least she wasn't stumbling over her words.

Cody cleared his throat. "I noticed the poster is still in the lobby."

Heat crept along her neck. "Oh, um, I haven't had a chance to talk to Bram yet."

"I thought you two were always together." There was another frown. This was even more exciting than the smile. "That's what Sandra in accounting says."

"We are, I mean, not always, I mean . . . " The words got all tangled up. Frustration shot through her veins, heating her cheeks. Instead of the polished, professional person she wanted to be, she was being typical, scatterbrained Aisha. The Aisha that she knew wouldn't interest Cody. Calling her nice wasn't the same as calling her smart or competent. "I had a lot of work to do yesterday, so I didn't see him all afternoon."

Cody nodded, like he approved of her working hard, and it sent bubbles whizzing around her chest.

Taking a deep breath before she opened her mouth again, Aisha slowed down her words. "If you see Bram first, I'm sure it's fine if you ask him."

"Ask me what?"

Aisha let out another yelp of surprise and turned toward the voice, catching the edge of a very familiar smirk.

TEN

BRAM

This was not the way Bram liked to start his day. Finding Cody in close conversation yet again with Aisha was like a sucker punch to the gut. Especially when he'd gotten there even earlier than usual, hoping to have a few minutes alone with her. He hadn't entirely given up on his idea to ask her out, but this felt like a sign he just wasn't meant to have her. Yesterday he'd wished to spend more time with her, but today he found Aisha and Cody together in front of Stella's tank.

Whoever's wishes Stella was granting, it wasn't Bram's.

Cody wasn't a terrible guy, or terrible-looking based on how other women at the aquarium looked at him. He just . . . wasn't right for Aisha.

Look at him standing there, all buttoned up and serious. Pants and shirt ironed to creases so stiff they looked like they could cut you. Opposites could attract, but Bram had literally never heard Cody talk about anything other than fish. Sure, they worked in an aquarium, and it was his job. But Bram had asked him once about his favorite books and movies, and the guy had listed all nonfiction and documentaries, all about fish. When he asked what he did for fun, Cody looked at him like he was the weird one for not spending his weekends immersed in a podcast about the intricacies of dolphin mating rituals.

Cody was, in a word, boring.

Boring was fine. Most of the people who came to the parties Bram's parents threw were epically boring. His siblings were all boring. Boring was safe, and there was nothing wrong with it.

But Aisha wasn't boring.

Even now, staring at him with a look that was half-nervous, half-relieved, her face held more interesting details than all the paintings in his parents' house.

"Ask me what?" he repeated when a full minute passed and she hadn't answered him.

A brief look that passed between Cody and Aisha, and Bram's already sour mood got impossibly worse. This was what he got for skipping breakfast, hoping for another secret madeleine raid with Aisha before the office got busy.

"Um, nothing." Aisha's hands went to the clips in her hair. "What's new with you?"

He bit the inside of his cheek. He'd get whatever it was out of her later, when she wasn't being this meek mouse. Cody couldn't hang around her all day.

Could he?

"I need to plan a gala for the end of next month."

At this, Aisha's face brightened. "A gala. That sounds like fun."

There she is. A smile spread across Bram's face. This was exactly the kind of energy he'd been hoping for from her.

"Why would we do that?" Cody pushed his glasses up his nose.

"Fundraising." The word was clipped, and Bram made no effort to hide his irritation.

"We just did that," Cody said as another look passed between him and Aisha. It felt like a rock from Stella's tank shot right into Bram's chest.

They were sharing looks now. What happened yesterday in her office? An invisible clock was ticking, counting down the

Cody-free minutes that Bram had left in his daily life at Lowcountry Research Aquarium. Just because the scientist hadn't shown much interest in anything but fish until now didn't mean that would always be the case. Once Cody was as hooked on Aisha as Bram was, there'd be no peace. The bespectacled doctor would be hanging around all the time.

So what? It's not like she's shown any interest in you.

The words hit him like a punch in the gut. And of course they were in his mother's voice.

"Yes, we had a very successful fundraising campaign, and we should capitalize on it." Bram kept his voice steady even as the blood felt like it was draining out of his body. "People like to give to successful endeavors, to be part of that success."

Some more than others.

"So you'll keep the fish poster in the front lobby a while longer?" Aisha's voice was small, timid, like she wasn't really sure of what she was saying. He hated hearing her talk like that and hated the man standing next to her who made her think she had to.

She was even wearing gray for the first time ever, he realized. A dark gray skirt suit that hit right below her knee. It looked like something his mother would wear.

Or something Cody would.

At least her earrings were still something fun, but they were tiny little stars. Nothing like the giant, colorful jewelry she usually wore.

"I'm not sure." Bram crossed his arms over his chest. "Why?"

"It's just . . . " She shifted on her feet, the black flats nowhere near as fun as her usual bright sneakers, and avoided his eyes. "That campaign is over, so we can probably move the poster. So people can see the plaques behind it better."

"Oh." That wasn't what he thought she'd say.

Her eyes darted to Cody's, and Bram had to bite his tongue to stop himself from saying something rude. If Cody had asked, of course Bram would have teased him and made it a running joke.

With Aisha, he was physically incapable of denying her anything she wanted that was within his power to give, even though she never directly asked him for anything. Until now.

"That's fine. I'll go grab it now."

"Thanks, Bram." The smile Aisha flashed him was one of her smaller ones, but he still put it with the others in his collection. Every smile that was just for him, he kept.

Okay, fine, he kept some of the ones she sent to others too. At least she hadn't sent too many Cody's way. Yet.

As he turned away, Bram expected to see a smirk on Cody's face, some hint of his triumph. Instead, all he saw was relief. The guy wasn't angling for attention from Aisha. He just wanted more attention for what he'd done at the aquarium. Like that would change the fact that he'd gotten the job thanks to his mother.

Hypocritical much?

This time the voice in his head sounded like Darcey.

Once Bram retraced his steps the short distance back to the lobby, he sighed as he removed the poster from its stand. It wasn't even attached that securely. Either Cody or Aisha could have done it, but Bram had grown up with this kind of convoluted politicking. This was how it had to be done to make everyone happy. If Cody took it off himself or asked Bram directly, then it would look like he wasn't playing nice with the development department. By getting Aisha to ask, it made it look like a marketing request and within their normal sphere of collaboration.

Cody was smart, there was no denying it. But Bram had been raised in a pit of vipers and knew how to scheme with the best of them.

As he made his way back to them, Bram plastered on the same fake, wide smile he'd used with his parents the previous night. "All set." He handed the poster to Aisha. "You want to keep it in your office to remind you of how successful your idea was?"

Her entire body turned scarlet at the praise. She never seemed to seek it out, which made him want to give it to her all the more.

"Um, sure. Thanks." She took the poster from him and shifted on her feet. "Tell me more about this gala idea."

Next to her, Cody let out a sigh. "I need to get to work." His tone made it clear that he didn't think the gala was real work, which irritated Bram more than anything else had so far this morning.

Before Bram could say anything back, Cody stalked off in the direction of the labs. Which was probably a good thing, since the only responses in Bram's mind were the opposite of polite.

Finally, it was just him and Aisha. It may not last, and he shot a quick glance at Stella in her tank, wondering if it was worth wishing none of their other colleagues decided to take a stroll through the tanks before starting work.

The starfish waved an arm at him, whatever that meant.

It means nothing except she's a starfish who moves around sometimes in her tank.

He turned his attention to Aisha, grateful to be alone with her, whether it was because of a magical starfish or not. "I was thinking it's time we held a member's gala, as kind of a thank-you, but also a fundraiser."

"The aquarium's never done a gala before." She bounced a little on her heels, excitement vibrating from her despite her drab work attire. "Like a red-carpet formal dinner, or just a drinks and hors d'œuvres kind of party?"

"I don't know much yet, other than the date." He sighed and ran a hand through his hair. Partly because he was exasperated, and partly because he knew how good it looked when tousled. Something Cody's hair definitely couldn't do. "And the location. We should definitely have it here."

"When is it?"

"September 14th."

That was barely six weeks away. "I haven't done something like this before on such short notice."

"Do you need help? Not that I've ever planned something like this." That hint of coral was back on her cheeks. "But I've helped my friend Brooke with events for her animal shelter."

He'd heard her talk about the shelter, but not about the events. "Oh yeah?"

Of course he'd need her help with the marketing, but if she wanted to get more involved, that would mean even more time together. He glanced at the starfish, who'd wriggled her way closer and was now right above Aisha's head.

"They do monthly adoption events, and there was a big firefighter raffle last year."

"A raffle wouldn't be a bad idea."

"With firefighters?"

Bram snorted. "The last thing I need is a bunch of muscled heroes parading around this place outshining me."

"Stop it." She shoved his arm. "Like anyone could outshine you."

His breath caught in his throat. Was this their regular teasing coworker banter, or something more? The way his skin burned where she'd touched made it clear what he was hoping for.

Tilting his head, he leaned against Stella's tank. "You do. Almost every day without even trying."

This deepened the flush on her cheeks, and everything inside his chest started to tap dance.

"So why've you turned yourself down from an eleven to a two today?" he asked, with a nod at her outfit.

She looked down at her depressing suit and bit her lip, her face reddening even more. "I'm just trying something different."

Jealousy flickered hot in Bram's chest. This had to be because of Cody. But short of blurting out his feelings for her—that he'd been too good at hiding behind teasing and ridiculous office competitions—there was no way to ask her about Cody without sounding like a jerk.

Time to get back to a safer topic.

"I really like your raffle idea. Maybe with something related to fish."

He knew this had been the right direction to take things when she looked up at him with a smile, clearly relieved not to be talking about her clothes anymore. "I'm sure you'll think of something. You're really good at what you do."

The tap dancing in his chest turned into an Olympic-level sprint. If she complimented him again, there'd be a real risk of cardiac arrest.

"Thanks, but I appreciate any help you can give me. You want to grab lunch together and help me brainstorm?"

"We always eat lunch together."

"I want to take you out." He inhaled sharply when Aisha's eyebrows shot up and he realized what he'd said. "I mean, we always eat here. Let's go out instead."

Her eyes lit up. "That would be fun."

"Great." It was a struggle to keep his voice even and to avoid showing how excited he was. A few teasing compliments for him didn't erase the looks Aisha had been sharing with Cody.

"Come and get me whenever you're ready. I have a ton to do this morning."

As she pranced off, her steps as light as ever despite her heavy clothing, he looked up at the tank, and could have sworn Stella was winking at him.

"Is this your doing?" More time with Aisha, just the two of them, had been all he could think about lately. And now he had it.

Maybe his wishes were coming true, after all.

Lunch with Bram isn't a big deal. We do it every day.

Despite repeating this to herself all morning, Aisha struggled to concentrate on her work. Between the conversation with Cody and then Bram's invitation to lunch, a lot had happened in the span of just ten minutes. What she wished she could do was take out a canvas and get lost in a painting, but the closest thing she had to that was tweaking the graphics on the next newsletter for aquarium members.

Unfortunately, that didn't absorb her the way that painting did, so she started cleaning up and organizing her desk. This kept her hands busy, leaving her mind mostly free to munch on all the questions that popped up.

There was no way that Bram was suggesting this was more than lunch . . . right? He'd corrected himself pretty quickly, but he'd also said so many nice things about her.

Then again, he was always saying nice things, the way Krista and Brooke did. That's just what friends did.

Would Cody stop by? He hadn't thanked her for the poster yet. Should she leave her door open so he could come in if he passed by or keep it closed so he'd think she was busy working? She settled on half-open.

By the time noon rolled around and Bram popped his head into her office, Aisha was exhausted from hours of mental gymnastics.

"Hey, ready to go?" The smile on Bram's face gave her the same heart palpitations it always did.

"Yes." She jumped out of her chair before she could let herself spiral into whether or not it was the same friendly smile he always had for her or if it meant something more . . . and before he could question why she was finally cleaning up her desk.

He'd already asked about her clothes, so he was sure to notice her mission to be more organized. It should have been a good thing. It meant her goal of changing how she was seen by others was working. Yet, for some reason, it didn't feel like a victory to have Bram say she'd gone from an eleven to a two.

So what? A two is what I need to be for Cody.

She smoothed out the gray skirt and hurried past Bram and into the hallway. If she kept moving, then maybe her thoughts would finally quiet themselves. "Where do you want to go?"

"I was thinking that Italian place in town?"

"That sounds fine." She walked next to him down the hallway. "Are you driving? Do I finally get to see this magical electric car?"

There was an undertone of excitement in her voice that she didn't even try to hide.

Bram's cheeks turned pink, and he rubbed the back of his neck. "I don't talk about the car that much, do I?"

A laugh burst out of Aisha's mouth before she could stop it, but she quickly cut it short, realizing how mean it might sound. She cleared her throat. "Um, maybe a little. But it's cute you're so excited about it."

"You mean you're not?" Getting a bit of his swagger back, Bram led her out of the aquarium to the back parking lot where the two electric charging stations were. Thanks to his nonstop yapping when he bought the car, Aisha knew they'd been installed by the city. A shiny gray sedan was connected to one, the sleek lines of it both familiar and futuristic.

Aisha let out a low whistle. "Very pretty."

"I didn't get it because it was pretty." Bram harrumphed, but she caught the twitch of pride in the corners of his lips. "I got it because it has a range of three hundred miles on a single charge."

"I didn't realize they're almost the same size as regular gas pumps." Aisha took a closer look at the way the car connected to the kiosk. "Adamsville doesn't have any charging stations yet."

The aquarium was situated right on the water, halfway between Adamsville and Beaufort. Even though Riverton was smaller than Aisha's town, it was better developed, with a cute main street that was built to look like a typical Lowcountry small town. It was fun to spend a weekend afternoon window shopping, but the boutiques here were all a bit out of Aisha's price range.

"I hope you get them soon. This is the future." He held open the passenger door for her, and she slid inside with butterflies in her stomach. Holding doors was just something Bram did. It didn't make this anything more than lunch between colleagues.

Not that she even wanted that. Cody was who she wanted, who she actually had a shot with.

"You sound like a salesman," she teased as he got into the driver's seat. "Do you own stock in the company or something?"

"Would that be a bad thing?" His eyes flicked to hers, and she sucked in a breath.

He'd always danced around this, pretending he didn't have money when it was so obvious he did. It was a tricky topic for Aisha, and while she had thoughts—so many thoughts it was hard to even know where to start—she also didn't want to offend Bram.

Maybe my next wish is for Bram to be honest with me.

"Not necessarily," Aisha said carefully. Outside the blue bubble of the aquarium, talking with Bram felt weightier. He was her work friend, but lunch in town pushed them over the line into the territory of real friends, which she didn't cross with many people. When you only worked somewhere for a few months, you didn't have a chance to develop deeper friendships. Like office politics, she didn't know all the rules about work friendships outside of work. How much backstory was too much, too soon?

"I think it's great when people use their money to support the causes they care about." She shifted in the leather seat as her eyes danced over the smooth screens on the dashboard that made the car feel like it was part spaceship. "Assuming what they care about isn't like banning books or something."

Bram chuckled softly, but didn't say anything, leaving Aisha to wonder if he had his own complicated history he wasn't telling her.

Of course he does. Everyone has weird family stuff.

Part of the reason Aisha, Brooke, and Krista were such good friends was because they all had absent mothers for one painful reason or another. Aisha's particular baggage involved a ridiculously wealthy mother who'd only provided the minimum legally required monetary support until she was eighteen and then stopped all contact.

Clearly Aisha wasn't a cause the woman cared much about.

They drove out of the parking lot, and the trip was thankfully a short one. It was blazing down through the windshield, making her sweat in her suit jacket.

"This is nice. I don't think I've been out for lunch since I started full time."

"If we had more time, we could go into Beaufort." Bram turned onto the road leading into town. "There're only two options here. Italian or barbeque."

"Adamsville isn't too far. We could go there next time."

He smiled at this, and her heart jumped in her chest. Next time *as friends* is what she'd meant.

Right?

They pulled into the nearly full parking lot in front of the restaurant.

"I didn't realize it would be this busy," Bram said when they got out of the car. "I didn't think to call for a reservation."

"I don't think it's the kind of place that takes reservations." Not that Bram would even need to make them. Aisha was sure tables just appeared when he snapped his fingers.

Except he didn't seem like a snapping-fingers kind of guy. In the few months she'd known him, he'd never once been anything other than kind and considerate. Well, and irritating whenever Cody was around, but that was just some weird guy thing, and had nothing to do with money.

In the late summer heat, when just stepping outside made you want to melt, Bram *was* the kind of guy who still managed to look perfect. His sun-kissed skin glowed, and his dark waves had gone curly at the ends. On anyone else—on Aisha in particular, if her waves weren't held back with clips—it would look messy. Bram was flawless. Aisha's fingers itched to paint him, the colors so stark and bold against the bright-blue summer sky it was like a pop art masterpiece.

"Shall we?" Bram asked, breaking her out of the daydream of a new painting in a style she'd never attempted before. The heat must be getting to her head. He was holding the door to the restaurant open, waiting for her. Stepping into the cool dark interior was a relief. The suit was professional but not intended for a South Carolina summer.

Despite the packed parking lot, there were still tables available inside the large dining room, and they were seated right away. Bram held out the leather chair for Aisha, and she slid in, taking in the one long brick wall and how it contrasted with the dark-green paint on the other walls. There were cloth napkins laid on top of the plates, making it just slightly nicer than a typical quick lunch spot.

As they were listening to the server go through the lunch specials, Aisha heard her name called and turned around.

"Krista!" She blinked away her surprise and stood up to hug

her friend. The server disappeared, saying she'd get them all some water.

It was a merging of her two worlds that Aisha hadn't expected. Of course she was thrilled to see Krista, but she wasn't so thrilled that Bram was meeting her.

Which was ridiculous. Bram was her colleague. Her friend. Why shouldn't he meet one of her best friends?

Who just happened to be a brilliant, beautiful lawyer with bouncy curls the color of sunshine and a smile that could power a whole fleet of electric cars.

While Aisha's heart thundered away, the surprise still running through her, Bram stood up and held out his hand. "Hi, I'm Bram Howard."

Krista's eyebrows rose a fraction of an inch, and her eyes flicked to Aisha for the briefest of moments. Translation: *who is this and why have you never talked about him?*

That was an excellent question, and not one Aisha had an answer for. After all, as far as her friends knew, the only guy she worked with was Cody, who she'd been talking about for months.

Unlike Aisha, Krista was able to hide her surprise. There was no indication on her warm, open expression that she was anything other than delighted. She clasped Bram's hand. "Nice to meet you. I'm Krista Waters."

His eyes lit up. "Oh, the famous Krista. I've heard plenty about you."

"All bad things, I hope." She winked, and when Bram chuckled in response, something inside Aisha's chest roared in protest. "Do you work at the aquarium too?"

"In development. I couldn't do what I do without Aisha, our marketing guru." He beamed in her direction.

That familiar heavy pressure made its way up Aisha's neck as her hand traced the edge of her plate. "I just do whatever you tell me you need."

"The Wish Upon A Starfish campaign was entirely your idea."

His gaze landed on her face, and the pressure increased so much her knees threatened to buckle.

"It was just a silly video that went viral." She waved a hand. He was giving her too much credit. "It's not like you can control those kinds of things."

It was part of why she liked social media marketing, honestly. The chaotic, unpredictable nature of it meant that success or failure was entirely out of her hands. The buzz of making a huge splash was big enough to tide them over when other things didn't work out as well. And as long as she followed the basic rules, she could expect steady growth for the account, even if nothing ever went viral again.

It was completely different from art. You could work for years and never make so much as a drop, let alone a splash. After seeing what her dad had gone through, she'd never even been tempted to try for that life. She might like a little chaos and unpredictability, but she wasn't totally reckless.

Krista was the one to save Aisha from more compliments she didn't deserve. "It was a great campaign." Her firm tone let Aisha relax the way she always did whenever Brooke or Krista took control of things that Aisha had somehow managed to muck up.

"Are you here with a client?" Aisha asked, looking around the restaurant. The tables had started to fill up, chatter humming through the dining room.

"Just meeting a friend from law school. This place is halfway between our offices, so we come here every few months." Krista was in a suit similar to Aisha's, but she looked much more at ease in it. The fit was slightly looser, the light-blue material sleeker.

Aisha tugged at the bottom of her jacket. "Is this the Barrister Bunch?" They were friends Krista talked about all the time, but since most of them lived and worked in Charleston, far away from Adamsville, Brooke and Aisha had never met them.

"Just one of them today." Krista smiled, a brilliant flash of white teeth. Next to her, Bram sucked in a breath, and Aisha's heart sank. Everyone had that reaction to Krista's smile.

It doesn't matter. He's just a friend.

"You know Darcey Yates?" Bram asked.

"Yes, she's the one who came up with the name." Krista looked past their table and waved. "I take it you know her too?"

Clearing his throat, Bram shifted on his feet. "Family friend."

Aisha's eyes snapped to him, but he avoided her gaze. There had to be more to it than that, based on how uncomfortable he looked. It was usually easy for Aisha to brush things off, to look past any awkwardness, but this was too obvious to ignore.

"Wellington." A beautiful red-haired, ivory-skinned woman in a beige dress with crisp lines looked delighted to see him. "I didn't know you'd be here."

"It's right down the road from the aquarium." He raised an eyebrow.

"Well, what a small world." She turned her laser-focused gaze on Aisha. "Hi, I'm Darcey Yates."

"Aisha Jackson." She bit her lip. The woman was from the same small, affluent world as Bram, that much was clear. "Is Wellington a family nickname?"

"No." Bram's eyes darkened as a look passed between him and Darcey. "Just something she calls me."

"Well, I'm not going to call you Bramwell like your mother." Darcey rolled her eyes. "Even if it is your name."

Aisha's mouth popped open. "Is it really? I always thought Bram was short for Abraham."

Despite working together for over three months, there was still so much she didn't know about him. He probably knew eight thousand times more about her, thanks to her nonstop chatter.

"Should we all sit together?" Bram asked, and the roaring in Aisha's chest was back.

Stop being silly. This is a lunch between colleagues, not a date.

"We would, but this is partially a work meeting." Darcey met

Bram's eyes again, and another look passed between them. "I need to get Krista's opinion on a few things about a case."

Though she might not know his full name, she did know Bram's face. Yet despite the dozens of expressions she'd seen on his face at work—boredom, frustration, joy—none of it fit into what his face was doing right now.

Was he disappointed?

It doesn't matter if he wants to sit with Darcey. He's just a friend.

Her racing heart, however, didn't seem to be listening.

TWELVE

BRAM

It was only because he'd known Darcey since they were both in diapers that Bram didn't strangle her the second her back was turned.

The look she'd given him could only mean one thing: she was here to talk to Krista about the Lowther case. Something must have happened, but she couldn't tell Bram, that much was clear.

Whatever was happening with Aisha next to him, however, was much less clear.

The second Krista and Darcey walked away, the cloud that had been darkening Aisha's expression since she'd spotted her friend suddenly disappeared, like the sun coming out again after the rain. She turned to Bram with a slight chuckle. "I'd much rather be talking about fish than about law stuff, wouldn't you?"

"Were we talking about fish?" His lips ticked up, grateful to be here with her and not on his own. Alone, he would have spent the afternoon brooding about Darcey's not-so-subtle hint that the case against Lowther Yachts was getting serious. With Aisha here, she'd pull him out of his funk in a matter of minutes. "I hope you weren't planning on ordering any. Seems a little bit like cannibalism."

Her face scrunched up as she wrinkled her nose. "Would you

laugh at me if I told you I haven't had fish since I started working at LCRA?"

She'd never been more adorable, and he was sure it was obvious on his face what he was thinking. A quick glance at Darcey revealed a smirk on his friend's face that let him know she could tell. Darcey could always tell.

His eyes slid back to Aisha, and he fought to keep his smile small and not grin like a fool the way his heart wanted to do. "As long as you don't hate me if I tell you that I have."

Aisha's laugh rang out in the small restaurant. People must have been looking, but Bram was too focused on her to notice. Something about seeing her outside of the aquarium's offices made her even more expansive, more full of life. Full of everything he wished he could have more of. She was free in a way he could only hope he could be. Even in that horrible gray suit she was clearly uncomfortable in.

A server came by to take their order, and they both got sandwiches. Made from cows, not fish.

When the woman walked back into the kitchen, Aisha turned to Bram, her eyes alight with mischief. "So . . . Wellington?"

He groaned and hid his face behind his hands. "Is there any possible way you'd forget you ever heard that?"

"Nope."

Face heating, he peeked through his fingers. She looked thrilled.

When he didn't say anything, she started to stand. "Should I just go ask Darcey about—"

"No, don't." Instinctively, he reached out to grab her arm and stop her. The warmth of the contact took him by surprise, and he pulled his hand away like he'd been burned.

It was the first time he'd been the one to initiate contact. Every other time was Aisha's exuberant hugging. He wondered if she even noticed. "I'll tell you."

She settled back in her chair and placed her chin on her intertwined fingers. Eyes and smile wide, she looked like she was waiting for the gift of a lifetime.

He took a deep breath. "I went through this phase when I was four or five where I only wore rain boots."

There was a moment of silence, then she blinked and drew her eyebrows together. "That's it?"

"Exactly. I only wore rain boots. Nothing else."

Her dark eyes widened, and that same bright, bold laughter echoed again around the restaurant. Twice in one day.

Despite the vice of embarrassment tightening around his chest, Bram had to laugh as well. "It was only in my room, so my parents didn't really notice. But one night they had a dinner party, and I came downstairs like that, and they, uh, didn't take it so well." He left out the part where he'd escaped from his nanny, the third in three months, and that his mother had fired her on the spot in front of everyone. A rare breach in the smooth civility she always projected that still stuck with him decades later. "Darcey wasn't even there, but she remembers her parents talking about it, so she gave me the nickname."

"I wish I had a nickname." This was said the way Aisha said a lot of things, in a dreamy, faraway voice, while her head was still perched on her hands. With little curls that had escaped her hair clips floating like a halo around her face, she looked like some Renaissance angel.

"I like your name." Hmm, when had his voice dropped an octave? He cleared his throat. "It suits you. It sounds like a song."

This lit up her eyes. "Did you know it's a French song?"

He shook his head.

Pulling out her phone, she scooted her chair closer to him. Trying to focus on that and not the smell of her shampoo invading his senses, Bram peered down at it. A track called *Aïcha* was on the screen.

"It's not spelled the same." She held out a wireless earphone. "You want to listen?"

"Sure." It was ridiculous to get this excited about her sharing a song with him. She always had music playing in her office, but this was different from the fast-paced dance music she played when focusing on a design on her computer, or the slow classical she preferred on Mondays.

"I can explain what the lyrics mean, if you want."

"I'll be ok." He considered mentioning he spoke French almost fluently, thanks to summers in Europe and a parade of au pairs once he was past the age for a nanny, but this didn't seem like the right time to bring it up. "It's very . . . French."

She giggled, and he handed back the earphone. "And very nineties. It came out a few years after I was born, so everyone in France always sang it to me when they met me."

"Did that annoy you?"

She raised an eyebrow, a smile tugging at the edge of her lips. "To have people burst into song when they meet me? What do you think?"

Shaking his head, he let out a low chuckle. It seemed she'd always been this fun. Had always been allowed to be, unlike him. His mother had banned rain boots entirely from the house after the "incident."

"So why is your name not spelled like the song, if that's the French way?"

Something in her eyes dimmed just a little. "My mom was Algerian, like the singer. It's what she wanted, but my dad said spelled that way would be too hard for Americans to pronounce." She let out a short, hard laugh he'd never heard from her before. "She fought with him about everything, even my name. But he was just thinking of what would be easier for me later on."

Goosebumps prickled up Bram's arms, and he leaned back in his chair.

This was the first time he'd ever heard about this. In the few short months he'd known her, Bram had heard all about her friends, and her dad, and the animals at the shelter. Literally every-thing and everyone else, except her mother.

Their food arrived, which gave him a moment to think about what to say. It was hard to picture Aisha mad at anyone, or holding a grudge. But that cold little laugh let him know there was more to the story with her mother than her cheery demeanor would like for him to believe.

Maybe she wasn't as free as she seemed. Maybe she'd actually understand his complicated family dynamics.

Maybe she'd actually like me despite all the reasons she shouldn't.

Aisha bit into her meatball parm and groaned. "Oh, this is much better than fish."

"How would you know if you haven't eaten it in over a year?" When Bram tried his own sandwich, he let out a similar involuntary sound. "Okay, yeah, this is amazing."

They ate in silence for a few minutes, concentrating on the unexpectedly good food.

"So, um, how long have you known Darcey?" Aisha bit into a fry, like she might be worried about the answer.

Something in Bram's chest lit up. *Was it possible she might be jealous?* "My entire life."

Her expression went dreamy again. "That must be nice. I didn't have friends until I moved here."

"Really? I find that hard to believe."

She popped another fry into her mouth. "I mean, I had friends at school and everything. But my dad didn't speak French that well, so he didn't really talk to the other parents. I never went to anyone's house."

"He didn't speak French?" He took a bite of his sandwich.

She shook her head. "He didn't need much French in Paris. There were enough English-speakers for him to get by."

"What did he do there?"

She wiped her mouth with a napkin and took so long answering he wasn't sure she was going to. "He was an artist."

"An artist?" That made so much sense. She had a great eye for design, and he'd watched her sketch in the corners of her notebook during boring staff meetings. But she'd never mentioned it before. "I thought he worked in insurance."

"You remember that?" Her eyes sparkled. "I mentioned it like, once, ages ago."

"I remember everything you tell me."

She snorted and rolled her eyes. "You must have a memory the size of Fort Knox. I tell you a lot of things."

There was also the fact that Bram's grandfather had been the one to start the insurance company where her dad worked, but that didn't seem like the way to introduce her to his complicated family history.

Everyone always changed when they found out he was a Lowther. Either they wanted something from him, or had some reason to hate his family, or they thought they knew all about him already. Or all three, in the case of one particularly nasty ex.

Which was why he didn't want to think about how Aisha might react to finding out. For months she'd known him as Bram Howard, not Bramwell Lowther. Telling her about his family would inevitably shift something between them that he wasn't ready to change.

"I'm sure Krista and Brooke remember everything too. Why wouldn't I?"

There was a slight flush to her cheek, and she concentrated on picking out another fry, discarding one that was too small, and another that was too long. Bram waited, hoping the silence would let her know that he had the space to hold whatever chaos she was holding inside of her. There was so much empty space inside of him, just waiting to be filled up by her exuberance.

"I've just had a lot of jobs." She kept her eyes on her plate. "Made a lot of work friends. None of them ever seemed as interested in me as you are."

"Oh?"

Her head shot up, her eyes wide. "Not interested like, *interested* in me. Obviously."

"Obviously." The smile on his face appeared without him thinking, the same friendly, teasing one he always seemed to have around her. "Horrible bog creature that you are."

She threw a napkin at him and he laughed. Running a hand over her hair, she did that move of hers where she checked that the clip that tied back her wavy hair was still in place, and then smoothed out her hair over one shoulder.

It absolutely killed him every time.

"But seriously, I've never had a work friend like you before," she said.

"You mean one that no one else can outshine?" Heart pounding away in his ears, he put on his cockiest smile.

With a snort, Aisha sat back in her chair and shook her head. "I shouldn't have said that. It's not like your big head needed any more compliments."

"Excuse me?" He held a hand to his chest in mock offense. "I'm the one with the big head? And what about Doctor Don't Block My Super Important Plaques With Your Fundraising Poster?"

It was like he'd thrown a light switch. Her eyes landed on her plate, and she fiddled with her napkin.

Yikes, even the mention of his name makes her dim that sparkle. He did his best to tamp down his jealousy and stay in playful friend mode.

If he'd had any doubt before today that her heart was set on

Cody, then this confirmed it. She wanted to become this other person for him, and there was nothing Bram could do about it.

Well, maybe not nothing. She was here at lunch with him, after all, not Cody.

"I'm sorry. I didn't mean to tease you about Cody. It's not fair." He ran his hands through his hair, making it extra tousled. "I'm just thinking about this gala I'm supposed to plan. My head isn't feeling big right now. It's feeling full and stressed."

"Yes, the gala. That's what we're here to talk about." Looking at her watch, she made a face. "Except we probably have to get back to the aquarium."

She waved to the server, who brought over the check, then she pulled out her wallet from her purse. Unlike her drab gray suit, the whale-shaped blue bag was still typically Aisha.

"I've got this."

"No, it's fine." Her gaze was steady, more serious than it usually was. Like the mention of her mother, he was taken aback by the unexpected shift in her tone. "I can pay my own way."

He backed down immediately with a shrug that he hoped was nonchalant. "Okay."

Her shoulders relaxed, as if she'd been ready for a fight. She pulled out a few bills and shook her head. "We didn't talk about the gala at all, thanks to me and my big mouth babbling away."

"I don't mind. I'll figure it out."

"No, we need a brainstorming session. A real one."

More time with Aisha? "I'd like that."

"An hour wouldn't have been enough anyway."

Had it already been an hour? It was easy to get wrapped up in Aisha. The time had flown by in what felt like minutes. It was only the worry of the gala hanging over him and Darcey's sneaky glances at their table that kept it from being a perfect lunch.

Well, that and the fact Aisha was as uninterested in him as she thought he was in her. There'd been little hints that maybe she was jealous of Darcey, but based on what Aisha had shared with him, it was more likely she was jealous of the childhood he'd had. Not because of his wealth, which he knew he'd have to figure out a way to tell her about soon, but because he'd had a friend.

If all they ever were was friends, Bram could be happy with that. Really.

Though he couldn't help but wish for more.

Maybe he'd stop by Stella's tank once they were back at work. One more wish couldn't hurt.

FOURTEEN
AISHA

On the drive back to the aquarium, Aisha was determined to help Bram with his gala. They spent the short trip brainstorming, discussing themes and checklists, things that had worked at his previous jobs and things that hadn't.

The marketing for this would be different from anything Aisha had done before. It targeted their existing members, but it would also be open to the public to buy tickets.

Aisha's jaw hit the floor when he told her how much he thought they would charge.

"For one ticket? No one can afford that."

He shifted in his seat, his gaze not wavering from the road in front of him. "The kinds of donors we want to attract can afford it. It'll be tax deductible."

Embarrassment spread hot and thick through her chest. Of course this wasn't for someone like her. This was for the kind of people who tried to pay the least amount of tax possible by supporting causes like this.

She shouldn't care, especially not when Bram belonged to that world. For whatever reason, he was still trying to hide it. Between the casual references to places in Europe he'd been and owning one of the most expensive electric cars on the market, it hadn't taken long for her to piece it together. Then, a few weeks ago, she'd overheard someone in accounting refer to Bram Lowther, and the final piece of the puzzle had clicked into place. She didn't know who the Lowthers were, but if he went by Howard at work, there had to be a reason.

She'd opened up a little more than she'd intended at lunch, unable to stop the words from flowing. There'd been a vague hope in the back of her mind while babbling away that maybe he'd finally tell her about his family. About being a Lowther, whatever that meant.

Instead, she'd made it awkward with that whole "you're not interested in me" thing, which he'd been quick to make a joke about to spare her any more embarrassment by confirming it.

Of course he wouldn't be interested in her. The nearly inaudible hum of the absurdly expensive electric car they were currently in was evidence enough of how different they were, how differently they'd grown up. It didn't mean he was anything like her mom, but in her experience, that world didn't easily welcome someone like her.

Race was a part of it, without a doubt, but it was more than that. With her features a blend of her Algerian mother and half-Black father, Aisha's light-brown, tawny skin and hair that fell in waves instead of tight curls meant she was often mistaken for Italian. She knew she passed through life differently than those with much darker skin, and often stumbled when asked where her family was from. Her dad was from South Carolina, so that's what she usually said. But she'd been born in France to an Algerian mother, and leaving that out of her story sometimes felt like a lie.

Until she remembered her own mother's upper-class family hadn't wanted her despite looking more like them than like her father. Why would Bram's be any different?

They hit a bump in the road, and it knocked her back into the conversation. Whatever her feelings about the wealthy families in this state, it was her job to tell them about this gala. "I'll start working on some ideas for invitations and online promotion."

This brought a smile to Bram's face. Not the big one that would crinkle the corners of his eyes, but a smaller one. "Thanks, Aisha."

He inhaled slowly, like he was going to say something important. She braced herself for the revelation he'd been holding back from her.

"Would you be willing to help me out with more than just the brainstorming and marketing?"

"Oh." She wasn't sure what to say. They'd arrived back at LCRA, and he pulled into his parking spot next to the charger. When he turned off the car, his azure eyes met hers, and her stomach fluttered. "You mean like helping organize things?"

"I know you have a lot to do, so if you don't have the time, I totally understand." His hands flexed on the steering wheel.

"It's not that." She sat up a little straighter, which made her skirt ride up, and she tugged it back down. "I've just never done something like this before. Brooke and Krista are the planners. I'm the creative one."

That's who she was, who she'd always been in their little trio. The flighty, expressive one to balance out Brooke and Krista's more serious tendencies. The one who showed up fifteen minutes late but brought a hundred helium balloons. The one who'd had fifteen different jobs since graduating from college and no retirement savings.

Turning to face her, Bram raised an eyebrow. "Because all the social media posts and website updates and email campaigns and everything else you do doesn't take planning?"

"That's different." When he opened his mouth to argue, she rushed on. "Like, I'm still just going by someone else's plan. How often to post, which keywords to use, updating the tracker for finance. The rules are already there. I'm just following them."

Her art was more spontaneous. Sometimes she'd go for weeks without painting at all, then make five canvases over a single weekend. Her dad had been the same way, and he'd eventually had to get a real job. Even if none of them had lasted, Aisha had always had jobs to pay the bills. Did she wish she had more time to paint and draw? Of course. But in no version of her messy life did she want to rely solely on her art to pay her bills. So she avoided the temptation entirely and had never even tried to get paid for it.

Bram smirked. "I'm pretty sure you'll be able to handle it. It definitely requires an artistic eye. The colors, the tablecloths, the seating arrangements."

Oh, he wasn't being fair. "That does sound pretty fun . . . "

"The food."

She laughed. "Okay, you've convinced me."

"Really?" He sounded thrilled.

"Yeah. And I think it'll help with Cody."

He frowned at this. "You mean with his research? Yeah, that's the whole point of the gala."

"No, I mean helping you plan something like this will show him my more serious, organized side."

There was a beat of silence in the car before Bram raised an eyebrow and his lips curved up.

She rolled her eyes. "I know what you're thinking. I don't even have a serious, organized side." It's what she'd been trying to show for weeks, whenever Cody was around. It was why she'd spent two hours that morning cleaning up her desk, though she hadn't made much progress.

"No, that's not what I was going to say." Eyes fixed on hers, Bram's voice was soft. "I was going to say, if he doesn't already see how great you are, why spend the effort trying to be something else?"

A fluttery whisper trickled through her stomach. It was something Krista would have said in her logical way, or Brooke in her encouraging, soothing voice.

It felt entirely different when Bram said it, looking at her like that.

He's a friend. That's why he said it. If he'd been interested, he would have made a move by now. In previous jobs, the guys she worked with hadn't waited months to ask her out. They'd do it within the first few days, first week max. And that was usually about how long it took for things to fizzle out. Since she never stayed anywhere long, it wasn't an issue. Most guys she didn't even bother mentioning to her friends. It was all just for fun. Like Aisha.

Now she wanted something serious. With the kind of guy who'd stick around longer than a few weeks, who made her want something to last more than a month. The kind of guy who wasn't eight billion miles above her in the stratosphere like Bram was.

Aisha shifted in her seat. "It's not just for him. This is the longest I've had a job."

It didn't used to bother her. In her thirties and having never been at a job longer than half a year was just who she was. But something had shifted in the past few months since she'd gone full time at LCRA. "I've been wanting to feel settled in a way I never have before."

While Bram's quiet contemplation filled the space between them, she smoothed her hair back over her shoulders. The car was getting hotter the longer they sat in it. "That probably sounds so silly."

"Nothing about you is silly." He reached out a hand like he wanted to put it on her arm, but then pulled back to rest it on the steering wheel. "You can be fun and organized. You can be whimsical and serious. They're not mutually exclusive. It's more interesting to be lots of things rather than just one."

Though he hadn't outright said *she* was interesting, it still felt like a compliment.

She took a deep breath. "So you agree. Helping you will show Cody the other side of me he hasn't seen yet." She stuck out a hand, like he'd done when meeting Krista earlier. "I'm in."

Lips fighting against a smile, he raised an eyebrow and shook her hand. "Glad to have you on board."

FIFTEEN
AISHA

On the way back into the aquarium, Aisha stopped to get her water bottle out of her car. If she was going to spend another five hours in this stuffy suit, she'd need to stay hydrated. It made her afternoon much more comfortable, and it passed in a flash sitting next to Bram as they continued to work on the gala. He'd done these kinds of events so many times, so he had multiple checklists, which was a relief. It was harder for Aisha to mess things up if they were already laid out for her.

Still, her heart beat nervously the more and more tasks he gave her. Like he trusted her completely. Like he thought she could do it.

It must be the suit. He'd said it toned down her sparkle, but that didn't mean he wasn't also taking her more seriously now. Hopefully Cody was thinking the same thing.

Then she got back to her car at the end of the day and discovered she'd left a door cracked. The interior lights had been on for hours, and the battery was dead. Unlike Bram's fancy electric model, Aisha had a used car so old it still had crank windows, but none of the features that would have prevented this.

Typical Aisha. Changing her clothes and organizing her desk wouldn't change who she really was.

On her slow, defeated walk back into the aquarium, Aisha perked up. This might just be Stella answering her wish for more time with Cody. He usually didn't leave until after she did, so maybe she could ask him for a ride. That was a normal thing for a colleague to do, right?

She took the long way around the offices, walking past the tanks in the back where the public couldn't access. This was where the researchers did their experiments and observations. There was a space for their technology as well, and Aisha had done a few videos for social media showing off what they were working on. It was even colder back here, so she was glad to be wearing her suit.

Cody was nowhere to be found, however. Other than passing Sandra from accounting on her way out, the entire area was empty. With a sigh, she made her way back to the offices, considering her options. Brooke and Krista would give her a ride, but they both worked late into the evenings most days. Bram had left before her, and she didn't want to bother him—even though a niggling voice in the back of her head whispered he probably wouldn't mind.

Realizing the only thing to do would be to call a rideshare, she decided she needed a snack first.

Coming into the kitchen, there were a few stray coffee cups still on the Formica tables, but the cramped space was empty. Perfect for getting the madeleines from the top cabinet. She pulled a chair over and stepped onto it.

Being alone wasn't something that bothered her. As an only child, it had been her normal whenever she wasn't with Brooke and Krista. Though her apartment had two bedrooms, she'd never had a roommate. The solitude was nice when she wanted to focus on painting, and being by herself meant she could play whatever music she wanted.

When things were too empty, however, it started to feel like a scary movie. Her imagination would go wild. Especially in the aquarium. Yes, the animals were all in tanks, and none of them were particularly dangerous.

But what if one of them escaped? What if there was something lurking at the very back of the cabinet, and she didn't see it—

"What are you doing?"

With a little yelp, she turned, wobbling dangerously on the chair. In an instant, Cody was at her side, holding the chair steady. Her heart shot into her throat at the thought of falling and him catching her. How romantic would that be?

"Nothing." She smoothed a hand over her hair, checking that her clips were still in place. She may have a massive crush on him, but she wasn't ready to share her madeleines with him. They were just for her and Bram. "I just thought I saw something up here."

Cody took a step back and held out a hand to help her off the chair. Her heart burst into a million tiny pieces that started fluttering around her chest.

When she took his hand, however, the fluttering all stopped. It was nothing but a hand. No electricity, no zing at the contact of their skin. Nothing like the rush of heat she'd felt earlier at the restaurant when Bram had grabbed her arm.

It must be the adrenaline still coursing through her that blocked her from feeling anything else.

"Thanks." Safely back on the floor, she pushed the chair back under the table, squeezing it between the others.

"What did you think you saw?" Cody was looking at the cabinet, not her.

Oh, right, that had been her reason for yelling. Not her imagination running wild, telling her she was about to be attacked by one of the turtles who'd somehow eaten a radioactive mushroom. "Um, a spider."

"Any particular patterns? What shape was the abdomen? What color?" For the first time since he'd started working here, Cody sounded excited.

"I don't remember. It could have just been dust."

Cody frowned, but kept scanning the top of the cabinets.

"I didn't know you knew so much about spiders." She twirled the end of a strand of hair around her finger, then dropped it, worried it made her look vapid. "I thought your specialty was starfish."

"Sea stars." His eyes darted back to hers, criticism lacing his tone.

You didn't work at an aquarium for over a year without learning this was the correct term, but she'd gotten used to calling Stella a starfish for the social media campaign. Marketing was about meeting the public where they were. "Wish Upon A Sea Star" didn't sound nearly as good as "Wish Upon A Starfish."

"Sea stars," she repeated dutifully, her breath catching to see how he'd react.

Nothing. His attention was entirely on the cabinets. "During my zoology degree, I considered entomology as a specialty. I didn't focus on echinoderms until my doctorate."

"What made you decide to focus on them?" This was the longest conversation they'd ever had. Her pulse had picked up again.

"There was a guest lecture about Antarctic sea stars and how they influence the population of sea sponges, and it was simply fascinating."

"Isn't that great how one little thing can change how you see things?" Like how she hoped these little interactions would lead to Cody seeing her differently. Helping with the gala would speed that up even more. First, he had to know she was even doing it.

"You mean like the butterfly effect?" He turned, his gaze now finally on her.

"Exactly." An idea popped into her head. "That'd be a great theme for the gala."

Instead of the excited response she'd have gotten from Bram, all Cody did was furrow his brow and push up his glasses. "We don't have any butterflies here."

"Yes, but it's not about the animal, it's about the impact." Now that the idea was there, she had to let it flow. "When people think of the butterfly effect and see it at the gala, they'll know their small participation made a big impact for us. Don't you see?"

His lips turned down. "Not really."

As much as this stung, she tried not to dwell, tried not to think about what Bram had said in the car. *If he doesn't already see how great you are, why spend the effort trying to be something else?*

But he'd also said she could be lots of things, including organized and serious. This was her chance to show that side of herself to Cody.

"You will once you see it. I'm helping with the gala, all the organization and planning, not just the marketing."

"Oh." He considered this. "Is that your job?"

"Not really, but I want the event to be a success." She took a deep breath, calming herself so she sounded less scattered. "This is a big opportunity for the aquarium to fund our research. So that your important work can continue."

This was meant to be a compliment, but he sighed and rubbed the bridge of his nose beneath his glasses. "I know we have to have these kinds of events, but it's just not my thing. Making small talk with all those people sounds terrible."

Warmth spread through her chest. He'd never shared anything personal like that with her before. She was suddenly very aware of her hands and had no idea what to do with them. Worried she'd start flapping them around like a butterfly, she settled for clasping them behind her back.

"I'll make sure you have fun. Don't worry."

Then, he smiled at her. Smiled!

Trying to look and sound as casual as possible, she leaned against the counter. "Do you live anywhere near Adamsville?"

"Not really. Why?"

The words were on the tip of her tongue, and she opened her mouth to ask, but at the last second, she snapped her lips shut. One personal tidbit didn't mean he liked her. One smile didn't mean he'd agree to drive out of his way just to help her out. On the zero to ten scale of falling in love, this interaction was about zero point five. Barely a start.

Besides, she wasn't really that important to anyone outside of her friends and her dad.

And maybe Bram?

"Oh, I was just curious." She stood up straight and cleared her throat. "I volunteer at an animal shelter there, and we're having an adoption event in a few weeks. In case you're in the market for a new pet."

His expression was unreadable, a blank canvas while his eyes still roamed the shelves, searching for the nonexistent spider.

"I'm allergic." With a nod, as if he was finally satisfied there were no spiders lurking, he turned toward the door. "Have a good night."

Before she could even reply, he walked out. Expecting to feel upset about missing her chance to ask him for a ride, she was surprised at how relieved she was to avoid more stilted small talk. The interaction had been what she'd wished for, and she'd learned a little more about him. But that drive to impress him, to catch his attention, had cooled.

Typical Aisha. If she'd been anyone else, it would be unnerving to realize her feelings could shift so suddenly.

What was actually unnerving was the desire to call Bram and ask him for a ride instead.

SIXTEEN
AISHA

The mural was finally done.

Only four days later than planned wasn't too bad. Thursday instead of Sunday. It was a delay, which was typical for her, but her shortest one ever. That was progress, wasn't it?

Aisha stepped back to take a picture of the finished piece to send to her dad, pleased with how the colors had turned out. Lately she'd been obsessed with a very particular shade of blue that filled the tanks at the aquarium when the lights hit them just right. It was also almost the same color as Bram's eyes, but that was just a coincidence. After working with him all afternoon on the email campaigns for the gala, it was only natural that his eyes would be on her mind.

The sky in this mural was definitely the color of water, however, not his eyes.

"This looks great." Brooke slung an arm over Aisha's shoulder. It was just her tonight at the shelter, while Ethan was out for drinks with his old firefighter crew. "Your best work yet, I'd say."

"Thanks." It was hard to disagree when Aisha was already so proud of how it turned out. That didn't happen with all of her pieces. "I'm sorry it took longer than planned."

Her friend waved the apology away, then crossed to the built-in desk that separated the reception area from the back of the shelter. A stack of mail lay perfectly perpendicular to the keyboard. There was nothing else on the desk, no stray papers, no knick-knacks waiting to topple over a cup of hot chocolate.

"I mean it." Aisha followed Brooke, then put her elbows up on the counter and propped her head in her hands. "I'm trying to be better about things like this. More organized."

Even after two days of cleaning, Aisha's desk at work still didn't look this nice. There were piles of things everywhere, mostly on the floor, while she sorted through them. Neat piles, at least. Well, neater than they'd been last week.

With her grandmother's letter opener, Brooke ripped open the first envelope on the stack. "It's really fine. I wasn't on any particular timeline." Her eyes scanned the contents of the letter, then darted to Aisha as she laid it to one side. "If you'd have let me pay you, there'd have been a contract with a deadline. Is that what you want?"

"Yes." Sighing, Aisha dropped her head into her hands. "I mean, no, I don't want to be paid. But I do want deadlines."

Since she was old enough to hold a paintbrush, Aisha had never wanted to be paid for her art. Even as a kid, she'd seen how much stress it was on her dad to wait to see if a piece he'd spent weeks on would sell. The money didn't matter to him when he'd been with Aisha's mom, but it had mattered a lot once she'd left. Then there hadn't been much money at all until they'd moved back to South Carolina. Once he'd taken the job with the insurance company his brother worked for, Aisha had never seen him paint again.

"I'll remember that for next time." A funny little smile danced across Brooke's face before she looked down at the pile of mail again and picked up the next envelope. "Where did this sudden urge for organization and deadlines come from? Is this Cody's influence?"

"In a way." Smoothing her hands along the counter, Aisha was impressed but not surprised at how dust and animal-hair free it was. Was there some special product Brooke used to keep it from coming back, or did she just clean multiple times a day? Knowing Brooke, it was probably the latter. "More like, I need to be more organized so that he'll take me seriously and notice me."

"I thought he already did notice you." The letter in Brooke's hand joined the previous one as a neat stack began to form. "He asked you for that favor a few days ago."

"Well, yeah, he notices me. Just not the way I want him to."

Do you still want him to? The coolness that had started to creep in after the spider incident in the kitchen was still there. Spending more time with Bram was making it hard to remember why she'd been so fixated on Cody for months.

Be serious, Aisha. The only reason she was around Bram more was for work. It wasn't romantic. He wasn't an option, and she'd only end up heartbroken if she let herself think otherwise. Cody was the safer choice, the more reasonable choice. She couldn't abandon her efforts now, or she'd be no better than she'd always been. Flighty, changeable, unsteady. That's not who she wanted to be anymore.

"I don't think being more organized will change anything." There were now three different tidy stacks of opened mail in front of Brooke. "If he doesn't already see how great you are, why spend the effort trying to be something else?"

The floor beneath Aisha's feet dropped away, and she leaned against the counter. It was the same thing Bram had said in the car. To hear her friend say it was just more proof Bram hadn't meant anything more by it.

More proof that she had to go all in on pursuing Cody, no matter how lukewarm his hand on her arm had left her.

"Cody's the one I want," she said, not sure if she was trying to convince Brooke or herself. When Brooke looked up from her mail sorting, her gaze lingered on Aisha's serious face, and she lifted her chin in response. "I want something steady and real, like what you have with Ethan."

Brooke snorted. "Things didn't exactly start out that way."

A smile spread across Aisha's face. "You mean because of how you met or because of the love potion?"

There was a flush to her friend's cheeks as she rolled her eyes in response. "Both." She turned away from her neatly sorted mail and tapped on the keyboard.

"I don't mean just Ethan. I mean everything." With one hand, Aisha gestured around the shelter. "You took this place from the brink of disaster to something amazing."

"I had a lot of help."

"I have help with Cody." Uncertainty trickled through her chest. How much should she say about Bram? "I'm helping someone at work plan something big."

"Oh?" Pulling her eyes away from the computer screen to look at Aisha, Brooke's eyebrows shot up. "What is it?"

Relief washed over her that she hadn't asked about *who*. "A gala. I'll make sure you and Krista get all the details."

"I'm sure it'll be great." Her gaze returned to the computer and then she frowned. "As long as I don't have to work. You're not available Saturday morning by any chance, are you?"

Safely away from the topic of Bram, Aisha would have said yes to anything right now. "Sure, what do you need?"

"Can you work a shift?" Brooke tapped on the keyboard. "Our regular person just emailed to say she needs to go out of town for a family emergency. Ethan will be here, but it's our busiest day with five families coming to look at animals so I don't want him to have to be on his own, and I have to be in Beaufort to pick up a new litter of kittens and—"

"Brooke, it's fine. I'm happy to help."

It had taken her friend so long to accept that she couldn't do it all herself that it still took some reminding that she wasn't alone in this. Aisha always seemed to have the opposite issue. Too many people around her taking care of her messes.

It was time for her to start cleaning them up on her own.

"Let me just put away this paint, and you can fill me in on what you need me to do Saturday." She turned away from the desk and headed toward the mural.

"Don't worry about it." Brooke was already beside her, scooping everything up. "You already did so much, painting this whole thing on your own. I'll tidy up."

Aisha hesitated, but only for a second. Keeping the shelter clean was Brooke's job. It didn't mean she didn't think Aisha could handle it.

"Okay." She gave Brooke a hug goodbye. "I'll be here Saturday."

"Thanks. I knew I could count on you."

The words should have given her a boost, but fear followed Aisha out to her car, balling tight in her belly as she drove home.

After months of hearing about the animal shelter in Adamsville, Bram was surprised to see just how small it was. The impression he'd gotten from Aisha's stories was of a huge center with dozens of animals and a constant buzz of activity.

Instead, it was quiet and cozy, with flowers in planters outside and big windows that bathed the reception area with light. A rug patterned with paw prints on top of a bright-blue concrete floor and a clock in the shape of a cat with a swishing tail were just what you'd expect to see in an animal shelter.

The mural, however, was unlike anything Bram had ever seen.

It took up the entire wall facing the door. The colors were bright, and the style was semi-abstract. He could recognize the grass and the trees and the sky, but it was all just a little bigger or smaller than it would be in real life, the colors two or three shades off from what you'd see in nature.

It was breathtaking, and so clearly Aisha's work, Bram had trouble breathing for a moment.

"Hi, Bram!" Aisha bounced into view, her blazing beauty the only thing that could have stolen his attention away from the impressive mural. Her earrings today were large daisies, and her shirt was a bright yellow. She looked like a sunny summer day that Bram wanted to bask in for hours.

Today he'd actually get the chance to do that. After planning what he could at the aquarium itself for the past few days, it was time to start visiting vendors for things like tables and flowers.

Could he have done this on his own during the week? Probably.

Did he push it until the weekend so that Aisha could come with him? Obviously.

So here he was in Adamsville on a Saturday afternoon, picking her up from her shift at the animal shelter he'd heard so much about. Though she'd never mentioned the mural.

"Is this yours?" He gestured to the wall, his voice unusually shaky. Despite practically screaming Aisha from the swish of brushstrokes to the blue that reminded him of the aquarium tanks, he might be wrong.

"Yeah, I finished it up a few days ago."

"I didn't know you painted. You never mentioned it." Of course she was always sketching, but she studied graphic design and worked in marketing. This was something beyond that, something that spoke to years of study and practice. She'd said her dad was an artist, and Bram wondered if he painted as well.

Her hands went to her hair, like they wanted to adjust clips that weren't there. Today, her dark waves were loose and flowing free over her shoulders. "It's just something I do for fun, for friends. Did you see the little paw prints along the bottom?" She bounded over to point out the only true-to-life details on the wall. "Your fish fundraising poster gave me the idea. Every time an animal gets adopted, their paw print goes on the wall."

"That's brilliant."

She straightened and tucked her hair behind her ears. "It was your idea for the poster. I just adapted it for the shelter."

It was infuriating sometimes how humble she was. At first he thought it was just something she did in front of Cody, but it was honestly all the time. While today's main mission was to get some final rental details finalized, Bram now had a new, secondary one: get Aisha to see how amazing she was.

"It's incredible."

She beamed, then reached behind the counter to grab her purse.

"Let me just tell Ethan I'm leaving. He'll be on his own until Brooke comes to pick him up later."

While Bram knew who Ethan was thanks to all of Aisha's stories about her friends, it was still a shock to see the tall, extremely muscled former firefighter walk into the reception area.

"Hey." He stuck out his hand, and Bram shook it, pretending not to notice how very small his own hand felt as Ethan wrapped it in his firm grip. "I'm Ethan."

"Bram. Nice to meet you."

In college, Bram swam and played tennis, and had kept doing both through his twenties. Now in his early thirties, he thought he still looked pretty good. But there was a big difference between staying in shape and whatever Ethan was.

"You work at the aquarium with Aisha?" Ethan was giving him the same kind of look Bram used to give Darcey's dates when they were in high school. A blend of suspiciously protective and mildly threatening.

Swallowing back his sudden urge to puff up his chest, Bram nodded. "We have some work to do to prepare for an event in a few weeks." He turned to Aisha. "Ready?"

"Yes." She stepped toward him, then turned on her heel. "Wait. I just want to say goodbye to one little guy. Come meet him."

When he opened his mouth to protest, Aisha grabbed his hand and pulled him into the back. He glanced at Ethan, who just shook his head with a smile on his face. It was an expression Bram could fully understand. Trying to escape Aisha's whirlwind was point-less, and it was easier to just go along for the ride.

He also had no intention of letting go of her hand.

Aisha led him into a large hallway lined with kennels. They were all full, mostly dogs but a few cats as well.

"Look how cute this one is." Still holding his hand, she brought him in front of the largest kennel, where a light-brown dog with black ears was sleeping with his head on his paws. The little paw-print shaped chalkboard on the kennel read "Brownie – male, possible German shepherd/bloodhound mix." Unlike so many in his parents' circle, Bram's family had never had dogs. This one looked . . . big.

"He is a very handsome animal."

Aisha snickered. "Is that how you talk about dogs?"

"How am I supposed to talk about them?" His hand was on fire where it touched hers. It was amazing he could even talk right now, let alone speak sensibly about an animal he'd never seen before.

She rolled her eyes. "You say he's the cutest doggo. Obviously."

His lips twitched. "Obviously."

She dropped his hand and squatted so her head was level with the cage. The dog woke up and yawned.

"Careful." He had to stop himself from pulling her away.

She stood up and tilted her head. "Are you afraid of dogs, Bram?"

"Not afraid, exactly." He rubbed the back of his neck. "I'm just not used to them."

"Your family never had dogs?"

"No. You seem surprised at that."

"It's just . . . " She tilted her head the other way, mimicking some of the dogs in the other kennels who were watching them closely. "You seem like the kind of person whose family had a few generations of purebred hunting dogs. Not the mutts most people around here have."

It was dangerously close to the truth. At least she'd gotten the vibe right, even if the animal wasn't.

"My parents don't hunt." Shifting on his feet, he bit his lip. She didn't sound jealous or insulted about it, but that didn't mean she wouldn't be. Everyone was, eventually. "Though they do have some horses."

Her eyes lit up with delight. "I bet you look really good in riding boots."

Something in his chest swelled, and fire prickled along his arms. "Thanks."

Her hair had fallen into her face, and she swept it back over her shoulder. "So you're not scared of horses, even though they're way bigger than dogs."

"They don't bite and jump on you." He paused. "Well, not usually."

"Is there a 'my horse bit me during a polo match' story I need to hear?" She clasped her hands together in anticipation.

Now his skin was practically burning. She was so close to the truth, should he just blurt it out? "I didn't play polo."

She waited, still petting the sleeping dog, with a small, mischievous smile on her face.

"My brother did."

"Ha! I knew it." She shook her head, the smile still on her face, but her eyes had turned shrewd. "You don't have to hide all that from me."

Panic laced through him. *This is it.* "Hide what?"

Aisha's sunny expression turned serious. Not in the dimming, minimizing way it did around Cody. More like she was hurt or angry or both.

He would give anything to never see that look on her face again.

"Bram, I know your last name isn't really Howard. I overheard Sandra in accounting call you that once when she was talking to Cody. I don't know why you feel like you can't be yourself at work, but if you trust me enough to help you with the gala, I hope you can trust me with this too."

Guilt licked at his chest. He'd been dancing around it long enough. It hadn't been lying exactly, but if he answered with anything other than the truth right now, it would be.

"I don't like hiding, but I feel like I have to." Rubbing his neck, he let out a sigh and leaned back against the wall, as far from the kennels as possible. The ever-present boulder in his stomach from avoiding the topic with Aisha was rolling around uneasily. "People tend to treat me differently when they know my family, uh, isn't exactly struggling."

This was how he was raised to talk about it. Once when he was little, he asked his parents if they were rich, and you'd have thought he'd said a swear word. "We do well enough for ourselves" was how his mother had phrased it then. Over the years he'd picked up all sorts of euphemisms.

"You mean they ask for favors?" Aisha's eyes were still narrowed, but she waggled her eyebrows a little. "Like donating a million dollars to an animal shelter her friend runs?"

He chuckled, some of the tension leaving his body. "Something like that. Or they ask for a yacht."

Her face scrunched up in confusion at this.

"My family, um, makes yachts. You've heard of Lowther Yachts?"

"I know the name from the donor lists." She raised a sardonic eyebrow. "But yachting isn't really something I do much of."

"Me neither, not since I learned about all the pollution it creates." He shifted and let his hand rest on the nearest cage. The cat inside it glared at him, but stayed put. "It's getting better, with more eco-conscious practices, but it's still being out in the water when you don't really need to be. Hurting marine life."

She was quiet for a moment as she stroked Brownie and considered what he'd said. "It must make things awkward with your family that you work at the aquarium. Is that why they donate?"

His stomach twisted. "It's a little more complicated than that."

Suddenly, there was a chorus of barks as a squirrel appeared in a nearby window. The noise echoed in the small space, and both Bram and Aisha put their hands over their ears, laughing a little at just how loud it had gotten.

Ethan appeared, probably to check what was going on, but Aisha waved him away. It took another few minutes for all the dogs to quiet down. Brownie had remained mostly calm throughout the whole thing, letting out a single low howl, more like he was telling off the other dogs than joining in their commotion.

"Well, that was fun." Aisha dropped her hand from her ears

and brushed her hands on her paint-splattered jeans before snagging Bram's gaze. "You shouldn't assume people can't tell you come from money, even if you don't say anything."

His throat tightened. "How did you know?"

"Probably the same way you knew about my crush on Cody." A smile ticked up at the corner of her lips. "I pay attention."

At the mention of Cody, Bram felt his face pull down automatically into a frown. "Am I really that obvious?"

"Let's just say I'm more attuned to it than others, given my history." A flush spread across her cheeks, and she looked unsettled, like she'd said too much. "There were hints, but not enough if you didn't know what to look for. The car. The shoes. The madeleines flown in from France."

Something in his chest lit up at the mention of the snack. She had no clue it was all for her. "I avoid asking them for favors unless I know it'll help someone else. I haven't touched my parents' money since I graduated from college, but I do spend what I earn myself on things that matter to me."

"That makes sense." She smiled and trailed her fingers along the edge of a cage for a kitten to bat at. "That's part of why we're friends. If you *had* flaunted it or been a jerk about it, I'd have ignored you from day one. I have zero tolerance for uppity rich people."

He laughed again, but he was now beyond curious about what in her history had turned her off to what his mother would call "families of substance." An ex-boyfriend who was gross about money? Fired from a job because of an acquisition? There were endless ways people like his family could ruin lives.

"I'm glad someone finally appreciates my humility. I work so hard on it."

That got a bark of a laugh out of Aisha that scared the kitten she was playing with.

Bram looked at his watch. "We should probably get going."

"Right." She dropped her hand from the kitten's cage then

glanced between Bram and Brownie. "Aren't you going to pet this handsome animal?"

Heart thumping for reasons entirely unrelated to Aisha, he raised an eyebrow. "Was I magically supposed to get over my fear in the past five minutes?"

"I knew you were actually afraid." She gasped, then got that look on her face he was so used to seeing. The one that meant she had a brilliant idea she just had to share with him. "You can volunteer here. Then you'll see how great dogs can be."

"Aisha, don't volunteer people without talking to Brooke first, please." Ethan's voice rang out from the reception area, in a tired kind of way that let Bram know this wasn't the first time she'd done this.

"Well, I had to try." She shrugged and gave Brownie a final pat on the head. "Now I'm ready to go."

Without looking back, she headed back out to the reception area. Only once she was gone did Bram bend over and slowly put his hand out. The dog's big ears twitched as he leaned his nose forward to sniff Bram's hand. Apparently finding it acceptable, Brownie licked it. Which Bram actually found a little gross, but Aisha had also made him pet some of the little sharks at the aquarium, and it wasn't that bad in comparison. Bram stroked his hand between the dog's floppy ears, and the animal gave a little satisfied sigh. Something in Bram's heart broke to see that such a small gesture could make the dog so happy.

He'd always liked the horses his family had. There was a reason so many of his development jobs had involved animals.

But this was something different.

"You do seem like a good boy," he said softly to Brownie. "If you're still here at the next adoption event, I'll take you home with me."

The promise came out of nowhere, but as it settled into the air around Bram, it felt right. He might not use his parents' money anymore, but there were plenty of ways they still influenced his life. The fear he'd had most of his life had more to do with the constant refrain from his mother about the hair and mud they tracked everywhere than any actual bad experiences with dogs.

While getting a dog wasn't quite the same as cutting ties with his family the way he should but knew he'd never be able to do, it was at least a start.

Brownie was such a sweet dog, there was every chance in the world he'd be adopted within the week, and he wouldn't go home with Bram. But like his pointless wishes to Stella, Bram couldn't help but let himself believe, just for a moment, that what he truly wanted was actually possible.

NINETEEN

AISHA

A shivery, excited energy ran through Aisha's veins as they drove away from the shelter. As if she didn't have enough reasons to adore him, overhearing Bram's promise to Brownie made her heart melt into a puddle the size of Stella's tank.

Focus, Aisha. Bram is out of your stratosphere. You're here to help him with the gala, so you can get Cody's attention. That's what she wanted, after all.

Right?

"So what's our first stop?" Aisha asked when Bram made the left turn onto the road toward Beaufort. They had a list of vendors to visit, but as usual, she'd left all the finer details to someone else. Just coming along felt like a huge step up in responsibility.

"Renting the table settings."

"You really need my help picking out plates and tablecloths?" Something snagged at the back of her throat, and she coughed.

There was dark black smoke coming from the pickup truck in front of them. Frowning, Bram reached into the console between them and pulled out a bottle of water and handed it to her.

At the brush of Bram's fingers against hers, the shivery excitement in Aisha's veins prickled along her skin. She took a grateful sip. "I'd have thought you'd be an expert at fancy dining."

"More so in my professional life than personal in the last few years."

"You don't see your family that much?"

"I eat dinner with them every week, but I don't go to any of their parties unless I absolutely have to." His lips turned down a little, and she sucked in a breath at the way the light hit his dark waves through the windshield.

Now that she finally knew who his family was and what they did, it was clear why they were important. Yachts–and the kinds of people who bought them—weren't all that common in Aisha's part of South Carolina, but the islands up and down the coast were full of them. She could easily imagine what it meant to be the family that made them for everyone else.

It was just as easy to imagine that a family like that would discard her, the same way her own had. Bram was friendly now, but that didn't mean he always would be. Dinner every week meant they were close, even if he didn't use their money anymore.

Which doesn't matter, since Cody is the one for me.

Convincing herself of this fact would be a lot easier if Bram didn't keep glancing over at her with a worried look in his eyes every time she coughed.

She took another sip of water. "How many of these events have you done?"

Hands gripped tight on the steering wheel, he changed lanes to pass the truck. "Dozens. Each one is different enough to keep it interesting."

"Any favorites?"

As Bram launched into a story about a very wild night at a zoo fundraiser, Aisha relaxed back into the leather seat. Maybe if she kept the conversation focused on work, she would be able to shove her growing feelings for him back into the little hidden part of her where they'd been living for the past three months.

They were colleagues and friends. That was it.

By the time they got to the nondescript warehouse, she'd mostly succeeded. When Bram opened the car door for her, he reached out a hand to help her out. That lingering, shivery, excited energy thrumming through her body wanted her to grab his hand and never let go.

Instead, she slid out on her own and made a beeline for the front door, reassuring herself she had to be imagining the look of disappointment on his face.

A little gasp escaped her when she walked in. From behind her, she heard him chuckle.

"Wow, this is . . . " She spun in a slow circle, taking it all in. "It's like we're inside a genie's lamp."

This got her another chuckle. "I thought you'd like it here."

The exterior might have been bland, but inside was beautiful. Soft white fabric draped across the high ceiling, making it feel like a tent, and a dozen round tables were each set up with different tablecloths, dishes, and beautiful bouquets. Calla lilies reaching for the sky above gold-plated flatware. A vase spilling out sunflowers was set between mint green plates and tiny little silver dessert spoons that glowed yellow from the reflection of the flowers. Roses and candles floating in a bowl of water surrounded by perfectly white china.

It was beautiful—and expensive. Taking it all in, Aisha's pulse ticked up, the way it always did whenever she went somewhere that felt too fancy for her to be there. "I hope I don't break something just by breathing."

Next to her, Bram hummed and let his hand trace along the edge of a dinner plate with an intricate shell pattern that made her think of the bag of madeleines they'd finally polished off the previous day at work. The ones his brother had probably flown in from France while sitting in first class. Maybe even a private jet. Just how much money was there in yachts? Krista would know.

"This is nothing. You should see my mom's collection of

Tiffany lamps. It takes up a whole room, and I've only been in it once, then was never allowed in again."

"Because you broke something?" A little tremor went through her. Now that Bram had finally admitted what Aisha had always suspected—that he was rich in the owning-horses-and-multiple-properties kind of way—she both wanted to hear more about his family and worried that too many details would just bring back bad memories. Like the one time she'd had dinner with her mother's parents and spilled juice all over a silk tablecloth not unlike the one on the table they were standing next to.

"Not even. I just touched it, and she said my oily fingers were going to damage it." He shook his head. "I thought that's what they were for, you know, lighting up a room, but apparently not."

Aisha giggled, her nerves slowly seeping out of her. Even though she now had confirmation that Bram was used to things like this, it sounded like he'd never felt like he really belonged in that world.

That was something she could understand.

"I should have worn something nicer." She looked down at her outfit, which had felt like the right thing that morning but now felt entirely out of place.

"Why? You look great."

"My pants have paint on them."

"Darcey has a similar pair that cost—" He looked down at the plate in front of him. "More than this china set."

The little sticker next to the place setting displayed an alarmingly high price for a single dish. Aisha swallowed her nerves.

Somehow, she knew that if they broke anything, all it would take was a call to his parents and everything would be sorted out. Even if Bram didn't flaunt his wealth, his family was still a part of his life. They were donors to the aquarium. His brother brought him treats from his trips. He'd had dinner with them weekly.

Meanwhile, Aisha hadn't spoken to her mother in almost fifteen years.

As much as she wanted to share part of her own story with Bram, voluntarily living your life apart from the upper echelons of society you were born into was not the same thing as being discarded by them.

Her mother not only came from money, but from the family whose name was synonymous in Algeria with one out of every two non-alcoholic drinks sold. Just like her first name, Aisha's parents had fought over her last name. Her father had wanted to double-barrel the names, giving Aisha a link to both sides of her heritage. Jackson-Kateb. Her mother had insisted on only Jackson.

It was as if she'd already planned to cast aside her daughter at the first opportunity.

Would Bram do the same? No matter how much she might like him, she could never put herself in the position to find out.

Aisha shoved her hands into the back pockets of what apparently could be mistaken for designer pants and reminded herself, for what felt like the hundredth time today, that she was only here as a way to impress Cody. "Are you sure this place is within the budget?"

Running his hands over another plate, this one with a vine pattern, Bram nodded. "I know the guy. We'll get a decent price."

"A family friend?"

Bram's eyes flicked to hers, and his cheeks tinged pink. "Maybe."

An older man appeared in the back of the room and approached them. His exact age was hard to tell. Though he had salt-and-pepper hair, his sun-kissed white skin was pulled just a little too tight to still be naturally wrinkle-free.

"Bram, how nice to see you again," he said in a booming voice. The smile on his face seemed a little too wide to be entirely sincere.

"Nice to see you too, Mr. Lee." Bram held out his hand and shook it.

"How's your mother?"

"Fine, fine."

"Say hello to her for me, will you?"

"Of course."

"And your father? How's his golf game?"

"Ah, not sure I should tell you, or you'll be after him for a makeup game. He's still grumbling about your last one."

"Can't blame a man for trying, can you?"

This was all performed in a hypnotic ballet of handshakes, head nods, and shoulder slaps. Aisha was unable to do anything other than watch, completely mesmerized. The dance of the wealthy, she liked to think of it. A way they could recognize each other without being too obvious. A way to keep people who didn't belong on the outside.

Which was fine. She didn't want to be a part of that world anyway. It didn't want her, and she didn't want it.

Social ballet complete, Bram finally turned to her. "This is Aisha Jackson."

Aisha held out her hand. "Nice to meet you."

Mr. Lee's face was brighter than a Christmas tree as he shook her hand. "Ah, I should have realized that's why you were here. Congratulations."

Bram laughed, but it was a tense, humorless one. "No, no, nothing like that."

It took Aisha a moment to catch up, and when she did, her chest filled with a million candles all lit up at once.

"Aisha is a colleague," Bram said, running a hand along the back of his neck and not quite meeting her eyes. "We're here about an event at the aquarium."

"A gala, actually." Smiling widely at Mr. Lee, she knew her voice was too loud for the small space but had lost all control of it at the moment. "For the aquarium."

Not a wedding, like this guy was clearly hoping for.

It hadn't even crossed her mind that that's what people would think, but now that it was in her head, it was hard not to picture. It may not be her profession, but after nurturing her creativity for years, she was able to take a single spark of an idea and in mere seconds turn it into a full-fledged fantasy. Like how a single nod hello from Cody on his first day had blown up into a massive crush. Now, the mere suggestion that she was Bram's fiancée sent her heart spinning on its axis.

That would be completely ridiculous. Clearly he thought so, too, given his awkward laugh and how he continued to avoid her eyes.

Aisha barely followed the conversation, her head so full of outrageous images.

Bram in a suit, standing next to an Elvis impersonator in a rhinestone-studded shirt. Aisha in a short white dress with daisies in her hair and in her hands. The bright lights of Las Vegas visible from the window of the little chapel they were in.

Whoa. Her mind had quickly gone overboard, taking this from spark to a chandelier's worth of candles burning bright over the most ridiculous—and romantic—fantasy she'd ever had.

"Well, I think that's something we could manage," Mr. Lee said, and Aisha realized in a panic that in her daydreamy haze, she'd entirely missed everything Bram had said.

Typical Aisha.

"What do you think, Aisha?" Bram looked at her, clearly wanting to include her.

She plastered on a smile, visions of Bram in a tux still dancing behind her eyes. "That all sounds great."

"How many people are you expecting?" Mr. Lee directed his question at Bram.

Instead of answering, Bram's eyes flicked to Aisha, and somehow, she was able to pull the information from the chaos in her brain. "We're hoping for at least eighty, maybe one hundred."

"And the date?"

This time, Aisha was ready with the answer without any prompting from Bram, but that was all she was able to do. The older man barely looked at Aisha while he and Bram finished up discussing the details. He'd probably downgraded Aisha from fiancée to clueless intern thanks to her meager contribution to the conversation.

After saying goodbye, Aisha followed Bram back to the car, embarrassed at how distracted she'd let herself get with a fantasy that had as much chance of coming true as her winning the lottery.

"I'm sorry I wasn't much help." A surprisingly cool breeze for August whipped past them, and she tucked her hair behind her ears. "You didn't even really need me here. You knew what you wanted already."

Their feet crunched on the gravel of the parking lot. "I'm still glad you came."

A few of the candles that had flickered out while she's been standing there silently flickered back to life.

"Really? Why?"

"Because." He held open the car door for her, and she slid inside. Then he made her wait until he was behind the wheel before finishing his thought. "The next stop is flowers, and I needed you to see the plates to be able to tell me what will work best."

"Oh." That did make sense, in a way. "I do like flowers."

He grinned widely as he started the car, the nearly silent hum of the engine still odd to Aisha's ears. "I know you do. Daisies are your favorite, right?"

The candles in her chest burst into a single, hot flame.

"How do you know I like flowers?" Aisha peered at Bram from the passenger seat, arms folded across her chest.

Because I'm obsessed with you.

It had been hard enough to admit the secret about his family that he'd apparently not been great at hiding. Too many revelations in one day would make him shatter into a million pieces.

He decided to pull out Darcey's favorite tactic for avoiding answering things.

"You mean besides the daisy earrings you're literally wearing right now?" Answering a question with a question always worked.

Aisha put her hands to her ears and gasped. "I totally forgot I had these on. How could you let me walk in there like this? That guy knows your parents."

Bram laughed and pulled onto the state highway. The florist his mother liked was further away from the aquarium than was really practical, but this whole thing was about making Evelyn Lowther happy. He knew she'd expect him to make the effort—and would notice if he tried to cut corners.

"You look great. You always have fun earrings or a cool shirt." He changed lanes to get around a particularly slow pickup. At least this one wasn't spewing poison into Aisha's lungs the way the one earlier had been. "Well, you used to until this week."

He let that hang in the air, to see if she'd give a reason for her sudden one-eighty this week on her work clothes. Even her desk was more organized, he'd noticed.

Which wasn't a bad thing, if that's what she really wanted. Bram had his doubts, however. If it weren't for a certain head researcher with an equally tidy desk and equally boring clothes, there was no way she'd be changing everything about herself.

Aisha shifted in her seat and looked out the window at the passing cars. "When I started working at the aquarium, I thought it would be temporary, like every other job I've had. Now that I've been full time for a few months, it just doesn't feel like I can keep dressing like this every day."

Oh. That wasn't what he'd been expecting.

"Why not?"

She shrugged. "It's not professional."

"Says who?"

"Bram." Her tone was more irritated than he'd ever heard it before. Not the teasing, fake annoyed that she used sometimes. "Don't pretend like you're not as smart as you are pretty. Some of us can't afford to be that naïve."

The vibration in his veins at her calling him pretty was quickly snuffed out by the sting of chastisement hitting right in the middle of his chest. They pulled off the highway, and he stopped at a red light. When he peeked over, her arms were folded so tightly across her chest, it looked like she was trying to squash herself into noth-ingness. Eyes back on the red light, Bram rubbed his hands over his face.

Of course he knew it was different for women, for people whose skin wasn't white like his and whose families weren't as well-off as his. That didn't mean he understood what it was like. Bram's hardest choices in getting dressed were which color polo shirt to wear, never once worrying that a wrong choice would make someone see him as less professional. How many fun, oversized earrings had Aisha passed over this week for something more subdued, all so she could settle into a role that had taken her months to get?

Turning to face Aisha, it took all of his self-control not to reach up to brush her hair back to see the daisies dangling from her ears. If he'd told her about his parents before today, told her the vendors they'd be visiting knew them, would she have chosen something different? "I'm sorry. I should have given you more details about who we were meeting. I shouldn't assume I know what looking professional means for you."

Her arms relaxed a bit, and she gave him half a smile. The urge to reach out to her grew even stronger, and he gripped the steering wheel tight.

She's only helping me to impress Cody. "All I meant was that I think you always look great, and you shouldn't have to hide who you are."

A beat passed, then she raised an eyebrow in a familiar incredulous look. "Isn't that what you've been doing, Mr. Howard?"

He inhaled sharply. This wasn't about him. This was supposed to be about lifting her up, making her see how amazing she was. He'd meant to do some of that back at the warehouse, but Mr. Lee had thrown him off with his assumption Bram was there for his wedding.

With Aisha.

Instead of letting Aisha lead things the way he'd planned, the picture of her in a white dress with daisies in her hair had suddenly filled his mind, and it had taken every ounce of concentration he had just to order his usual setup.

The light turned green, and he pulled into the intersection. "Well, for this next part, neither of us needs to hide anything. You'll love this florist. Even though she's my mom's favorite, I've known her for years, so we can just be ourselves."

"Hmm." It was the quietest response he'd ever gotten from Aisha, but he wasn't sure what else to say.

After making his way through streets lined with oaks covered in Spanish moss, he parked in front of a nondescript low brick building on the corner in a residential neighborhood. The sky was a perfect summer blue, and it was the perfect summer Saturday afternoon in South Carolina. In some other world without Cody, this might have been a real date.

Aisha peered through the window. "This is the florist?"

"Oh, are we being judgy now?"

With a click of her tongue, Aisha shoved his shoulder, and he laughed. "You said she's your mom's favorite, so I just figured . . ." She bit her lip, as if unsure how to finish her sentence without proving she was, in fact, being judgy.

"One thing you should know about rich people is that they never pay more than they have to for things, even though they could."

"Oh yeah, I know that already."

Her tone was unexpectedly sharp, cutting through the space between them. Before he could ask her what she meant, she got out of the car.

Walking into the small space, the moist, cool air was what hit Bram first. Then the smell, a combination of earth and flowers and something specific to florists he couldn't quite describe but was in the background of countless childhood memories of fancy dinners and events. The main shop only had a few bouquets, something for those hurrying home might stop to grab if they'd forgotten an important anniversary. Bram knew the real store was beyond the sliding door behind the counter, in a refrigerated area that smelled like dirt and rain.

"Oh, Bram, hi, honey!" The silver-haired black woman behind the counter exclaimed the second she spotted him. She didn't waste any time coming out from behind the counter and wrapping him in a hug. "Sheila said you'd be coming by today."

"Hi, Martha." Whenever Bram visited this shop, he couldn't keep the smile off his face.

Then, just like Mr. Lee had, Martha's eyes lit up when she saw Aisha. "Well now, who is this lovely young lady? Must be someone special if you brought her here."

"Good afternoon, ma'am, I'm Aisha."

Martha looked a little too happy to be shaking her hand. Bram almost choked in his rush to explain.

"We work together at the aquarium."

"Hmm, is that all you do?" Martha winked at him.

In an instant, electricity licked across his entire body. Why did everyone think they were a couple? Was it the way he looked at her? He'd have to be more careful. Failing at hiding his wealth had turned out okay. Better than okay, really. For the first time in a long time, it felt like someone might actually be his friend because of him, and not because of what he or his family could do for them.

Failing at hiding his feelings for Aisha, however, wouldn't go as well. Not when she was only helping him out to impress another guy.

"Would we get a better price if we told you we were engaged?"

At Aisha's question, both Martha and Bram whipped their heads around to stare at her. She was smiling in that perfectly bemused way she always had, clueless that she'd just set every single one of Bram's nerve endings on fire.

Then Martha let out a short, loud laugh, and Bram forced himself to join her.

"Oh, I like her." Martha shook her finger at Aisha. "Just for that, I *will* give you a better price."

Narrowing his eyes, Bram crossed his arms over his chest. "You'd do that for a wedding that isn't even real but not for a nonprofit dedicated to saving the local aquatic wildlife that makes our great state so unique?"

"Well, if you'd started with that instead of getting all my hopes up, maybe." Martha moved behind the counter, where she picked up a pad of paper and a pen. "Now, tell me what you need."

Aisha turned to Bram, her eyes full of questions, but he'd brought her here for a reason. Lifting his palms to the sky, he gave her a wink. "I'm just here to drive her around. She's the one who knows what'll look good."

That got an appreciative hum from Martha, and a satisfying flush on Aisha's cheeks.

"Do you have any celosia?" The excitement lacing Aisha's voice was hard to miss, with the familiar enthusiastic look painting her features. "Maybe we could do something that looks like a coral reef."

It was unbearably satisfying to see Aisha take charge. Even though Bram knew plenty about flowers, as the two women chatted, it was obvious they had the same kind of creative spirit that understood color and texture in a way Bram could only pretend to.

It was only when Martha waved them into the back to look at even more flower options that Bram realized he'd left out the most important part. "My mother will be at the event."

At this, Aisha's eyebrows shot up, but only for a moment. Her face quickly smoothed out, and she shivered in the cool refrigerated back room.

"I figured as much. Otherwise, you wouldn't have come all the way out here." Martha started pulling out vases full of flowers and setting them on a table in the middle of the space for Aisha and Bram to look at.

"Lowther Yachts is one of the aquarium's donors, so that means your mom?" Aisha leaned in close to ask him this softly in his ear.

Now he shivered in the cool room. "My parents, yes."

"They're one of the bigger donors, right?" She picked up a pink dahlia and brought it to her nose, but her gaze was on him.

Bram bit his lip. "The biggest."

Her eyes widened, and she dropped the flower back onto the table. "So if this event doesn't go well . . ."

She didn't finish, but she didn't need to. Bram shook his head. What else could he say? Now she knew it all. What was at stake, not just for him personally or professionally, but for the aquarium as well.

After a quiet moment running her fingers up and down a step, Aisha squared her shoulders and looked up at him, a familiar competitive glint in her eye.

"Well then, we'll have to make sure it's perfect, won't we?"

If he hadn't already been half in love with her, he'd have fallen right then and there.

TWENTY-TWO
AISHA

Krista didn't even say hello when she walked into Aisha's living room the following afternoon and set her bag down on the goldfish-shaped coffee table. "So how long have you been keeping Bram a secret?"

Brooke was right behind her carrying her own bag, which was gigantic today. "Can you at least wait until we've had something to drink before cross-examining her?"

Krista clicked her tongue. "Like you're not curious."

Leaning against the doorway to her small kitchen, Aisha crossed her arms over her chest. "I thought this was movie night, not gossip night."

"Are you sure?" Brooke tucked her straight dark hair behind her ear and pursed her lips, trying not to smile.

The point of movie night wasn't actually the movie. The point was seeing her friends. It used to happen every week once they'd all moved back from college, then it got more irregular while Brooke was opening the animal shelter last year. Now they'd settled into a new routine where it was every other week—and on a Sunday afternoon, since none of them ever managed to stay awake past nine-thirty now that they were in their early thirties.

"Of course I'm curious," said Brooke, setting her overstuffed bag down next to a pile of shoes in the hallway. "When Ethan told me someone from the aquarium picked you up yesterday from your shift, I thought it was Cody and was so excited for you. Why have you never mentioned Bram before? Should I still be excited?"

This was Aisha's cue to turn around and escape into the kitchen, just a few steps away from the living room but behind a half-wall that half-hid her from the curious and eager stares of her best friends.

"Are we drinking red or white tonight?" She opened the fridge. "Actually, scratch that. We're drinking red. I have no white."

"I brought some."

Turning, Aisha saw Brooke pulling some out of her bag, along with a bag of carrot sticks and a Tupperware of cookies.

"If you're going to provide all the food, why don't we just do this at your house like we usually do?" It wasn't in Aisha's nature to grumble, but something had shifted in the past few days, and she was annoyed by the same take-charge attitude from her friends that she normally welcomed.

It wasn't hard for Aisha to pinpoint what had shifted. After being mostly ignored by Mr. Lee thanks to her own runaway imagination, Bram had let her take the lead at every other vendor. It had been scary at first, but by the end of the day, she'd felt capable, in a way she almost never did. The florist, the caterer, and the stationery store all deferred to her as the one who was making all the decisions, and Bram hadn't told them otherwise.

Every single one had also assumed they were there for a wedding at first, which had just made it that much harder to stay professional.

And yet she'd still managed it, daisy earrings and all. The bumbling, forgetful, chaotic personality she worked so hard to suppress around Cody was still there, just muted. Not like she was hiding, just letting other things shine. There'd been an effortlessness she hadn't felt since . . . well, ever.

This wasn't what she'd wished for from Stella. As she was passing the starfish's tank on Friday on her way out of work, she'd put her hand against the glass, closed her eyes, and thought *I wish he'd see things differently thanks to planning the gala.*

The only person who saw things differently was Aisha. Apparently Bram had always seen her in this professional, capable way, which she wasn't sure yet how she felt about.

Actually, scratch that. She knew *exactly* how she felt about it, and it had kept her up all night.

"You said you wanted to host it here." Krista's eyebrows furrowed, and she exchanged a glance with Brooke. "When we agreed that Brooke had been feeding us enough over the past year."

Right after Brooke's gran died, the three friends would have breakfast together almost every day at her house. While that still happened occasionally, Ethan had moved in with Brooke a few months ago, so now it felt awkward to be there so early. Sometimes he came to movie nights, which was totally fine. Aisha loved Ethan. He was the perfect balance of chill to Brooke's more anxious tendencies. It used to be Aisha who'd provided that balance, but now she recognized that her role was the chaos monster that kept Brooke feeling useful.

Ethan made her feel safe.

It was this balance that Aisha would get with Cody. How could she not, when he was so serious all the time? Not even his hand on hers could get her pulse racing. He would keep her calm and focused, the way she wanted.

The way she'd somehow still managed to be yesterday, with Bram.

"If we have it at my apartment, that means I do all the things." Aisha waved her hands around the kitchen, painted green at the moment but six months ago it had been red. "I got snacks. I got wine. Just not white wine."

"I'm sorry. I didn't mean to upset you." Brooke put everything back into her bag. "I just knew you'd be busy yesterday with the shelter in the morning and then working all afternoon—"

"Wait, you spent the entire afternoon with Bramwell Lowther?" Krista whirled to face Aisha. "A midweek lunch between colleagues is one thing. Spending your Saturday together is something else."

Aisha wrinkled her nose. "Nobody calls him Bramwell. Or Lowther, at least at the aquarium. He's always been Bram Howard to me."

At this little nugget of information, Krista narrowed her eyes. "That doesn't change who his parents are."

Heat flooded Aisha's face. Krista was without a doubt the smartest of the three of them. Top of her class in law school, she could have gotten a job in New York or Atlanta, but she'd come back to Adamsville to take care of her dad. After a clerkship for a federal judge, it had only taken a few years for her to become a junior partner at the firm where she worked, and it was probably only another few years before Krista became a state judge.

It wasn't surprising that Krista would know about Bram's wealthy and connected parents. Hadn't Aisha even hoped for it the previous day, wondering if Krista would have some idea about just how rich yacht makers were?

Today, however, Aisha was just irritated.

"Why does it matter who his parents are?" Aisha went to the cabinet where she'd stashed the snacks she'd bought for this afternoon. Pretzels were her favorite, cheese puffs were Brooke's, and sour cream and onion chips were Krista's. "That doesn't change who he is as a person."

Except his family still impacted his life, just like her mother's wealth still impacted Aisha's. The apartment they were standing in was bought with the money her mother had sent every year until she turned eighteen. Her dad had put it all aside, letting her make her own choice about what to do with it.

Did using it instead of giving it all away make Aisha any

different from people like the Lowthers? The question had been floating around in her head since Bram had told her he didn't use his family's money anymore. That didn't mean he hadn't taken advantage of other things, like the name or the status or the connections.

When she turned to get serving bowls out of another cabinet, she caught the apologetic tilt of Krista's eyebrows. Her friend's voice was softer now, and she leaned against the doorway to the kitchen. "I know it doesn't change how you see him. But you know some people will only ever see him as a Lowther."

Heart hammering, Aisha kept her hands busy opening the bags of snacks and dumping each one into a separate bowl she'd set out on the white Formica countertops speckled with paint.

Of course she knew that. She'd spent hours yesterday coming to terms with the fact that no matter how much she liked Bram, it was never going to be possible to separate his place in the world from his family's. Just like she'd always be marked by her exclusion from hers.

It had been fifteen years since she'd spoken to her mother. The embarrassment for the wealthy Kateb family of their daughter having a child out of wedlock with a poor American artist had been easy to fix with enough money from an ocean's distance away.

It was like a scar Aisha carried around, the word "unwanted" branded across her face. Bram would see it eventually. The Lowthers would surely be able to see it, if she ever met them.

Which, she suddenly remembered, she would at the gala.

"Well, I don't see him that way, and I don't want to talk about his family anymore." Aisha looked up from the bowls to see both of her friends frowning at her. "If that's okay with you?"

In an instant, Krista's face smoothed out. "Of course. I didn't mean to be gossipy."

Brooke snorted from behind her in the hallway. "Yes, you did."

Defeated, Krista raised her hands in the air. "Guilty as charged. You know I can't talk about anything at work the way you two can, but I can totally talk about everything and everyone else." She put her elbow on the counter and rested her head in her hand. "So let's talk about Bram and why you were with him yesterday."

"If you want to gossip, you could tell us who 'J' is." Aisha fanned her eyelashes at Krista, while Brooke cackled from the hallway.

"Oh no, don't turn this back on me. Bram is the topic of the evening."

With a defeated sigh, Aisha picked up the bowls and headed into the living room. Getting information out of Krista when she didn't want to give it was impossible. If she hadn't drunkenly gone on a rant about "guys with J names being the worst" last summer, she and Brooke wouldn't even know his first initial. Despite pressing for details at every opportunity, Krista remained a steel trap. Great for her clients, terrible for her friends.

Today definitely wasn't the day they were going to get the full story about the mysterious "J," but that didn't mean Aisha had to tell them everything about Bram. "I'm helping him with the gala at the aquarium."

"Where did you go?" Krista flopped onto the worn lavender plaid couch, with Brooke beside her, both practically salivating for details. "What did you do?"

"It was just for work." Nudging aside Krista's bag with her elbow, Aisha set the bowls on the low coffee table. She'd had the goldfish-shaped table long before she'd started at the aquarium. The turquoise shag rug underneath, however, was partly inspired by her endless hours over the past year surrounded by gently undulating waves. Sometimes she even dreamed she was swimming in the ocean, which had inspired a whole series of paintings that were hidden away in her second bedroom she used as a studio. "We had to see vendors about plates and flowers and stuff. It wasn't that interesting."

"Spending the entire afternoon with a guy from work who is not Cody is definitely interesting." Brooke popped a cheese puff into her mouth. "Do you still like him?"

"Of course." Aisha frowned and sat at the far end of the couch. That didn't feel entirely true, but changing her mind after so many months wasn't the kind of person she wanted to be.

"Has he asked you for any more favors?" Grinning, Brooke waggled her eyebrows.

"Favors for Cody, helping Bram on a weekend." Krista shook her head, her blond curls bouncing as she sat back with her arms crossed. "Why are you doing these guys' work for them? You know the rule. If they're not serving you, they're not for you."

"Since when is that the rule?" Brooke raised her eyebrows. "I don't remember you saying that when I started talking to Ethan."

"He had a puppy. Puppies trump all other rules."

As usual, there was no arguing with Krista's logic.

Aisha grabbed the remote and turned on the TV. "What movie are we watching?"

Leaning forward, Krista snatched it out of her hand. "The one where you tell us more about Bram."

With a sigh, Aisha gave in. There would be no escape from the cross-examination—and no movie—until she had satisfied the lawyer's curiosity.

"I don't usually tell you two about the people I work with." She shrugged and grabbed some pretzels from the bowl. Curling her legs underneath her, she munched for a moment before continuing. "Since, you know, I never stay anywhere very long. But Bram's been my friend since he started a few months ago."

"A few months, and this is the first time we've heard about him?" Brooke's eyebrows were sky-high.

"Exactly." Krista narrowed her eyes. "Until I saw you two at the restaurant, I had no idea he even existed."

A knot was starting to form in Aisha's chest, somewhere between her heart and her stomach. Breathing around it proved difficult.

"He's not important."

Well, that had been a mistake. There was no fooling her friends, and from the look they gave her, they knew she knew she'd messed up. She shrank back into the soft, worn cushions of her couch in a desperate attempt to either disappear or suffocate herself. Whatever it took to avoid dealing with what was coming next.

"Not important?" Krista punctuated her rhetorical question with a raised eyebrow that was sharper than the lines on a legal pad. "So I guess you spend your weekend afternoons with unimportant people. Brooke, did you know we were unimportant?"

"I had no idea, but it makes sense." Brooke nodded sagely, her lips twitching a little. "The less important someone is to Aisha, the more time she spends with them."

"Ah, stop, please." Sinking even further into the cushions, Aisha felt her face heat to what had to be a shade of red never before seen in nature on skin that wasn't already rosy pink like Krista's. "I didn't mean it. I'm sorry."

"Don't be sorry. It's fine to have a crush on more than one guy at a time."

"That's not what this is."

How could she explain it to them without sounding self-pitying? Her friends knew her story about the reasons her parents split up, why she lived in South Carolina and not in Paris. Along with her dad and Brooke's late grandmother, they were the only people on the planet who didn't seem to see her "unwanted" scar. They made her feel totally loved.

Which was why they wouldn't be able to understand this burning desire she had to be someone different. They'd just tell her she was perfect the way she was, that she shouldn't have to change for some guy—just like Bram had said.

"A crush on Bram isn't an option. Cody is who I should be with."

"Why?" asked Brooke, her eyebrows tilted with curiosity.

"He's serious. I need a serious boyfriend."

"Why?" asked Krista, wrinkling her nose in disgust.

"Because I do." She grabbed the remote back from Krista and turned on the TV. "Can we just drop it?"

She could feel Krista's icy gaze on one side of her face and Brooke's softer one on the other as she flipped through the options on the screen.

They'd known each other since they were in elementary school, but Aisha had always been different. Brooke and Krista were both already seen as smart, responsible kids. Meanwhile, Aisha was the kid with the artist dad and an accent, who came to school in mismatched outfits and liked weird food. It hadn't taken long before she'd stopped trying and leaned into her creative, aimless, free-spirited side. That's the role she held in their little trio. Krista was the brains, Brooke the planner, and Aisha the fun.

How could she tell them that she wanted that to change? That it had to change if she wanted to finally be settled the way they were? With grown-up jobs that gave them purpose and direction. Her dad had done the same thing when she was a kid. Given up the uncertainty of the artist's life that had broken his heart for something more serious and stable.

None of them had been where she was. None of them knew what it was like to be discarded, rejected early on and then constantly trying to meet expectations. It was easier not to try at all.

Now that she actually wanted to try, she was terrified they wouldn't let her, preferring to love her just the way she was.

Whenever his mother had something she knew Bram wouldn't like, she asked him to meet her at their country club. That way she knew he wouldn't make a scene. Bram scoffed as he parked his car in the middle of a row of luxury vehicles that cost more than his annual salary. In his mother's world, showing emotion was worse than swearing or wearing the wrong tie to an event.

Conveniently, Bram had forgotten a tie today. His chinos and button-down were just nice enough not to draw any attention, but casual enough he knew his outfit would annoy his mother.

Would he have done the same thing a week ago? Probably not. Aisha's explanations about her sartorial transformation at work had reminded him there was another way to tease apart his life from his family's. On his way to the country club, he'd stopped by his parents' house to pick up all the clothes he had there. The next time his mother invited him to something last minute, she'd just have to deal with his LCRA polo.

As Bram strolled across the patio full of people perched at little tables drinking pre-lunch cocktails, he nodded at everyone he knew and tried to keep his breathing steady. This was the absolute last place he wanted to be right now, but there was nothing useful he could be doing for the gala today. Thoughts of Aisha had been plaguing him since dropping her off the day before.

When don't they? The dark-haired beauty was never far from his mind.

This was more than normal, however. This was constant. The need to know what she was doing, the desire to see her reaction to things. It went beyond whatever meager crush he'd been nursing for the past few months. Yesterday had shifted things irrevocably, but he shouldn't assume that they had for her as well.

Walking through the wide pocket doors open to the patio, he steeled his shoulders. Scanning the sunlit-drenched dining room, he found his parents tucked into a corner table inside the restaurant, perfectly framed by a potted palm tree. It was his mother's favorite spot. Visible, yet not at all approachable.

With calm, even breaths, he made his way toward them. It was unlikely that his mother had decided to forgo the gala entirely. She loved a good party and a chance to be seen. If she'd gotten a better invitation somewhere for that weekend, however, before he'd even gotten a chance to send his out . . . well, that was a different story.

"Bramwell, thank you for joining us for lunch on such a lovely day." His mother smiled widely, and she reached out a tanned, toned arm to pick up her glass of wine.

He raised an eyebrow and sat down. "Am I staying for lunch?"

"Yes," was his father's curt reply. Unlike his mother, Bram's father was not one to indulge in useless chatter. He peered at his watch through his glasses. "I've got a one o'clock tee time, so make this quick, Evelyn."

Holding back a sigh, Bram's fist clenched on his thigh below the table. "Hi, Dad, nice to see you too."

"You look different." His mother narrowed her eyes at him once he'd given his drink order to the server, who'd appeared approximately three seconds after he sat down. Nobody wanted to keep the Lowthers waiting for anything.

He swallowed hard, trying to banish thoughts of Aisha to the trunk of his car, along with the boxes of clothes, where his mother wouldn't be able to see them. "I'm just a little tired. I was running around yesterday talking to vendors."

These were the magic words. Her face lit up with something that might have been pride.

"Well, that's nice to hear. I've already filled out our table, and I told everyone it'll be incredible."

While he was relieved to hear she wasn't abandoning the event, unease still thundered away in his chest. "The invitations aren't even going out until tomorrow."

She waved that away. "Just make sure the tables seat ten."

Biting back a reply that would have ruined the mood, he took a sip of water and smiled. "Of course, Mother. Anything else you'd like to see at the gala?"

Now she raised an eyebrow. "Don't take that tone with me. This is to help you."

What would have helped him was if she'd kept her donation without him having to jump through these hoops, but he didn't say that either.

Most of the time he spent with his mother was spent not saying the things he really wanted to say. Maybe that's why he liked being around Aisha. Her unfiltered enthusiasm filled his days with a brightness he didn't know he'd been missing. Would she still dim herself in front of Cody this week at work? It was probably too much to hope that she'd be any different after spending her Saturday afternoon with Bram.

"I'm sorry. That's not what I meant." He leaned back in his chair and looked around the restaurant, wishing he could be at any other table right now. Even if they were filled with all the same kind of boring, polite people talking about golf and investing he'd been avoiding his entire life. "Truly, I'd like to know what you want to see at the gala, so I can be sure to arrange it if possible. I want you and your friends to have a good time."

"Hmm." His mother looked him up and down, as if looking for

something to critique about his outfit. Everything he was wearing was something she'd bought him, so other than the lack of tie, there was nothing she could say unless she wanted to insult her own taste. "No dancing. I know you probably can't fit a string quartet in the space you have, so you'll have to get a DJ. Find one who won't play anything loud or fast. We should be able to talk and mingle, not shout over club music."

"That shouldn't be a problem." It would mean more time for people to walk around the aquarium and see the animals. The more they saw, hopefully the more they'd donate.

"Hmm." His mother gave him that look again, but he was being perfectly pleasant, his tone the epitome of graciousness. Just like she'd taught him.

His heart still thrummed a mile a minute, as if she were about to bite his head off. Another sip of water kept his hands busy but did nothing to calm his racing pulse.

Why did it matter so much? He'd been planning events and galas for years. He knew what he was doing. There'd never been a single event that didn't raise the target amount, and most of them raised more. He was good at his job; he knew that.

But how much of that was because he was a Lowther? Everything he'd learned growing up in this life meant he knew how to act and what to say to get what he wanted. He could move his stuff out of their house, but there was no separating his family from his success in his career. If the Lowther money and name went away, would he really be able to do it on his own?

Without the support from his parents, however, he knew he wouldn't be able to help these causes nearly as much as he could with their support.

So he stayed silent. It was beyond frustrating that he was still following his mother's instructions and bending to her every whim like when he was a kid.

I have my own house. Paid with money I earned, not money I was given just for being born.

These regular reminders helped soothe his doubts, but not as easily as they used to. Something big had to change, and soon, or he'd float out to sea on the current of the Lowther name and lose sight of the shore entirely.

"Who are you using for flowers?" his mother asked.

"Martha Montgomery."

Her eyebrows popped up. "The aquarium can afford that? I'm not paying more than three grand for tickets. It's just fish."

"Endangered native species."

If Evelyn Lowther had been the kind of woman who rolled her eyes, she'd have done it then. "Yes, well, there are limits to what my friends will pay to stare at fish tanks all evening."

"I'll try to think of some other entertainment. A lecture maybe?" He could ask Cody, which he absolutely did not want to, but if that's what it took, so be it. The scientist and his team were the ones using all this money they raised, so the least they could do was help him raise it.

"No, that sounds dull. It's a shame you're not at the hospital anymore. I enjoyed bidding on art for the walls."

The combination of "art" and "walls" brought Aisha to his mind. Not that she was ever not on his mind. It was more like his mother's words brought his creative, artistic colleague to the fore-front yet again. An art auction would be a great way to raise money, but Bram didn't want to promise anything to his mother before he'd fully vetted the idea to know if it would work.

"Yes, well, the nails to hang the paintings would break the tanks." He shrugged, not expecting a laugh, but hoping for at least a polite chuckle.

Instead, he got that glare his mother had perfected. The one that made him feel like a silly little boy asking for a hug.

His father had been silent until now, his gaze fixed on the people coming and going on the patio, and he didn't even look at Bram when he admonished him. "Don't sass your mother."

"I hope you're taking this seriously. Your father and I still plan on shifting around our donations in the fall." The small, subtle roll of her shoulders was the only hint she was uncomfortable. "We need to make sure we're making the biggest impact we can."

His spine straightened. "Oh?"

This wasn't something he thought they paid attention to. Charity, to his parents, was about tax write-offs and rubbing shoulders with the right people.

"Of course. Lowther Yachts isn't some heartless, polluting conglomerate the way some people think. We're a family business that's been supporting the local economy for decades."

Ah, of course. He sat back in his chair, stomach in knots. It wasn't because his mother actually cared. It was just about looking good. This must have something to do with the case Darcey mentioned. What had Lowther Yachts done, if his mother was this focused on showing the positive impact their company could make? Asking Darcey was pointless, since she was a steel trap.

Like she'd somehow known he was thinking about her, Darcey appeared at their table.

TWENTY-FIVE

BRAM

"Mr. and Mrs. Lowther. How are you today?" Darcey's smile was bright, and she was dressed for tennis in a visor and short white skirt that just barely hid the tattoo she had on her upper thigh.

"Oh, Darcey, darling." His mother flashed her a shark-like smile. "I didn't know you were here today. Won't you join us for lunch?"

"Thank you, but I'm not dressed for that." She turned her gaze to Bram. "I actually need to steal your son for a moment. I hope you don't mind."

"Not at all." His mother looked thrilled. Even his father had glanced Darcey's way and given her an indulgent look.

Bram stood, and Darcey took his arm. "I'll have him back as soon as I can."

"Take your time." With a smug smile, his mother waved them away. His father didn't even grumble about missing his tee time. Even after all these years, they were still holding out hope for a Lowther-Yates merger disguised as a wedding.

Darcey tugged on his arm and hurried him away from the dining room and into the cool dark hallways of the club.

"You looked like you could use some saving," she said under her breath.

"Thanks, but it wasn't that bad." His neck strained to look back, to see how his mother was reacting to being interrupted, but she was just as likely to look thrilled that Darcey and Bram were together. He wasn't sure which one would be worse. "She was just telling me exactly what to do for the gala."

"Do you need any help?"

He gave her a wry look and she laughed.

"Okay, fine, not from me. From my assistant. She really is very good at planning these." Darcey winked. "And she's pretty cute."

They were heading toward the club's game room, a frequent refuge for them when they were kids. "Thanks, but I have someone helping me."

"Aisha?"

His stomach dropped and he held back a groan. "Let's hear it."

"What?" Darcey gave him a smug smile. "She's adorable. One of Krista's oldest friends."

"What did you find out about her?"

"Nothing that you probably don't know already."

"That might not be entirely true. Our relationship has been very professional until recently."

"Ooh, so it's more than professional now?"

They had made their way into the dark, carpeted game room. It was empty, just like it was every other time he'd been here over the past three decades. A stack of battered board games was in one corner, and a bookshelf filled with bestsellers from the previous century was in another. It was the one place in the entire club that wasn't updated every few years. Probably because nobody seemed to use it except for kids—or adults in their thirties—trying to escape their parents.

"No, that's not what I meant." He ran his hands through his hair and sat down on the couch that had already been worn and ancient when he was a teenager. It was oddly comforting how nothing had changed in here. "Just that we're finally spending some time together outside of work, but it's still for work, because it's for the gala."

"What about the lunch I crashed with Krista?" Darcey moved aside a Time magazine with Nixon on the cover to sit next to him.

"That was also to work on the gala." He glanced at her. "Though we didn't manage to do much, so that's why we were together yesterday afternoon."

Throwing up her hands, Darcey fell back into the plaid cushions. "Why don't you just make a move?"

"She likes someone else."

"Someone better than you?" With an exaggerated grimace, Darcey looked over her shoulder toward the door and lowered her voice. "I hope your mom didn't hear me say that."

Despite his twisted insides, Bram managed to laugh. "Don't get her hopes up. Aisha isn't exactly who she'd want me to be with."

There was a lot in that statement, and he knew Darcey wouldn't let him just let it hang there without pushing. Besides being his oldest friend, she was also a very good lawyer. "And why is that exactly?"

"She isn't from our world." It was the simplest way to answer that question.

"Neither are you," said Darcey. "Not anymore."

"Is that true though?" Bram gestured around them, to the room that even in its shabbiness spoke of wealth, inside a multi-million-dollar country club where people with watches that cost more than the aquarium's operating expenses played tennis. "I want it to be, but look at where I am. Look at what I have to do to keep going in my career."

"We all have to do things we don't like in life. Is hobnobbing at parties with our parents' jerk friends so that they give money to places that need it really so bad?" Darcey shook her head. "At least you're not involved in this case. It's going to be ugly."

"Do you know when it'll go to court?"

"It'll be better for everyone if we can avoid that entirely, but if not, then sometime this fall most likely." She lifted a shoulder. "Sorry. I can't really say more."

It was already more than enough to take Bram's anxiety about the gala from a four to a ten. Of course Lowther Yachts should pay for whatever horrible thing they'd done. Darcey would make sure of it. That didn't stop Bram from wanting to make his parents happy if he could. If that meant a glitzy gala where they could be seen as benevolent benefactors, then that's what he'd give them.

He loved them, despite everything. He wished he didn't. It would make his life easier.

Just like not wanting Aisha would make his life easier.

"You make it sound like I should move away."

"I thought you wanted to." Darcey tugged at her skirt. From all her griping over the years about the dress code, he knew it wasn't because she was embarrassed at showing so much of her thigh, but because it was riding up uncomfortably. "When I visited you in college, you couldn't shut up about lobster rolls and the American Revolution."

He had considered it before, though never seriously. Even if he'd only gone to Harvard because that's what Lowthers did, college in Boston had been a nice escape from the heavy climate and more conservative politics of the South. But it wasn't home. And now that things with Aisha were . . . well, not moving forward exactly but at least moving, he couldn't bear to think about leaving her.

He flashed his teeth at Darcey in a mocking grin. "If I move away, then who would you bother?"

She made a kissy face at him. "I'd be fine. Think about yourself for once."

Except that's what he'd been trying not to do since he was old enough to understand that he had so much more than so many people. All it had taken was one trip to the zoo as a kid. A little girl was crying over her dropped ice cream, and he'd given her his popcorn. The girl's mother had been so profusely grateful, he'd asked his nanny why she didn't just buy another ice cream. Her response had been hesitant.

"Not everyone can afford that."

"Popcorn?" It had only cost a few dollars. Something had stuck in his little brain—all the toys and clothes in his room that he'd taken for granted suddenly became evidence of something he'd never put a name on before.

"You're a very lucky little boy, Bram." The nanny smiled down at him as they waited in line for another popcorn. "And very sweet. I hope you stay that way."

When he'd gotten home, he'd told his mother they should give money to the zoo so everyone could get free popcorn whenever they wanted.

That nanny had been gone by dinnertime.

Ever since then, doing what was best for him had come second to doing as much good as he could for everyone else.

Even if it meant letting Aisha find happiness with Cody.

"You're thinking of doing something noble, aren't you?" Darcey rolled her eyes and leaned her head back on the couch with a groan.

"I'm not going to force myself where I'm not wanted. How many cases did you see during your internship of men doing the opposite?"

A shudder passed through Darcey as she sat up. "Don't remind me. There are many reasons I picked environmental law, and pissing off my parents was just one of them." She leaned over and brushed some lint only she could see off his shoulder. "If you ask Aisha out and she says no, I know you'll drop it because you're not a dirtbag. But I'm pretty sure she'll say yes."

Hope pinged through his chest. "You can't know that."

"Um, excuse me, I have eyes. There was definitely something going on at the restaurant."

"But she likes—"

"Someone else, you already said that." Darcey threw up her hands. "It's possible to like more than one person at a time. Has this other guy asked her out?"

"No, but—"

"So ask her first."

Shaking his head, Bram let out a sad chuckle. "If it were that easy, don't you think I'd have done it by now?"

Darcey considered this. She was his oldest friend, so she knew how he could be, knew that the confident facade he always had hid a lot of uncertainty.

"You're a brave man, Wellington. You may not always see it, but you are. You've done some extraordinary things when you could have had an easy life. You've dedicated yourself to helping others when the world only expects you to help yourself." A prickling, knotted feeling filled him. "So stop being such a chicken and ask out the girl you like. Or I will."

A laugh burst out of him. It was rare to hear so many nice things from Darcey, and he knew it wouldn't last.

"Okay, okay." He patted her knee, the closest they got to hugs, then stood up. A glance at his watch told him he was probably too late for lunch now, but he'd bet the rest of his trust fund his mother was still holding court at the table for whoever walked by. "I guess if I'm that brave, you're going to make me eat dessert alone with my mom, aren't you?"

He held out his hand to help her off the couch, and she grinned at him wickedly. "Of course."

As he made his way back to the dining room on his own, Bram realized Darcey was right—though he'd never admit it to her face. He'd done way harder things over the years than asking out a girl.

Had he ever liked one this much though? A rejection from Aisha wouldn't be something he came back from easily.

Sitting down next to his parents again with a forced smile, Bram wondered if the thing that finally pushed him to make a big enough change to leave South Carolina and his family for good wouldn't be something they did, but the heartbreak that was looming ahead.

TWENTY-SIX
AISHA

The morning stop at Stella's tank had no surprise interruptions. Aisha's heart couldn't decide if she was grateful or disappointed. Running into Cody was still something she wanted, but when she thought about what to wish for from Stella, it wasn't his face that came up first. It was Bram's.

You did spend Saturday with him, she reminded herself.

There'd also been the movie on Sunday. After a solid twenty minutes of bickering, she and her friends had landed on rewatching *Escape to New York* for the thousandth time.

It had come out when they were in middle school, about a teenage boy trying to hide from his jealous relatives in the city after he inherited a fortune, while also winning the heart of a pretty tourist. Of course the best part was Hayden Carmichael, the movie's dreamy star, but for Aisha there was also the reminder that money could change everything overnight. How people saw you, how they treated you, their interest in you. Of course in the movie, the pretty tourist didn't care that he lost everything, and she loved him anyway.

But that wasn't real life.

To change or not to change, that seemed to be the question. It wasn't one Stella would help with, and as Aisha watched the sea star slowly slide her way along the tank, she struggled to think of a wish that might actually get her what she wanted.

Maybe it was selfish to wish for so many things, but there was no denying it was working.

I wish I could spend more time with him. Just the two of us.

I wish he'd see things differently thanks to planning the gala.

Though she'd never thought Cody's name, it had been clear who she was wishing for.

Hadn't it?

Aisha peered at Stella, the twelve eyes winking at her through the glass of the tank.

Whether it had been Bram or Cody on her mind when making the wishes, her thoughts today were all for herself:

Give me a way to shine.

Watching Escape to New York always got Krista ranting about how annoying it was that the love interest in these movies had to be "quirky." Whether or not that was a bad thing was for the movie critics to decide. For Aisha, all it had reminded her was that there was one thing about her that didn't have to change to set her apart:

Her art.

Even if she never sold her work, she knew she was good at it. While she still needed to temper some of her more shambolic impulses to find love and success, there was no denying that making things with her hands came naturally to her. Drawing, messing around with clay, or painting—her favorite. It was just a hobby, and always would be, but it helped her focus in a way that nothing else did. When things got busy, it was how she relaxed. She had a lot of work to get through this morning, but during her breaks from staring at the computer screen, she sketched.

And kept her door open in case Cody walked by.

A few hours later, absorbed in one of these sketch breaks, Aisha didn't even realize she was no longer alone in her office until she heard Bram speak.

"That's really good."

With a yelp, her hands flew up. The pencil shot out of her hand and hit Bram on the side of the head, which made him take a step back. This knocked over the giant stuffed penguin Aisha still hadn't moved back into the storage closet, and of course it fell onto her desk, scattering papers and knickknacks everywhere.

A defeated groan escaped her. It had taken her hours to organize those papers, and the tidy row of figurines and novelty erasers she'd been so proud of was now in total disarray.

At least it covered what she'd been working on. The way Bram's hair had been shining in the sun that weekend, the darker brown waves shot through with hints of blond, had been too enticing not to try to get down on paper. So far it was just hair, and the curve of an ear, but once she unearthed it from the chaos on her desk, he might recognize it was him.

So there was no hurry to clean up this mess.

"Oh well, I guess that means it's time for a break." She stood up and stretched her arms over her head. When she dropped them again, Bram was staring at her, his gaze slightly unfocused. Then, like he'd been snapped out of a dream, he shook his head and cleared his throat.

"You were really concentrating there. Drawing anyone I know?" A raised eyebrow accompanied his teasing words, but there was a serious undertone. "Care to share with the rest of the class?"

Heat spread up her neck. "Nope."

"At least let me help you clean up your desk. It's my fault for scaring you." He reached over and pushed back her chair. She hurried to block him, shoving her body between him and her desk. When he turned left like he would go around her, she shifted, their shoulders brushing. Then he moved in the opposite direction, and her body followed, crashing into his.

"Come on, Aisha, I just want to help." A smile danced at the corners of his lips as he took a step back. "I promise I'm not trying to see your love poem to Cody, or whatever it was."

"That's not what it was." Cheeks on fire, she was having trouble breathing.

He feinted right and she fell for it. He snagged a few papers and pushed them together into a pile. "See? I'm helping."

With her heart in her mouth, she hip-checked him out of the way, but it didn't dislodge him completely from in front of her desk. Had he always been this tall and broad? Or had he grown bigger somehow since Saturday?

"No, it's my fault for leaving everything everywhere." She chuckled, trying to make light of it, hoping to distract him from the drawing—and herself from the prickles on her skin where they'd touched. Multiple times. "I know I'm a mess."

"No, you're not."

The breath stilled in her lungs at the earnest way he said it. Even Brooke and Krista would have laughed along with her. Aisha's role in their trio as the effervescent, funny, dependent one didn't seem to be the same with Bram.

Turning back to the mayhem on her desk, she absently picked up a few of the fallen papers, starting a stack that she knew she'd abandon halfway through.

Bram leaned over her shoulder, his breath hot on her cheek. "Can I please see what you were working on? I promise I won't tease you about it, whatever it is."

A quick inhale got her a lungful of Bram's smell, something she'd never noticed until now. Light and sharp, like the slightest hint of the ocean in a summer's breeze, she closed her eyes for just a moment to soak it in. Yesterday there'd been a million reasons why Bram wasn't an option, but today, with him standing close enough she could almost feel his heartbeat syncing up with her own, she couldn't think of a single one.

"If you can find it." She opened her eyes and instantly spotted it, then tried to nudge the drawing underneath her keyboard. Unfortunately, Bram was too quick and swooped in to pick it up.

She held her breath. This wasn't like the mural, which was

more abstract and she'd been given guidelines for. This was just her own imagination, running wild with the light and Bram's undeniably luxuriant head of hair. It could have been Cody's, except his was cut very short, with straight even edges. It didn't have any texture as far as she could tell. Not the way Bram's waves ran along the side of his head, sometimes falling over one eye. Then he'd push it up out of the way, which he did right now as he was looking at her drawing.

"This is really good, Aisha."

"It's just a sketch."

"It's a really good sketch."

She turned and started to clean up her desk again. "Thanks."

Bram was quiet for a moment, and she avoided looking at him by keeping her eyes on the mess in front of her. Papers in one pile, knickknacks in another, paperclips back onto the magnetic holder shaped like a cow Krista had given her back in middle school.

"What if we had an art auction?"

Aisha turned to him with a frown. "For what?"

"For the gala. That would raise a ton of money with this crowd. They love finding up-and-coming artists." He leaned against the desk and twisted his lips, like he wasn't sure how she'd react to this next part. "You could put some of your paintings up for auction."

"I don't paint."

"So the mural at the shelter was what? A hallucination?"

She clicked her tongue. "I mean, I paint, but I'm not a painter. It's a hobby, not my career. I'm a social media and marketing specialist." Her art was what set her apart, but in a fun way, not something serious.

"Aisha, you're an artist."

Hearing someone else say the words out loud who wasn't her friends or her dad felt like she was running naked along Adamsville's Main Street. Her hands stacked and restacked the pile of papers in front of her. She tried to imagine what her reaction would have been if instead Cody had stumbled across her in the middle of sketching. That's what she'd been hoping would happen, wasn't it? For him to spot her doing the thing that made her the quirky love interest in a movie.

Instead, it was Bram who'd caught her sketching, and now her heart wouldn't stop pounding against her rib cage like it wanted to escape into the next county.

"I'm not an artist. I've never been paid for my work. I don't make it with the intention to sell. It's just for me." Aisha bit her lip, thinking not just of the mural but also of the window paintings she did for holidays. Brooke's huge Victorian house was decorated extravagantly from mid-October through March. It used to be her grandmother's, and ever since middle school, she'd asked Aisha to paint the windows to fit whatever the theme was. "Or for friends."

"So paint me a picture, as a friend, and I'll sell it."

This wasn't what I meant by a way to shine! Aisha's wish to the starfish hadn't meant putting her art on display in a public way. She'd been thinking of something like the director asking her to design a new logo for the aquarium or something.

Of course, the director didn't know Aisha did anything other than the basic graphic design. If she had a painting at the auction, then the director would see it . . . and so would Cody. There was still a way he could realize she was his quirky love interest. Still a way this didn't end with her falling for Bram and having her heart undoubtedly broken.

"What do you say?" Bram's pleading eyes, the same color she'd painted the sky in the shelter's mural, met hers, and Aisha knew she was losing this fight, along with her heart.

"I'll think about it."

Aisha looked up at Bram and saw the little satisfied smile on his face. Halfway between a smirk and a grin, it was a wonder they only raised a million dollars from his videos and not a billion. "That's all I ask."

It felt like he was asking a lot more than that, but she let it slide.

Ignoring her racing heart, which hadn't slowed down once he'd walked in, she put a hand on her hip and shot him a silly smile. "Are you sure you're not just trying to butter me up, so I'll be your pretend fiancée and get better rates from vendors?"

"If that's what I was doing, there'd be nothing fake about it."

Her stomach dropped to the floor.

"Bram, you can't just say things like that." While her hands fumbled to push her hair away from her face, she stepped back, her legs hitting the edge of the desk. "It's not nice."

"I meant it."

Mouth suddenly parched, she licked her lips. When had he gotten so close to her? He'd been leaning on the desk a moment before, safely several feet away, but now he was right in front of her. It was impossible to look at him when he was that close, his eyes on her face making her skin heat.

"Aisha, I know we're just friends, but I was wondering . . ."

When he didn't say anything else, she looked up. He was right there. Close enough to touch. Close enough to kiss.

Her breath left her body in a single rush.

Kissing Bram was not something she'd ever thought about.

Now it sounded like the absolute best idea in the entire world.

What about Cody?

Cody who?

With Bram filling her vision, his light ocean breeze scent filling her nose, there was no room for anyone else.

Voice shaking, Aisha tried to focus on anything but his lips and failed. "Wondering what?"

He took another step toward her and—

The knock at the door was like a bolt of lightning, zapping the two of them apart.

"Aisha?" Cody popped his head in, his eyes narrowed behind his glasses. "Is this a bad time?"

"No, this is fine." It was impossible not to miss the frown that pulled at Bram's lips. Dragging her eyes away from his mouth, she turned to Cody. "What's up?"

Clearing his throat, he pushed his glasses up on his nose. The same move had made her heart patter faster than a hummingbird last week, but Cody wasn't the reason it wanted to escape its cage today. No, it was Bram's almost kiss.

Which she'd clearly imagined. There was no way he would have kissed her, if that's even what he'd been about to do. She glanced his way, on the other side of the room, arms crossed and face smooth like they'd just been talking normally. He'd probably just been going to ask for a favor, something even bigger than putting her art up for auction, and he'd gotten all intense because he wanted her to take it seriously. That's why he'd been looking at her that way, and why there was no hint of it now.

"Does that sound okay?"

Uh-oh. Her face had been turned toward Cody, but she hadn't heard a word he said.

"Sure."

His face lit up with a smile. It did warm her heart to see it, but it didn't quite hit in the direct center of her chest the way Bram's smile did.

"Great. I'll bring it by tomorrow."

With a silent nod at Bram, Cody left the office.

Aisha rushed to shut the door, then turned around and put her back against it, head in her hands.

"Okay, don't laugh."

"I will absolutely laugh."

She peeked through her fingers to see Bram already grinning like a manta ray at her.

"I was not exactly paying attention when he was talking." She dropped her hands and blew out a breath. "What did I just agree to?"

"Seriously? Were his dreamy brown eyes that distracting?" There was a sharpness to his tone, underneath the teasing. A slight tugging down of his lips that he tried to play off as nonchalance by crossing his arms over his chest and leaning against her desk.

Why had she never noticed how wide his chest was? The blue aquarium polo was tight across his pecs, the color making his eyes even more remarkable than usual.

"No, it wasn't that." Heart racing yet again—was she having some kind of a cardiac event or was it just proximity to Bram?—she ran her hand along her hair, checking her pins were still locked in securely. "I was thinking about, um, a painting that might work. For the auction."

His eyes lit up. "You'll do it?"

"If you tell me what Cody wanted."

"Oh, that." Bram waved a hand. "He just wants you to take a look at a presentation he's making and see if you can do anything to make the graphics stand out. Something Sandra in accounting asked him for."

"Really?" Stella had come through after all. "That's what I wished for."

"For Sandra to bug him instead of us about logging all our expenses?" Bram's eyebrows shot up. "When did you make that wish?"

"I didn't. I mean, I made a wish, like I do every day, but it wasn't for that." She started stacking papers again on her desk, and she kept her eyes on her hands. "Today I wished for a way to make me shine."

There was a long silence, so long that Aisha started to get a little nervous. Did Bram think she was silly? After everything he'd done on Saturday to make her feel like a professional whose opinion he trusted, all it would take was a single word to bring her confidence crashing back down. Not because he was a Lowther, and she feared the criticism of someone wealthy. Though that was a part of it and always would be, she feared.

The biggest part of it was because there was a fine line between quirky love interest and eccentric side character.

Aisha desperately wanted to be Bram's love interest.

"I've been making wishes too," he said softly, and her head whipped around to stare at him. He wasn't making fun of her. He was serious.

"Oh yeah?" Throat suddenly dry, she swallowed hard and tried to make her next words teasing. Getting back to their easy banter was what she needed right now. "About what?"

He flashed her a cheeky grin and waggled his eyebrows. "I wished I could see one of your paintings."

With a sigh of relief, she rolled her eyes. This was where the two of them belonged. Teasing friends, not whatever might have been happening before Cody walked in. That had felt too danger-ous, too much like it might hurt her later, no matter how much she wanted it. Like a sunny beach right before a tidal wave hit. This felt safer. A shallow creek where you could see your feet and watch the little fishies swim around your toes.

"Well then, come by my apartment tonight, and I'll show you one." Now that they were back in safe waters, why shouldn't he have one of his wishes fulfilled? Even if she was sure he was teasing. There was no way she figured in any of his wishes, if he even made any that weren't for her videos.

"Really?" His eyebrows popped up.

"I won't have time to make anything new for the gala. But I have a few that might work."

"Alright then. I'll see you tonight."

The grin he flashed threatened to reel her right back into those deeper, dangerous waves of impossible desire.

It was hard not to hope that the invitation from Aisha meant something more. The simmering tension had been so high in her office, he was surprised he hadn't burst into flames. If Cody hadn't shown up when he had, would Bram have kissed her? Did she want him to?

The answer was most assuredly no. Not after the way she'd acted around Cody, so distracted she hadn't even heard what the scientist had said. The invitation to her house was just a practical thing for her. There was a painting she wanted to show him, it was at her apartment, so she invited Bram there rather than drag it into work.

Of course, Bram's heart didn't seem to be paying attention to any of that. He stopped by Stella's tank on the way out of the aquarium that evening. Aisha seemed to think they were working for her and Cody. It was time for him to use some of whatever magic the starfish had too.

Stella was half-hidden behind a plant, with only two of her arms visible.

"So are you really magic, or is it all just coincidences?"

The starfish obviously didn't answer him. Just like she obviously had nothing to do with Aisha's supposed success with Cody. The truth was that the scientist was just finally taking notice of Aisha after keeping his head buried in research for the past six months. It was bound to happen eventually, but Aisha was the kind of person who believed it happened because she wished upon a starfish.

Bram didn't believe, but was the kind of person to fall hopelessly in love with the kind of woman who did.

The dim lights of the closed aquarium danced across Stella's tank, giving her a dappled, wavy coloring. Today, Aisha had wished for a chance to shine, not something specifically about Cody. Maybe Bram had more of a chance than he realized. After all, he was the one giving her a way to publicly show off her art. That was a much better way to shine than helping stupid Cody with his stupid graphics.

Plus, that sketch she'd been hiding looked way more like him than Cody.

Putting a hand against the tank, he asked Stella for the same thing he always did.

I wish she felt about me the way I feel about her.

A few hours later, Bram waited outside Aisha's apartment building with sweaty palms. Whatever happened today wouldn't prove one way or another that Stella granted wishes. It was just another chance to spend time with Aisha, away from the aquarium.

Except this time, she'd been the one to ask him.

The door buzzed, and he pushed it open to enter the vestibule. It was a small space, with just six mailboxes. The door to the right of them opened, and Aisha was there, smiling, dressed in a paint-splattered green hoodie, pink plaid pajama pants, and fluffy bunny slippers. Her wavy hair was tied up in a bun on top of her head. It was the opposite of the plain white button-down and gray slacks she'd worn at work. It was also the opposite way she'd be dressed if this were any kind of date.

Yet Bram struggled to swallow.

"You're early." She raised an eyebrow.

"I can come back."

She giggled and waved him in. "It's fine. I knew you would be."

This little hint that she knew him better than he realized was the most hopeful sign yet.

He followed her inside the small apartment, a smile instantly spreading across his face. His eyes darted from the fish-shaped coffee table to the bright pink walls and the paintings there, then down to the blue-green shag rug.

"I know it's a mess—"

He held up a hand, knowing exactly what she was about to say. She was going to try to excuse the bright but cluttered space as some sort of personality flaw. He'd watched her diminish herself in front of Cody for months, first with her words, then her clothes, but he wouldn't let her do that here, in her own home.

"It's perfectly you, and it's great."

The slow smile that spread across her face still didn't quite reach her eyes. "It's probably smaller than what you have."

It was like she'd taken a hot poker and stabbed it into his chest. This was what happened when people found out he was a Lowther. "Why does that matter? Do you think I pick my friends based on how big their apartments are?"

"We're friends?" There was a teasing lilt to her voice.

Of course they were friends. But were they more?

"What would you call us?" His hopeful heart stuttered in his chest.

"Colleagues . . . with potential." She grinned, the light sparking in her eye again.

"Only potential?" He crossed his arms over his chest and shook his head. "Wow, it must be tough to make the cut."

"You have no idea."

"So what would help push me over the edge into a friend?"

"More compliments about my house wouldn't hurt." She batted her eyelashes at him, and he chuckled.

"I'd need to see more of it first."

She gestured around the living room, with its squishy couch and wide windows facing the back of the property rather than the parking lot out front. "This is pretty much it." She pointed to the kitchen, its green cabinets visible over a half-wall. "That's obviously the kitchen. Down the hall, there're two bedrooms and a bathroom."

"Two bedrooms?" His stomach did a somersault. "Do you have a roommate?"

She grimaced. "No, I have a lot of stuff."

"How long have you lived here?"

It was a simple question, or so he thought, but Aisha grew quiet. She shoved her hands into the pockets of her hoodie and leaned back against the wall. "I bought it when I was eighteen."

"Oh." That wasn't what he'd been expecting.

"My mother . . . " She sighed and looked up at the ceiling. "I haven't seen my mother since I moved here from France, but she sent money until I was eighteen. My dad never used it. Said it was mine. I didn't know what to do with it, and Brooke's grandmother said buying property would be a good idea. I rented it out when I was in college to help pay for classes, then moved in when I graduated."

Hundreds of questions flooded his brain, and he could barely hold himself back from asking at least one of them. This desire to know her more, to know everything about her, had always been simmering under the surface. The only way he seemed to get information, however, was by not trying too hard. If he kept it light, let her know this didn't change anything for him, then maybe she'd keep talking.

He let out a low whistle. "Look at you, a real estate queen."

She laughed, but it was short and hard, so unlike her usual

tinkling, airy laugh. "Hardly. If I were smart, I would have sold it ages ago and bought something nicer." She ran a hand along the doorway to the kitchen, where the bright-pink paint was chipped. "But I like it here."

"All your stuff is here."

Now she gave him a real smile, and his shoulders relaxed. His gaze roamed around the living room again and landed on the canvas hanging over the television.

"Is this the painting you wanted me to see?" He stared open-mouthed at the burst of colors on the canvas. It was somehow both a meticulous depiction of a tree and the ocean. It shouldn't have been possible to show two things so well, but she'd captured the essence of the different settings with the colors and brushstrokes. "It's incredible."

"Oh, that?" She looked over her shoulder and shook her head. "That's just something I did back in high school."

High school? "If this is how good you were in your teens, why didn't you go to art school? Didn't you say your dad was an artist?"

Her lips were twisted to the side, like she wanted to respond but wasn't sure how. Bram recognized something in her face that he often felt. A pull between family loyalty and your own desires.

"Did he . . . not want you to be one?" Bram asked carefully.

"He wants me to do whatever makes me happy." A soft smile tugged at her lips. "He would have loved for me to go to art school, but I saw how hard that life was for him after my mom left."

Things were clicking into place, questions he'd been wondering about for days finally getting answers. A wealthy mother she hadn't seen in years. An artist father who'd shown her that a creative life wasn't a stable one. This desire she had to be seen as professional may have been new, but the fear motivating it was an old one.

"I can totally understand not wanting to end up like your parents."

Now the smile was directed at him, and everything inside of him lit up.

"I bet you can." She waved him over. "Come on. The piece I want to show you is in here."

He followed her down the short hallway lined with more artwork to a closed door. When she turned around, her face was red. "So this room is messy."

"Yes, I've seen your desk." He fought back a smile.

"No, I mean really messy." The color in her cheeks deepened. "Krista and Brooke don't even come in here. They say it gives them hives."

"So you don't show many people this room?"

She shook her head, and something glistened in her eyes. Not quite tears, but they weren't far away either. Had she ever been this vulnerable with him before? Talking about her parents was one thing. He could tell that there was more to the story than the little tidbits he'd gotten, but everyone had complicated family stuff. This was something else. This was her opening up the most private part of herself to him.

They were definitely more than colleagues with potential.

He cleared his throat. "You can just bring it out to me. I don't need to see the room."

"Well, you might not like this one, and it's just easier if you see them all, so if there's another one you think will be better you can see everything at once."

She was babbling. Not the excited, fun kind whenever she was excited about an idea. This was nervous babbling, something she hadn't done around him since their first week working together.

"That sounds good." He reached out a hand and put it on her shoulder. She seemed to relax into it. "Thank you for trusting me."

Now her eyes met his, and she reached up to take his hand in hers and lead him into the room. The contact with her skin was hot, like fire lacing her palms. He sucked in a breath, trying and failing to get his heart to beat in a regular rhythm instead of the erratic grasshopper jumps it was doing now.

They walked into the room, and the frantic beating of his heart stopped entirely. It was all so overwhelmingly Aisha, Bram didn't know where to look first. Every single wall was covered with paintings, and more were stacked on chairs. Piles and piles of art, bright sweeps of color over zoomed-in photographs, canvases entirely filled with paint, with others half-finished in what was almost a frustrated way. There were flecks of paint splattered on the carpet and wall, and a long desk in the back of the room was crammed with mason jars full of paintbrushes.

"This is . . . " He shook his head, the words not coming. How could he ever hope to describe his reaction to this? It was like being inside of her technicolored brain, inside of her bright and expansive soul. He wanted to curl up in a corner and never leave, just spend his life watching a genius at work.

"A mess, I told you." She shifted like she was going to release his hand, but he squeezed it tight, and pulled her to his side, her bunny slippers brushing against his sneakers.

It was definitely messy. Of course it was. But that's not all it was.

"It's wonderful."

Red spread up her neck and along her cheeks. She squirmed, trying to release her hand from his, but he held tight.

"I hope you know how incredible you are." The words didn't quite feel right, but they were the best he had right then. "I meant what I said the other day. You shouldn't have to change."

"But I want to." At this, he released her hand and took a step back to take her in. She rubbed her forehead and sighed. "I don't like feeling unsettled or messy. I want to be something, someone, else. Not just who everyone thinks I am."

"I get that." He did, more than she probably realized. The conversation with Darcey had been swimming around in his head all day. Short of moving away, there didn't seem to be a way out. He needed his parents' support for the aquarium, for everything. Their lives would always be intertwined.

"With my parents being who they are, people judge me before I even open my mouth." He shook his head and leaned back against the wall, reaching out to intertwine their hands again. Absently, he brushed a thumb along her palm. "I don't like feeling like that's all people see in me."

"Well, I don't know them, so I've only ever seen you." The smile she gave him was so electric, it was a good thing he was already leaning against something.

"And I don't see a mess when I look at you." She turned away with a frown, and he pulled on her arm to bring her closer to him. Her hoodie was soft and worn, like she'd had it for ages. "Really. It's hard to describe you, but unsettled or disorganized are not words I'd ever use. You're . . . " He bit his lip, aware of the warmth of her palm in his hand, the slight tingling from the touching of their skin distracting him almost as much as the vulnerability in her eyes. "You're so full of life and beauty and creativity. It's like working with the sun."

A smile played at the edges of her lips, her eyes not quite meeting his. "Is this just your effort to edge into friendship territory?"

"I want more than that."

She sucked in a breath at his words, and he almost did the

same. He hadn't planned on saying that. They were standing barely a foot apart, her hand in his, her eyes locked on his face, and all he could hear was the pounding of his heart in his ears.

"Look, I know you like Cody, and if he's who you really want, I won't get in the way of that." The words were bitter on his tongue, but he meant them. "I just thought you should know how I feel. It might make things awkward at work, but I can't keep pretending I don't like you as more than a colleague, more than a friend."

This went way beyond asking her out, which was all he'd been intending to do when Cody interrupted them that afternoon. There was no chance of that now. Only the urgent, desperate feeling that if Bram didn't say all of this now, he never would.

Several moments passed, and she was still standing silently in front of him. The longer she went without speaking, the more his stomach twisted into a tight knot. If there was one thing Aisha wasn't, it was quiet. The only reason she wasn't saying anything must be because she wasn't able to find the words to tell him nicely that she didn't feel the same.

Why would she? This bright, expansive world she lived in was so far away from his own limited life, he could only dream of being a part of it.

Finally, he let go of her hand and stepped back toward the door.

"I'm sorry, I didn't mean to—"

In the space of a heartbeat, she was wrapped around him, her lips on his, and his mind went blank from happiness.

THIRTY

AISHA

I'm kissing Bram.
Bram is kissing me.
We're kissing.
This is great!

The running commentary of what she was doing was hard to ignore, but Aisha did her best, wanting with every fiber of her being to stay in the moment and enjoy it. The feel of his luxurious curls between her fingers, the heat of his hand on her hip, the scratch of his stubble on her chin. And his lips . . .

Oh, his lips. Somehow soft and hard at the same time, giving her exactly what she wanted, like they'd been doing this for years. Like he'd been made just for her.

Had anything in her life ever felt this right?

If this were a painting, it would be bursts of color on a kite waving in the wind. This kiss couldn't be contained on a static canvas. It was floating high in the sky, touching the clouds.

The words he'd said rolled around in her mind and imprinted themselves on her heart.

It's like working with the sun.

No one had ever said anything like that about her, and she doubted anyone else ever would. She'd never felt so seen.

Eventually, they came up for air, and there was a brief moment when they stared at each other. Aisha's gut clenched, worried the kiss had been yet another impulsive mistake in a life full of them.

His lips, slightly swollen and red, turned up in a smile. "So I guess you probably like me more than a colleague too?"

Breathless, she giggled, and her shoulders dropped. "Something like that."

Still wrapped around each other, they grinned goofily, neither wanting to be the first to let go.

"Was there actually a painting you wanted to show me, or was this all a ruse to get me in here and ravage me?" He brushed a strand of hair that had fallen out of her bun off her face.

"Me?" She smacked his arm. "You're the one throwing out compliments like they're beads at a Mardi Gras parade. How did you think I'd react?"

He shrugged and bit his lip. "I dunno, blush?" He smoothed a finger along her neck and up to her cheek. "You get red here first, then it kind of creeps up into your face. It's adorable. Almost worth having Cody interrupt us earlier just to see it happen."

The name of her workplace crush, who was definitely not the person she'd just kissed within an inch of his life, hung in the air between them.

"Just so you know, I've liked you since the second I met you." The heat in her cheeks bloomed beneath his fingers. "But I knew you were out of my league."

"Excuse me?" He tsked. "If anyone is out of someone's league, it is you out of mine."

"Don't be ridiculous." Though with his arms wrapped around her, her lips stinging from his kisses, it was easy to feel like all her worries really were ridiculous. "I know what wealth looks like, and I know that I'm not part of that world. I don't want to be."

The next words out of her mouth should have been some

explanation, but she didn't even know where to start. How could she sum up everything in a single conversation about her mother? It felt impossible to put words to being discarded like a broken toy, to being taken away from the country she grew up in, to watching her dad give up his art. All because some spoiled rich girl got tired of being a mom and her family was embarrassed she'd had a child with someone they considered beneath her. The last words from Aisha's mother had been that she'd never even wanted to be one.

There was no explanation she could give Bram right now that would make him understand how very far away she wanted to stay from the whims of the wealthy.

"You feel like Cody's from the same world?" Bram's brow was wrinkled, and he spoke slowly, like he wanted to understand but couldn't connect the dots.

It was no surprise he couldn't, when Aisha was bending over backward to make the logic work. For months, she'd had to remind herself of all the reasons she didn't want Bram. Clinging to her lukewarm crush on Cody had felt like the solution to everything. Someone more attainable as well as someone to give her a reason to be more grounded and professional.

She'd been lying to herself to avoid looking too closely at what it would mean to actually be with Bram. She didn't want to start lying to him too.

"Do you really want to talk about Cody right now?" She raised an eyebrow, hoping to distract Bram.

It worked, a slow grin spreading across his face. "Not really, no. I'd much rather see the painting you wanted to show me. If there even is one."

She laughed and took a step back, then gestured around the room. "Oh, don't worry. I've got plenty of paintings."

"You said there was one in particular you had in mind for the auction."

"Actually, a few."

There was a stack of canvases in one corner that Aisha had

painted right after she started at the aquarium. The colors and animals had invaded her dreams for weeks—when they weren't filled with the face of her beautiful new colleague, Bram—and painting had been the only way to get some sleep.

Bram looked through them, his face serious, eyes darting along the details of each one.

"These are gorgeous. What inspired them?"

Hmm, maybe I need to rethink that whole "I don't want to lie to him" thing.

"Um, the aquarium?"

A smirk pulled at his lips, and his eyes were sparkling when he looked at her.

"Oh yeah? Anything in particular there?"

The heat he loved to see creep up her cheeks was definitely doing that now. She let her hands wander over the desk, picking up stray paintbrushes and shoving them into the already overstuffed mason jars that were scattered around.

"Just you know . . . the animals . . . the people."

One particularly fat paintbrush did not want to go into the jar, and she turned toward it, using her other hand to rearrange the brushes already in there to make space. There was a soft swish of his feet on the paint-splattered carpet as he came up behind her.

His voice was low, and his hands were firm on her hips as he whispered in her ear, "I don't know if I want my parents bidding on a painting that's actually me."

"I never said it was you." She spun around, breaking his hold on her, and crossed her arms. He was tall enough that her gaze was more lip-level than eye-level. Lifting her chin, she glared as much as she could. "Someone has an awfully big ego."

That smirk was back, and he settled his hands again on her hips, pulling her even closer. "Then tell me it's not me, just like that sketch from earlier today wasn't me."

It was hard to breathe this close to him, and even harder to lie.

"Fine, they're all of you." She rolled her eyes, arms still crossed over her chest. "Happy?"

He leaned in and planted a kiss right below her ear, sending a shiver through her body that she'd be feeling for the next week. "I am, but now they definitely can't be put up for auction. What else do you have?"

"I literally have dozens of others." Aisha gestured around the room weakly with one hand, her arms having gone limp as seaweed as soon as he'd kissed her neck.

He took a step away from her, his own arms feeling a little wobbly as well. Turning toward the stacks of canvas around her, he kept a hand on the small of her back, not able to let her go just yet. To be able to touch her, to kiss her, after months of thinking about it was . . . well, it was a good thing this had happened here in the privacy of her home and not in her office earlier or they'd both probably be out of a job.

"Are there any others with sea creatures?" The grin he knew would be on his face for days widened. "Ones *not* inspired by me, if that's even possible?"

She let out a groan and dropped her head into her hands. "You're not going to let me live that down, are you?"

With a chuckle, he planted a kiss on her cheek just because he could. "Nope."

"There's nothing I'd want anyone to see, but there are a few older pieces that could work." Stepping away from him, she crouched down to a stack below a table that was covered with tubes of paint. They were all closed and grouped by color. It was cluttered but there was still a logic to things, it just wasn't what most people would think of as organized.

Bram found it adorable. Though his punch-drunk ecstasy from finally being able to kiss Aisha meant he would have found anything about her adorable right now. The girl he'd liked for months liked him too. There were things that she was uncomfortable with about his family, that much was clear, but there'd be a way around that. He'd find a way. Now that he had her, he was even more determined to find a way to disentangle himself from Evelyn and Richard Lowther.

Nothing was coming to him right now, but Aisha was bent over in front of him, so every brain cell was obviously focused on that.

"Here it is!" She popped up and turned around with a smile as bright as the sun. Ironically, that's what the painting seemed to be. On a canvas almost half her height, a bright-yellow background was streaked with oranges and reds in a swirling pattern that was somehow both the sky and the ocean. With only three colors, she'd painted an entire seascape.

"I hope you realize how incredibly talented you are."

"Yeah, yeah, I've heard it before." Her arms dropped so the painting could rest on the ground. There was that satisfying pink tinge to her skin that let him know his words had affected her. "Brooke and Krista always thought I should try to start a social media account, sell stuff on the side but . . . " She shrugged. "I didn't want to start to rely on that and then have it all be taken away."

"So you did a bunch of random jobs instead?"

She stuck her tongue out at him. "They weren't random. They were fun."

"Painting isn't fun?"

She pursed her lips, still red from their kisses, as she considered this. "It's more than fun. It's a part of me." She looked down at the enormous painting propped against her legs. "It felt safer somehow, to have these jobs I didn't care about than for people to judge my art. So I just do it for me, and for friends."

The significance of what she was willing to do, just because he'd asked, settled heavy on his shoulders. "You're really okay putting this one up for auction?"

Her hands gripped the canvas tightly and she rocked back on her heels. "I think so. It's for Stella, right?"

"I do have a lot to thank her for." Reaching out to the painting, he set it aside and then let his hands trail up her arms to rest on her cheeks. "All my wishes have come true."

There'd only been the same wish, over and over, but it was still unbelievable Aisha felt the same for him as he did for her. That she had since the beginning, but it had taken a spontaneous social media fundraising campaign inspired by a little kid to finally push them together.

They'd already settled on the butterfly effect as the perfect theme for the gala, and it really was perfect. One small thing could change everything.

"I don't think I could even have imagined this to be able to wish for it." Setting aside the canvas, Aisha made her way back into Bram's arms. When he wrapped them around her, she let out a little sigh, like this was the only place she wanted to be.

"It'll be my job now to grant your wishes." He placed a kiss on her forehead. "No Stella needed."

"What about our real jobs?" Her voice was softer than he'd ever heard it around him, and his tender heart pulsed in his ears, hoping he'd be able to put her at ease.

He brushed a strand of her hair off her face, and just that gentle touch of his fingers sent pinpricks of light along his skin. They both inhaled deeply in unison, and Bram chuckled a little on the exhale.

"You mean, do we need to say anything at work?"

She nodded, eyes full of uncertainty. He could feel her body stiffen in his arms.

"Do you *not* want to say anything?" The words were like sawdust in his mouth, but he forced them out.

"Maybe just . . . not right away?"

His chest caved in at that. There was no denying it rankled, the idea that nobody would know. That Cody wouldn't know. Did it really matter as long as Bram knew Aisha had picked him?

The silence stretched on, his brain and mouth not able to work together long enough to respond.

"Maybe not until after the gala?" she finally supplied.

He sucked in a breath. "That's still over a month away." Could he pretend that long?

You've been pretending to be Bram Howard for months. Pretending he wasn't the trust-fund child of millionaires.

"I just don't want people to get distracted by . . . " Aisha gestured at their embracing bodies. "This. The focus should be on fundraising. Not our private life."

"If that's what you want." It was the last thing he wanted, but he'd give her anything that was in his power to give. If she was willing to overlook who his family was, to give him a chance, then he could give her the privacy she wanted so they could focus on work.

He lifted her chin with his hand and kissed her again, and everything jumping around inside of him settled down. He'd waited this long to be with her. What was one more month?

THIRTY-TWO
BRAM

After a long week of pretending he wasn't deliriously happy, Bram decided to swing by Stella's tank Friday morning. He didn't know what he should wish for from the starfish—he only knew that he couldn't survive another month like this.

Thirty days to go.

The countdown to the gala Bram had been tracking in his head now meant something else entirely. Keeping things casual at work, making sure no one suspected anything was going on between him and Aisha, was proving just as hard as he'd thought it would be. She seemed to be doing much better at it, which he tried not to read too much into.

They'd both been busy that week and hadn't spent much time together at the office other than popping into each other's offices for quick updates on gala preparations.

Had Aisha confirmed things with the caterer? Had Bram finalized the program? Had the director approved the final budget? Had Sandra in accounting gotten all the receipts?

It was all politely professional. Other than the lingering gazes that promised their evenings would be much less professional. Bram was now very familiar with Aisha's technicolor apartment. It was like a burr in his chest to see her back in gray and beige business casual every morning.

Maybe he'd wish for her to go back to dressing the way she did before.

An arm poked out from behind a rock as Bram approached Stella's tank.

He shook his head. How she dressed was her choice, even if he preferred to see her in clothes that matched her bright personality.

"I suppose you're quite pleased with yourself, aren't you?" He grinned and put a hand on the tank. As the arm waved, the starfish slowly wriggled into view. "I'll take that as a yes."

There was a quiet moment as he watched Stella, her arms undulating gently in the water, the low lights reflecting off the glass, the layer of grime that had accumulated overnight that would be vacuumed away before the aquarium opened in a few hours.

"I really do wish your species will get saved, you know." He traced the outline of her shape with a finger, missing the mark half the time since she kept moving around. "I do care about endangered sea life. Not just my love life."

This seemed to please the starfish, and she wriggled in place, which made Bram laugh.

"This is ridiculous, talking to a starfish." He looked over his shoulder, but the main atrium was empty, the lights dimmed and the other tanks bathed in shadows. "I know it's not really because of you that I got what I wanted."

Did he have everything he wanted, though? A niggling worry had been eating away at him all week. Would Aisha have made the same request to keep things quiet with Cody?

Stella's mouth opened and closed, and Bram took a step back. Then he laughed at himself. It was even more ridiculous to be afraid that she would eat him from the other side of the tank. She didn't even have teeth. To eat, she would push her stomach outside of her body and wrap it around the prey she'd trapped in her arms. Though it was really cool, he'd only had to see it once before he decided that little factoid would not be going into any promotional materials. People wanted to donate to nice, happy animals whose stomachs stayed inside their bodies.

"Well, thank you for listening at least." He gave her a little salute. "I'll make sure the gala raises as much money as possible so there can be little Stellas for centuries to come."

"That's very sweet of you."

Mrs. Rhode's voice drifted over him, and his chest tightened. Plastering on a smile, he turned to face her. The director of the aquarium was dressed in dark navy slacks with creases so straight they looked ironed, her silver-streaked hair up in a tight bun at the back of her head. Nothing in her face revealed even a hint of how much she might have heard of Bram's one-sided conversation with Stella.

"You don't think our starfish is magical?" Normally when using such a casual, jaunty tone, he'd wink. This was not someone he did that with.

The older woman pursed her lips, looking so much like Cody it was hard to believe it had taken Aisha so long to realize the connection between the mother and son. She'd admitted sheepishly the night before she'd been unaware of it for the first few weeks after Cody started working at the aquarium, even with the same last name.

Last names.

Aisha's hesitancy to make their relationship public must have something to do with him being a Lowther. Attaching yourself to a family like his was no easy feat. The expectations that weighed on him daily would take Aisha's shining light—already dimmed so she could feel more professional at work—and snuff it out completely.

Maybe it was better this way, as hard as it was for him to hide how he was feeling.

"I think the money Stella has helped raise has been transformative. It feels magical to my researchers," Mrs. Rhodes said, dragging Bram's attention back to the aquarium.

"I'm glad to hear that." He gave her his most reassuring smile. "The gala will bring in even more."

"You're confident you'll be able to sell all the tickets?" A frown creased her forehead. "It's less than a month away."

"I've done it before with less time." The confidence that radiated off him came from years of experience, but he wondered if that's what Mrs. Rhodes saw, or just the Lowther connections he'd brought with him. "And Aisha's got a great plan for the marketing."

"Hmm." It was the same reaction Mrs. Rhodes always seemed to have about Aisha. It took all of Bram's control not to say anything. They were just colleagues, as far as the director knew, and if he went too intense in his defense, it might clue her in that there was something more going on.

"I understand she's helping you out as well outside of the marketing?"

Panic shot through him, and his easy, confident smile slipped for a moment. Were they supposed to have gotten her sign-off for that? He normally had quite a bit of leeway with how he did things, but this was the biggest event they'd ever had at the aquarium. It was to be expected that the director would want to be more involved than simply signing off on the budget. "Just getting her input on some of the design choices. She has a really good eye."

"She does." A sharp nod accompanied this, and Bram relaxed a little. "She helped Cody with the graphics for a presentation. They were good changes."

Coming from her, that was practically a standing ovation.

"I'll tell her you think so. She'll be glad to know she could help."

"She is helpful, isn't she?" Mrs. Rhodes sounded thoughtful, her eyes roaming over Stella's tank, now empty of the starfish. "I wasn't sure about her at first, but with the way Cody talks about her and the way things have been going lately, it was a good choice to bring her on full time."

How does Cody talk about her? Jealousy pooled in Bram's chest.

Mrs. Rhodes glanced up at Bram, like she'd forgotten he was there. "Not as good as bringing you on, of course." Not one to smile, the director's flash of teeth was totally unexpected. "I've never seen such large donations before. I hope this is just the start of what you can do for us."

Bram's stomach felt like it was going to eject from his body the way Stella's could. Like he really needed another reminder about how important this gala was.

"Of course." His smile was weaker than he'd have liked, but Mrs. Rhodes didn't seem to notice. She nodded at him, then made her way to the executive offices on the other side of the aquarium.

Turning to give Stella a final glance, Bram rushed toward the door that led to the staff area.

Please let her be here already.

It hadn't quite been a wish, but Bram silently thanked Stella anyway when he opened the door to Aisha's office and saw her standing in front of her desk. Her bag was on her chair like she'd only just arrived. The black pinstriped pantsuit was the most severe he'd seen on her yet, but he couldn't deny it did make her look incredibly put together.

Too put together.

The door closed with a bang when he kicked it with his foot, and her eyes widened.

"Bram, you shouldn't be in—"

Her words cut off when his mouth found hers, and she sank into his kiss like it was home. Less than twelve hours ago, they'd been doing the same thing on her couch, and he'd give anything to be back there now, where he didn't have to hide anything. Where he could just be Bram, and not Bramwell Lowther, and all the pressure and complications that brought along with it.

It took everything in him to pull out of the kiss, to disentangle his hands from her hair, and to take a deep breath that didn't shudder inside his chest.

"Are you sure you don't want to go to HR today?" His hands

were on her shoulders, his desperate gaze locked on hers. "Tell them we're together, let everyone know?"

Her eyes were hazy for a moment, her lips bee-stung red and puffy from the kiss. Taking a deep breath, she put her hands on his chest and pushed away. "It's been fine this week, hasn't it?"

"I mean, everything after work has been great, but I just wonder . . . " He sighed and rubbed his forehead with a hand. What he was really wondering was if he were anyone else, would she still want to hide, but the words wouldn't come. What if the one thing he couldn't change was the one thing she couldn't get past? "I just wonder how much longer I can still do my job when I'm this distracted."

Her laugh was a warm breath on his cheek, and his heart soared. "Am I really that distracting in this suit? I feel like I'm going to a funeral."

"You look great." He meant it with his whole heart, but she raised her eyebrow at him. "You do. I ran into Mrs. Rhodes by Stella's tank, and she had lots of good things to say about you."

Aisha sucked in a breath. "Really?"

"Those graphics you did for Cody's presentation seemed to impress her. Even if it was just for Sandra." The head of accounting was, impossibly, even blander and more serious than Cody, so the changes Aisha had made were actually to take colors out, not add them in.

"Oh, that's . . . that's good." A slight hint of panic laced her words. Before Bram could reach out with a reassuring hand on her shoulder, she closed her eyes and took a deep breath. When she opened them, she looked and sounded calmer. "I'm glad she's taking notice of what I can do. That was the whole point of helping with the gala."

"I thought you were doing that to get Cody to see you differently?" Bram's words were teasing, but jealousy licked at his chest.

A bashful smile swept across her face. "That's what I said, but it was just to spend more time with you."

What response was there to that other than to kiss her again?

When they finally pulled out of the embrace, they were both breathless and their cheeks flushed.

"Are you busy tomorrow?" Her eyes were hazy again.

"Not at all." He tucked a strand of her hair behind her ear. The clips she secured so carefully had been completely dislodged thanks to him. "My only plans are to spend as much time as possible with you. The whole day if possible."

Her bottom lip tucked under her teeth. "I don't know about the whole day. I'm helping Brooke with—"

"I'll come help too."

She giggled. "You don't even know what it is."

"Doesn't matter. I want to spend the whole day with you, whatever you're doing."

"We already spend all day together."

Pulling back one side of her hair, he fastened the clip the way he'd seen her do a hundred times. Worry balled tight in his stomach. They had been together a lot this week. All day at the office and then every night after work until late. It still hadn't been enough for Bram, but Aisha might not feel the same. "I understand if you need a break."

"I don't need one, but I thought . . . " She reached up and touched her hair, surprise flickering across her face when she realized there was nothing to adjust. "You might need one? It's been almost a week after all. That's usually when, um, well. It's usually when guys need a break."

This was all said in her small voice, the one he'd hoped he'd never hear again, and it had Bram seeing red.

Was that the reason she didn't want to tell people at work? Because she thought his interest might not last more than a week?

Only thirty days to go.

Then he'd be able to tell the entire world how he felt about her, and she'd realize this wasn't some passing fancy for him.

He wrapped his arms around her.

"The only break I need is from spreadsheets." He buried her face in her neck and breathed in the smell of her shampoo that was already as familiar as if it was his own. "If I need to look at that RSVP list one more time, I might explode."

Aisha laughed, and whatever lingering jealousy or worry Bram had left melted away.

Saturday morning dawned bright and cheery, a streak of sunlight peeking through the gauzy curtains in Aisha's bedroom to paint her walls red and orange. The humidity of the past few days was gone, along with the weight Aisha'd been carrying around. Trying to hide how she felt about Bram at work had been harder than she'd expected. Stuffy, uncomfortable clothes and dialing back her energy was a walk in the park compared to pretending she didn't want to drag Bram into a supply closet and kiss his face off every two minutes.

As hard as it was, she knew it was the right call. There was no way Mrs. Rhodes would have been so complimentary about her to Bram if she had known about their relationship. Finally making progress with her boss was worth it, right?

At least today she could just be the same Aisha she always was with her friends at the animal shelter. A smile spread wide across her face as she reached for the giant Yorkie earrings and cat-patterned shirt she always wore for these monthly adoption events. She loved helping Brooke, and until this month, the other main attraction was the handful of Ethan's firefighter friends there lending a hand as well. Not that she'd be noticing any of them today.

Bram was coming with her.

A shiver of excitement ran through her when the front door buzzed. Before she'd even told Bram what they'd be doing today, he'd said yes. It seemed like he'd say yes to anything she wanted, which was both thrilling and terrifying. There were other people in her life who'd do anything for her, but Bram was the only one with the kind of resources to actually do it.

No, he doesn't use that money anymore, she reminded herself as she flung the door open wide and wrapped him in her arms. His shoulders shook from silent laughter at her enthusiasm, and he planted a kiss on her cheek in greeting.

He's living a different life from his family, on purpose.

How long can that really last though?

The sleek electric car that drove them to the shelter was, if not exactly proof of a split from his family, at least proof that his values lay elsewhere. For now. As much as she wanted to trust that he wouldn't change his mind about Aisha at some point, the same part of her that had trouble believing he'd even be friends with her wasn't convinced he'd stick around now that they were more.

There was still that other, bigger part of her that believed in Stella's magic, and that anything was possible. Today, she'd try to listen to that part of her instead.

"So, what do you need me to do today?" Bram had one hand on the steering wheel and one on her knee, just below where her long denim shorts stopped. The heat of his palm on her skin was distracting enough that he had to ask her a second time before she managed an answer.

"Oh, um, I'm not sure." She reached up to smooth her hair away from her face. Without her usual clips, her waves had a tendency to go wild around her head, like swirling storm clouds. That's what his hand on her leg made her feel. Electric. Like she could run a marathon and still have energy left to swim to Florida. "I just do whatever Ethan and Brooke tell me to do."

"Hmm."

She couldn't tell if he sounded disappointed or not. With his thumb moving in little circles against her skin, she couldn't even tell what day it was.

"Will we have to stay long?" His eyes slid to hers, and the air in the car seemed to disappear.

"At least a few hours . . . " She leaned her head back against the seat. "Bram, I can't think with your hand there."

He chuckled and squeezed her knee. "This hand?"

"Yes." She squirmed, but not hard enough to dislodge it. That wasn't really her goal. After trying so hard to avoid touching each other all week at work, the ability to do it as much as they wanted when they were alone was intoxicating.

"I have no intention of removing it until I absolutely have to." The look he gave her was suddenly uncertain. "Or if you ask me to, of course."

There was silence in the car. The longer it stretched out, the wider and smugger Bram's smile got. Aisha had no intention of asking him, and he knew it.

A few silent, tingling, tension-filled minutes later, he pulled into a parking spot in the small lot in front of the shelter, his hand never leaving her leg. It was actually kind of impressive—and hot— how in control of the car he was with just one hand.

He even managed to put the car into park with his left hand, turning his body to face her.

"So." She looked down at her knee, and he gave it another squeeze in response.

"So." There was a laugh at the edge of his voice, and Aisha couldn't help but smile, a tight fluttering feeling invading her chest.

It was like their competitions at work, which they hadn't done in a few weeks. No lunchroom charades or paperclip battles in the hallway. Not with a gala to plan and Aisha's more professional work persona finally getting some attention.

"Are we just going to sit here until someone interrupts us?" She raised an eyebrow, the challenge made.

He leaned in closer, his breath hot on her cheek. "Or until you can't stand it anymore."

This was familiar territory, but taken up to an entirely new level. It was all the fun of their previous friendship, with an extra bite of something more.

"I can sit here all day." Lifting her hands behind her head, she leaned back in her seat.

The only response to that was for his fingers to start tracing little circles on her thigh.

I may have underestimated his competitive spirit.

A knock on the window sent a jolt through them both, and Bram's hand shot off her leg like it was on fire.

"Ha! I won." With a delighted snicker, she flipped her hair over her shoulder.

Rolling his eyes, he hit the button to roll down the window. "Doesn't count," he murmured.

"Sir, this spot is reserved for volun—" Ethan's eyes went wide when he peered in through the passenger-side window. "Oh, hey, Aisha. And . . . Bram."

There was the slightest tremble at the corner of Ethan's lips before his face smoothed out entirely.

"Hi, Ethan. We're both here to help." With a smile she hoped was bright enough to distract her friend from asking any questions, Aisha got out of the car as quickly as possible. "Just tell us what to do."

"Sounds good." He shook Bram's hand when he got out of the car. "But you've done as many of these as I have. You already know the drill."

For some reason, Ethan's comment sent a funny shiver through Aisha's spine.

All her recent efforts at work were finally paying off, but this was Brooke's event. Would her friends be able to see her as the capable person she was starting to consider herself?

While Ethan took Bram to go do that serious-faced, crossed-arms commentary thing that guys seemed compelled to do when faced with a flurry of activity that required nothing directly from them, Aisha looked around for her friends. Her stomach was in knots, but not because of the lingering traces of heat Bram's palm had left on her knee.

Neither Krista nor Brooke was out front with the dogs and cats. Since most people wanted puppies, the idea was to get them to walk past all the other adorable, but older, animals first. It worked super well, with nearly every adoption event ending with empty cages.

It had been Aisha's suggestion after the first event all those months ago. Something she'd learned during a marketing seminar.

This second reminder of how well she understood how things worked settled into her stomach, like she'd eaten something weird.

Had she even eaten anything this morning? She couldn't remember.

Typical Aisha. Making one suggestion that Brooke used months ago didn't change that.

Aisha found Brooke and Krista wrangling puppies in the special fenced-off area of the yard at the back of the shelter.

"Nice new ride you got there." With twinkling eyes, Brooke lifted a familiar dachshund puppy. Chip or Dale, there was no way to tell without looking at the collar. "Very eco-friendly."

"Very pricey." Krista raised an eyebrow.

"I, uh, came here with Bram."

This got a pleased gasp from Brooke and a smug smile from Krista. Putting the puppy into the arms of another volunteer, Brooke grabbed Aisha's arm and dragged her around to the front of the building with Krista following closely. Ethan now had Bram carrying out crates of cat food. The families who adopted got free samples to help ease the transition for the animals in a new home. This had been Brooke's idea, but Aisha had been the one to set up the partnership with the pet store for donations.

"Is he here as a friend or something more?" Krista said, her eyes only landing briefly on Bram before her gaze turned to the handful of firefighters who'd come by today. The inexplicable aversion she seemed to have for the profession had softened quite a bit once Ethan came into their lives last year, but she was still wary around them as a group. It was like with everyone else, she wanted to be adored, but with firefighters, she wanted to fade into the background.

Fading into the background right now would be nice, thought Aisha, but she knew it would be better to get this out of the way sooner rather than later.

"Well, I invited him over on Monday, and we've been kissing every day since then, so I guess that means something more?"

Letting out the tiniest of shrieks that still made a few of the dogs bark in concern, Brooke clapped excitedly. "What? That's great! Tell us everything."

"Right now?" Aisha gestured around. "Isn't there anything we need to be doing? Are the adoption forms printed out? Did you post this morning on social media?"

Brooke waved a hand. "Everything's running smoothly. These guys know what they're doing."

The change in Brooke from the first adoption event all those months ago was remarkable. Instead of being anxious about every little thing, clutching a clipboard with a schedule that planned everything down to the minute, Brooke was the epitome of calm. The "Ethan effect" is what Aisha and Krista called it, but they knew it wasn't just him. Losing the grandmother who had raised her had changed everything for Brooke, and it was only after talking to a therapist that things had truly taken a turn, and she'd gotten a better handle on this new, unexpected life she found herself in.

Though a supportive, sweet, gorgeous boyfriend certainly didn't make things worse.

Is that what Aisha had now too? The only reason she noticed all the things she'd contributed to this event was because of Bram. His gentle reminders all week that Aisha had the skills and knowledge to help him had settled into her brain and were hard to ignore now that she knew where to find them.

"He came over to look at a painting and—"

"You showed him your painting room?" Krista interrupted, her eyebrows sky-high.

"Well, yeah, that's where all my paintings are."

"And that's where it happened?" Brooke squeezed her arm again, distracting her from Krista's subtle criticism. For years, Krista had been trying to get Aisha to do something with her art, to show it publicly in some way, but Aisha had always resisted. Until Bram had asked.

Unease rippled through her. Did that mean she was doing what her dad had, relying on an affluent partner to get connected to people interested in their art?

No, this was completely different. Aisha wasn't an artist, not the way her dad had been. She never wanted to be. It was too unpredictable, too chaotic, even for her. With all his talent, her dad still had to give it up when they moved back to the States. It wasn't a viable option.

Words were suddenly getting blocked in the space between her brain and her mouth, so Aisha simply nodded in response to Brooke's question. A smile did manage to spread across her face, and Brooke did a little happy-dance next to her.

Krista's eyes narrowed. "Why was he looking at a painting?"

Words would be required now, unfortunately. Avoiding the question wouldn't work, not with Krista. Her finely honed lawyer senses would sniff out any attempts at masking the truth. "There's going to be an art auction at the gala, so I'm contributing one of my paintings."

This seemed to stun Krista into complete silence, an occurrence so rare that Aisha was tempted to take a picture.

Meanwhile, Brooke was beaming. "That's great. I'm sure it'll raise a ton of money for the aquarium."

Krista cleared her throat. "Make sure you get a receipt so you can claim the deduction on your taxes for donating the art."

Sneaking her arm away from Brooke, Aisha threw it over Krista's shoulder and hugged her tight. While on the surface it might not sound like an enthusiastic response, especially when compared to Brooke's, tax advice from Krista was giving her stamp of approval.

"This all happened Monday, and you waited until now to tell us?"

With a sigh, Aisha slipped her arm off her friend's shoulder. Accusatory Krista was back.

"We're keeping it quiet." Crossing her arms over her chest, Aisha kept her voice even. "I don't want anyone at work knowing."

Krista nodded, her eagle-eye gaze back on the firefighters, as if waiting for one of them to make a mistake. "That's sensible, especially before you know for sure where it's going."

If Krista agreed with her, then it must be the right decision. In all her prior dreams of being with Cody, Aisha had never considered the real impact dating someone at work might have on her career. After that first kiss with Bram, the potential fallout had suddenly hit her. The transformation to a more professional persona would disappear in an instant if people knew she was dating someone at work. People would assume she was just helping out her boyfriend because he asked, not because she had any skills in the area.

If things went sour, like they most certainly would at some point, then she'd be in an even worse situation at work than before. Things were finally going well, and she wasn't about to put all that in jeopardy.

"I don't think there's any doubt where it's going. Look at him staring at you." Brooke nudged her, almost vibrating with happiness.

Bram was over by the fenced-in pens with the older dogs, crouching next to Brownie but looking over at Aisha and her friends. It was true he was gazing at her with something that until now she'd only seen in Ethan's eyes when he looked at Brooke. That same tight, fluttering feeling from the car ride over here was back in Aisha's chest.

"I'm going to see if he needs my help."

As she made her way through the tamed chaos that was the monthly adoption event, Aisha tried not to feel discouraged. Even her friends were more focused on her relationship than on how she could be useful today. The decision to stay quiet at work was the right one, no matter how hard it was to keep pretending she wasn't as crazy about Bram as he seemed to be about her.

At least for now.

THIRTY-FIVE
AISHA

Bent over Brownie, Bram was whispering into the dog's ear when Aisha walked up to them, her heart hammering.

"Looks like you found your old friend." Luckily, her voice was steady enough so he wouldn't notice anything was amiss. Or that her heart was about to beat out of her chest.

Bram looked up at her, a small smile on his face. "I promised him last weekend that if he was still here at the next adoption event, he'd come home with me."

"You really meant it?" Her pulse was getting close to hummingbird speed.

"Of course." There was a slight crinkle between his eyebrows. "If I promise I'll do something, I will."

Even though she'd known him for months, had spent more hours with him than with any other guy in the past few years besides her dad, part of her still didn't believe him. She knew it was his wealth that made her not fully trust him, and she wanted to get past that, she really did.

After all, it was her mother that had caused it, not something Bram had done, or even his family. Not that the Lowthers were innocent of all wrongdoing, of course. No one with that much wealth ever could be. Bram was close to his family, so it wasn't fair to think he'd give it all up for someone who didn't even want to tell people they were together.

Not that giving up his family is what she wanted him to do, either.

What a mess. Typical Aisha.

This complicated web of thoughts and feelings wouldn't get untangled in a single day, but watching Bram cuddle Brownie was helping tease apart the tightest of the knots.

"That's really sweet of you." With emotions flooding her system, she didn't trust herself to say more than that. She bit her lip, unsure of whether she was holding back a smile or tears.

Bram stood up and looked around, a helpless but excited look on his face. "Are there forms I need to fill out? Will you come with me to buy all the stuff I need, or do you need to stay here? Can he go in my car, or will that scare him?"

Warmth spread through Aisha's chest, but something still held her back from fully sinking into the feeling. "Are you sure you've thought this through? A dog is a lot of work, a big commitment. He's a living being. You can't just forget about him and abandon him if you get bored."

Curiosity was brimming in Bram's expression, and Aisha was worried she'd revealed too much. Was her "unwanted" scar showing? When she blinked, however, the look was gone, and he flashed a familiar smirk.

"You of all people know I'm up for any challenge." He bent down again, reaching over the sides of the pen with the dogs to give Brownie another scratch behind the ears.

A smile tugged at her own lips against her will. "This isn't like seeing who can stuff more candy into their mouth or who can get more tourists to buy the ugly t-shirts from the gift shop."

Both had been unofficial competitions at work that he'd of course won.

"You're just upset I technically won earlier."

He stuck out his lower lip and pouted. *Pouted.* That must have been how he'd won the gift shop contest. Who could resist that face? "Interference from an outside source doesn't count."

Heat raced along her body, reminding her of what had happened in the car, but she narrowed her gaze at him and crossed her arms. This was much more important than any of that.

"Hey." Seeming to realize she wasn't kidding around when it came to an animal's welfare, Bram stood up and came to put a hand on her shoulder. He dropped his voice and leaned in close. "I'm taking this seriously. You can trust me."

A shiver ran through her as he gazed deep into her eyes, like he was trying to speak directly to her soul. Was he only talking about the dog?

Though she'd hinted at it, Aisha still hadn't told him about her mother, about all the fears she still had and the hang-ups around wealth that would probably always be there for her. She and Bram only been doing . . . whatever they were doing . . . for less than a week. There was no guarantee this was going to be anything more than the kind of fun work hookup that she'd had dozens of times before.

It was hard to let herself hope it could be more, after decades of disappointment.

"The shelter will give you a few things, but we can stop at a store nearby." She held out her hand, and he took it, letting her lead him to the table with the adoption forms.

Yes, he was serious about Brownie, and she trusted Bram was serious about owning a dog.

She simply wasn't sure she'd ever trust that he was serious about her.

Deep inside, she was still that abandoned little girl, afraid of being abandoned again.

Typical Aisha.

Having a dog was both easier and harder than Bram had expected.

Easy because Brownie wasn't a puppy, so he already knew to sit by the door when he needed to go out. Easy because he was calm and never barked. Easy because he seemed to trust Bram from the very start, like he'd understood the promise that day at the shelter and realized Bram came through on it.

All of the easy is what made it hard. Within days it was impossible for Bram to remember what his life had been like without a dog. The instant he stepped out of the house, he felt guilty for leaving Brownie alone. He had the urge to text the dog walker every five minutes to make sure she was still coming and wouldn't bail at the last second.

It was the same thing with his relationship with Aisha. Nothing was easier than their evenings together, walking Brownie, making dinner, watching a movie together afterward.

Then, twelve hours later, they'd be at work, and he had the impossible task of acting like nothing was going on. Only his years of Lowther training let him pull it off, but as the weeks went by, the harder it got.

Right when he needed to be focused on finishing things up for the gala, his brain was consumed by everything new and wonderful, everything easy yet hard in his life. A little over a week before the big night, he wasn't even sure he could tell you what time it was starting if you'd asked him.

At least Aisha was there to help. She'd been doing so much more than he'd ever expected, and she was doing it to perfection.

On Friday morning, with just eight days to go, she was sitting at the tiny table in the staff kitchen when he arrived at work. A notebook was open in front of her, along with a fresh bag of madeleines. His brother Stephen had given it to Bram at family dinner the previous Sunday. Apparently there'd been some meeting with a vendor in the UK, and Stephen had "popped over to France for a few days' vacation." Bram couldn't even remember his last vacation.

When Aisha looked up from her notes and smiled at him, his heart turned over in his chest. Once the gala was over, he'd ask about taking a few days off. With Aisha.

"How was Brownie this morning?" she asked. "Does he like the new leash I got him?"

After peering down the hallway to make sure it was empty, Bram swooped in to plant a quick kiss on Aisha's neck, right behind her ear.

"Bram!" She was pink in an instant, the color rising along her skin the way he knew it would, the way he loved to see. Like her entire body was being taken over by the emotion, too strong to keep it contained. "What if someone sees?"

"Nobody's here." He leaned forward and wrapped his arms around her, breathing her in. "What's the point of working with my girlfriend if I can't do this when nobody's around?"

She stiffened in his arms. "Girlfriend?"

They hadn't said the words yet, but it had been almost three weeks. "What else would you be?"

"A colleague with potential?" She snickered, but it quickly

turned into a happy sigh when he kissed her again, right below her ear.

When she leaned back into his arms, it was like all was right with the world. Nothing could ruin his mood today. They were going to raise millions for Stella at the gala and then he'd take a vacation with his girlfriend.

"Good morning."

Aisha let out a yelp, and Bram sprang back from her. Somehow, Cody had managed to make his way into the minuscule kitchen without either of them hearing or seeing him.

"Another spider sighting?" Cody's eyes were on the top of the cabinets, where the madeleines were usually stored.

"Um, yeah." Aisha turned her wide, panicked eyes to Bram, giving him a 'back me up here' look.

Grumbling to himself at the interruption, he played along. "It had a red spot. Is that bad?"

"A red spot? Are you sure?" Pushing his glasses up his nose, Cody moved a chair over to the counter to climb up and investigate closer. "I can't think of how a Latrodectus mactans got in here but—"

"A what?" Bram interrupted what was probably going to be a very long, boring science talk about spiders.

"A black widow. That's what you saw, isn't it?"

"I'm not sure. Maybe."

"Aisha, was it the same one you saw the other week? When we were in the kitchen, just the two of us, after work?"

Bram cut his eyes to his girlfriend, who was turning a bright pink.

"I'm—I'm not sure."

Cody stepped off the chair. "I'll need to talk to the director. With the one Aisha saw last week, that's two, and something we should definitely investigate."

Yeah, go have Mommy sort it out.

Okay, that wasn't fair. But Bram's hackles were sky-high at the moment. Aisha and Cody alone wasn't something he wanted to picture.

On his way out of the kitchen, Cody paused at the doorway. "I came in here looking for Sandra. If either of you see her, can you ask her to come by my office, please?"

"Of course." Aisha smiled at him, bright and wide.

The second Cody was gone, Bram turned to Aisha, lips pursed together, trying to keep his jealousy at bay. He leaned against the counter and crossed his arms. "Why is this the first time I'm hearing about a spider sighting while you and Cody were just hanging out together after work?"

"Well, I didn't really see one." She rolled her eyes but then avoided meeting his, her fingers tracing the cover of her notebook. "That day we went to lunch, my car wouldn't start when I got off work. I came back in here to see if Cody was around to give me a ride, and I got flustered, so I told him I saw a spider instead of asking him for a ride."

"Why didn't you ask me?" It was ridiculous to be jealous, not after what had happened in the past few weeks, but not as ridiculous as thinking Stella was granting his wishes.

Though he hadn't made any wishes lately. Maybe this was the starfish's revenge for ignoring her amid the gala preparations in her honor. He'd stop by her tank on the way out to make his apologies and wish for as much Cody-free time as possible going forward.

Aisha worried her bottom lip before answering him. "You were already gone for the day."

"I would have come back."

A silence stretched between them.

"I'll always come back for you." He stepped away from the counter, the distance between them suddenly feeling as wide as the Mariana Trench. "Don't you know that?"

She looked down and adjusted the pins in her hair. They were slightly askew thanks to the hug he'd given her earlier. "I didn't want to bother you."

"You could never bother me."

At this, she raised a skeptical eyebrow, and he laughed. "I mean it. All the things you think annoy everyone else just don't bother me. Okay?"

She didn't look convinced but nodded. He leaned down to give her another kiss, and this one she leaned into a little more. The kiss deepened, her hand coming up to lace her fingers in his hair, and she let out a little sigh of happiness that made the organ in his chest blow up like a puffer fish. He braced himself with one hand on the table, his legs threatening to collapse underneath him.

That nothing about her bothered him was an understatement. He was obsessed with her. Her joy, her laugh, her talent, her lips, her fussing over his dog, her multicolored apartment.

How could she not see that?

Her warnings when he'd adopted Brownie were etched into his brain. Of course, everyone who wanted to adopt an animal got the same lecture about responsibility, but did she still think he was the same kind of rich kid he'd grown up surrounded by? The kind who never learned how to work that hard, who let his parents take care of his mistakes, who threw money at problems until they went away.

That wasn't Bram, but it wasn't like Aisha was totally wrong. They wouldn't even be throwing the gala if he weren't trying to hold on to his parents as donors. It wasn't surprising that Aisha didn't expect him to be there for her, when he still needed his parents so much.

Though her lack of trust in him wasn't all due to Bram's family. There was some part of her story that he didn't know. Something to do with her mother, who'd given her enough money to buy an apartment but wasn't in her life at all anymore.

All it would take would be one slip, one hint that he wasn't one hundred percent committed, and she'd run. He knew it in his bones the same way he knew Brownie would be waiting for him by the door when he got home.

There had to be a way to show her he was as serious about her, about them.

"Darcey is having a party this weekend."

She blinked up at him, frowning. "Okay."

"I want you to come. With me." He hadn't been planning to go, but what better way to show her he wanted her by his side than to introduce her to all his friends? It might even help reassure her that not all rich people were jerks. "As my girlfriend."

She sucked in a breath. "Are you sure?"

"I am." He planted a kiss on the tip of her nose. "But there's one condition."

A flicker of doubt passed across her face.

"Please don't wear a suit." He smoothed her hair back over her shoulder. "I want them to meet you. The real you."

"I'm not sure who that is right now." She looked down at the notebook in front of her, filled with neat little boxes next to reminders, half of them checked off and the rest still to do.

"You're my girlfriend. That's all you have to be."

She looked up at him, doubt still tugging at her features, but she nodded. "Okay. I can do that."

Saturday afternoon, mere hours before the party, and Aisha had no idea what to wear.

"Just wear what you always wear, something bright and fun," Brooke said from where she lay on her stomach on the bed, head in her hands and feet kicking up in the air. With Krista there too, it could have been high school again.

How many nights had they spent together in her room, helping Aisha get dressed for a date? She'd always had so many more than they had. Not because more boys had been interested in her—that was Krista's crown to wear—but because she'd never said no to anyone. Dating had been fun, a chance to hang out with different people, which had continued well into her twenties.

Now it was something serious.

She was going to the party as Bram's *girlfriend*.

Krista clicked her tongue, hovering over her dresser and poking through her jewelry boxes. "Darcey would be fine with you wearing whatever, but I don't know about everyone else at the party."

"Why? Who's going to be there?" The nerves that had been

building steadily since yesterday were now threatening to engulf her.

I want them to meet you. The real you, Bram had said. As if Aisha even knew who that was anymore.

As she stood in front of her closet, she felt as helpless as her first day at Adamsville Elementary school as an eight-year-old with a French braid that had unraveled by lunchtime and who couldn't pronounce squirrel.

Picking out clothes used to be Aisha's favorite thing to do. Matching the unexpected colors, patterns, textures. It was like art on her body. That had all stopped when she'd started stepping things up at work. Changing herself externally felt like the next logical step after changing herself internally.

It had been easy enough to create the two different personas. There was her regular self, who wore whatever she wanted. Then there was "Work Aisha" who stuck to a more muted palette and accessorized with conventional jewelry. She even had two separate parts of her closet, so that she didn't accidentally mix them up in her early-morning grogginess. Gray and beige on one side, a rainbow explosion on the other.

Which side would "Bram's girlfriend" dress from? She'd never been someone's girlfriend before.

This was what she'd wanted, she reminded herself. Something settled and serious.

"I have no idea who'll be there." Krista held up the silver pair of Aisha's butterfly earrings—of course she had more than one pair—to her ears.

"Why don't you come too?" Something like hope sparked in Aisha. "You know Darcey. Did she invite you?"

"She did, but she lives so far away." Wrinkling her nose, Krista held up a pair of long, dangling earrings in the shape of a giraffe. "Don't you have anything without animals or flowers?"

"No." This hadn't seemed like a problem in her jewelry collection until right this moment. "You should come. We can give you a ride."

"I haven't seen my dad much this week. I want to check on him." The chronic health issues Krista's dad had been dealing with for a decade were mostly under control, but that didn't stop her from helping him however she could. "Besides, you're going back to Bram's tonight, since it's closer to her place than Adamsville."

"Oh, right." Darcey lived closer to Charleston, not too far from where Bram's parents lived on one of the islands that dotted South Carolina's coast. Islands full of the wealthiest people in the state. "So you really don't know who'll be there?"

"No, but it's not hard to guess. Her friends, people she works with. People like the Yates and the Lowthers that she grew up with."

Groaning, Aisha buried her head in the middle of her closet, one hand on a bright pink pleated midi skirt, the other on a pair of dark-brown slacks.

"Speaking of work," Brooke said from behind her. "Have you told anyone yet?"

Aisha shook her head, then wrapped her arms around as many clothes as she could and dropped them all onto the bed next to Brooke. The next step in the familiar date-night routine was Brooke helping her sort through everything.

"I'm waiting until after the gala." Aisha held up a bright-green dress with a seashell pattern, then tossed it onto the floor. When leaving work yesterday, she'd wanted to stop at Stella's tank to wish for this party to go well, but she'd walked out with Bram and hadn't wanted him to know how nervous she was.

Now she wished she'd made up some excuse to visit the starfish. Going in without that assurance things would be okay meant it was up to Aisha to do this on her own. "I don't want there to be any issues to distract people from the event."

Nobody at the party would have any connection to LCRA

other than through Bram, so it was safe to be there as a couple. If Aisha could ever find something to wear.

"Why would there be issues?" Now Krista was sorting through her necklaces, placing a few on top of the dresser as options for tonight. Letting Aisha choose her own jewelry for something this important was clearly out of the question. "Most workplaces are fine with it as long as it's not a supervisor dating a direct report."

"We all report to the director."

"Then you're fine." This was said in the same assured Krista tone that she said almost everything. Like the world made complete sense, and she understood everything about it.

It used to calm Aisha to hear her talk that way. Tonight it rankled. Aisha glanced at Brooke, who rolled her eyes and made her hold back a giggle. It released some of the tension Aisha was holding, but not all of it. Neither of her friends had ever been in her situation, so she was really on her own.

What advice could they really have about secretly dating a coworker whose parents were major funders of their workplace and who might pull out their money if the big event she was planning with the coworker she was secretly dating didn't go well?

At least she wasn't on her own picking out her clothes.

It took another half hour and one broken zipper that she'd been meaning to fix anyway, but they managed to narrow it down to two options.

There was a simple red dress that she'd bought at a flea market in college. It wasn't fancy by any means, but it fit her body perfectly. With a few gold accessories and her hair pulled back into a tight bun, she looked like she might actually belong at a party with people who knew the Lowthers.

Option two was a jumpsuit patterned with leaves and flowers, all bright-greens and pinks in a flowy material that was perfect for the South Carolina summer heat. The front dipped low, and with her hair down around her shoulders, she looked like the artist her friends always said she was.

"Are you sending Bram these options?" Brooke asked as she took a picture of Aisha in the red dress.

The rock rolled right over her heart at the thought. *I want them to meet you. The real you.*

"No. I can figure it out." The last thing she wanted was for him to think she didn't know how to handle herself at an event like tonight. She might not want to belong to his world, but he'd invited her into it. He didn't need any reason to kick her right back out.

"Are you sure?" The raised eyebrow from Krista settled it for her.

"Yes. I know what's expected of me."

The vaguest of memories she always tried to push away pushed itself into her mind. She was seven years old and dressed in a pale-blue dress. As a kid, Aisha didn't like dresses. She remembered tugging at it, kicking the ground with her black ballet flats. She'd wanted to wear her sparkly pink sneakers. She'd wanted to go to Parc Monceau with her dad and watch him paint like they always did on a Saturday.

It was the one and only time she ever met her grandparents. She didn't remember being particularly rude or unruly, but she definitely spilled something and didn't want to eat everything on her plate. Looking back now, she knew she'd behaved like any other seven-year-old. Yet she hadn't been acceptable to her grandparents, because shortly after that, her parents split up.

From things her dad had said over the years, she knew it wasn't just that one day that had decided things. Her grandparents were disappointed their daughter had a child with someone who wasn't Algerian, who wasn't French, who was mixed race, who she wasn't even married to. Before Aisha had even opened her mouth to say bonjour, they'd decided what they thought about her. All the pretty dresses in the world and picture-perfect behavior were never going to change that.

As much as Aisha didn't want it to be, tonight felt like a second chance. She might not want to belong, but she wanted it to be her choice to leave, not to have someone else expel her.

Especially not Bram.

"Maybe if tonight goes well, he'll ask me to dinner with his parents." She knew he went every Sunday and had been waiting for the invitation. But he hadn't mentioned it once. Tonight had to be a test. If she did well with Darcey and her friends as his girl-friend, then at the gala he could introduce her to his parents as the same.

Unless there was some other reason he didn't want her to meet them. Aisha could think of at least a dozen.

Even though Stella was miles away at the aquarium, Aisha closed her eyes for a moment to make the wish she should have yesterday.

Please let everything go okay tonight.

"I've made a terrible mistake."

Aisha's whispered words and panicked look took Bram by surprise as he led her into Darcey's apartment. The door was unlocked, and they followed the hum of chatter down a hallway lined with textured wallpaper and photos from Darcey's travels. Bram was even in a few of them.

Stopping next to Aisha before they reached the wide doorway that led to the living room, Bram put her hand on her lower back.

"Do you want to leave?"

Shaking her head, she looked down. "No, I don't mean about coming. I mean my clothes." She gestured to the red dress she had on. It was distractingly tight and with her hair pulled back, it was like some ballerina fantasy he didn't know he'd had come to life. Keeping his hands to himself in the car on the long drive here had been enough of a struggle. Getting through the entire party without staring at her the entire time would be almost impossible.

"You look incredible." The warmth and comfort he tried to infuse into the pressure of his hand on her back did little to stem the hot prickle of tears in her eyes.

"But you're in jeans. I totally picked the wrong outfit."

"It'll be fine. Just be yourself."

Slipping his arm around her waist, he led her into the living room.

"Is that really what you want me to be?"

Her words were so low, he wasn't sure he'd heard them correctly. Before he could ask her about it, Darcey appeared.

"Aisha, it's so nice to see you again." Darcey's smile was genuine.

When Aisha's shoulders relaxed a fraction of an inch, Bram let out a sigh of relief. The eyes of everyone else in the room swiveled to her, however, and under the scrutiny he could feel her shrink.

Though he still thought she looked amazing, Bram tried to see it from her perspective. Aisha hadn't asked about what to wear, and Bram realized with a tightening in his chest he should have mentioned how casual it would be. Everyone else was in jeans or khakis, and a few women were in flowy, summer dresses. Even Bram had gone less formal than what he'd wear for work, in jeans and a button-up with the sleeves rolled up.

He hadn't even thought to say something when he'd picked her up, too enamored by the way her red dress hugged every curve.

Bram narrowed his eyes on the men around the room appreciating the same thing. Though that wasn't what Aisha would notice. Assuming the party would be fancy, she'd tried to dress in a way that kept everyone from looking at her. Yet that's what they were all doing anyway, and she probably thought it was because she'd misjudged or hadn't thought things through.

Before he could think of a way to explain that every woman was jealous of how amazing she looked, and every man was jealous of him for being with her, she took a deep inhale and lifted her chin. He watched her transform, drawing on some internal reservoir of irreverence as she dropped her shoulders and returned Darcey's smile.

"It's nice to see you again." There was a brief hug with a cheek kiss between the two of them that Bram hoped was sincere. Darcey caught his eye over Aisha's shoulder, and she winked at him. He mouthed, "be nice."

And she was, in her Darcey way. She pulled Aisha away to introduce her to people, with Bram trailing behind, since he already knew everyone. It was the same crowd as always, a mix of their friends from high school, lawyers Darcey knew, and people they both knew from charities their parents were in. The overlap between these three groups was unsurprisingly large, so some fell into all three categories.

It warmed Bram's insides to see how his best friend made sure to explain who everyone was to Aisha. Then, as she led her to the next person, she'd whisper in Aisha's ear what Bram knew would be those little extra details that you could only know if you grew up in this world.

Feeling confident that Darcey had things under control, Bram made his way to the drinks table in the corner. A dozen half-empty bottles were arranged by height and alcohol content. Since he was driving, he poured some sparkling water into one of the tall glasses, then added a slice of lime from a bowl.

"Hey, Bram. What have you been up to? Still trying to save the world?"

He turned to see Anderson, a high school friend who was also a lawyer, though not at Darcey's firm. No, Anderson had made his family proud and gone into corporate law, protecting the same companies that Darcey would go after.

Like Lowther Yachts.

He reached out to shake Anderson's hand. "Doing my best. Just got a dog."

"Oh, yeah?" The guy's eyes lit up. "What kind? I have a French Bulldog named Frenchie."

Before Bram could even respond, the proud dog dad had pulled out his phone to show him pictures of the predictably named pooch in various outfits that likely cost more than Bram's car payment.

The smushed face was really kind of cute though.

Reciprocation was expected, and for once when dealing with his old classmates, Bram didn't mind the quid pro quo. He excitedly swiped through the dozen—okay, several dozen—pictures of Brownie he'd taken earlier that morning to find the best one to show off.

"I got him at a shelter a few weeks ago."

"Nice." Anderson nodded. "Smart to save some money. Purebreds are pricey."

That hadn't been Bram's reason for adopting, but it didn't seem worth it to mention.

"What are you doing these days? Still at Baker, Glenn, and Gunner?" It was the firm that represented his parents. Darcey wouldn't have invited Anderson if he'd been working directly on the case, but that didn't mean he knew nothing at all about it. While Darcey had been keeping annoyingly tight-lipped about it, not everyone here toed that ethical line quite as well.

"Yup, still there." Raising his glass of whiskey like he was toasting himself, Anderson gave him a smug smile. "Should be making partner next year."

"Wow, that's great." Not that Bram really understood how it worked at law firms, despite Darcey's repeated explanations over the years, but he knew enough to recognize "making partner" was the goal for a lot of lawyers.

Impossibly, Anderson's smile got even smugger, and he set his empty whiskey glass on a side table. "Yeah, I've brought in a lot of business for the firm."

Was that how it worked? It didn't sound all that different from what he did. His stomach turned a little at the thought that he was anything like Anderson.

Once a Lowther, always a Lowther.

"It helps to know the right people, doesn't it?" Bram nodded around the room, to all the friends and acquaintances who had likely given them both a leg up. The simple accident of birth made both of their lives infinitely easier. Was Anderson aware of that, or did he think he just had good luck?

Bram noticed Aisha talking to someone across the room and smiled. Well, grinned like a fool was more like it. There was an easy grace to her movements he'd never seen before. No sign of the nerves she'd had walking in. The total opposite of how she used to be around Cody.

Maybe Bram was the right guy for her after all, even if he couldn't change the fact that he was a Lowther.

Anderson must have seen Bram's dreamy gaze and looked over his shoulder, then turned back with a leer that made Bram miss the smugness.

"Nice." The guy nodded his approval, and Bram felt like barfing. "Where'd you meet her?"

Swallowing what he actually wanted to say, Bram let just a hint of menace into his tone. "We work together at the aquarium."

"Yikes." Leaning in close, Anderson lowered his voice. The scent of whiskey was strong on his breath. "Word of advice. Don't get involved with someone at work. It never ends well."

"Is that your professional opinion or are you speaking from personal experience?"

"Both." A sour look settled onto the guy's face. "I'll give you another professional opinion. Be glad you didn't take your parents up on that job offer all those years ago. It's a real mess over there."

Bram's breath caught in his throat, and he tried to stay calm. "I don't really discuss business with my parents."

"Like they'll even have much left once Darcey's boss is done with them." Anderson shook his head and leaned in closer. "One oil spill from a faulty piece of equipment is easy enough to handle. But fifteen in the past five years is something else entirely. Especially if you don't report any of them."

The floor seemed to fall out from under Bram's feet, and he leaned against a nearby couch to keep himself upright. No wonder Darcey didn't want to give him the details. It wasn't the worst he'd imagined, but it wasn't far off. This would definitely explain his parents needing to move around money, and his mother's desperation to show how environmentally friendly Lowther Yachts was through their donations.

"Like I said, I don't discuss business with my parents." Bram raised his empty glass. "I need a refill. Can I get you anything?"

Thankfully, Anderson said no and wandered off to talk to someone else, leaving Bram alone to attempt to hide his rising panic and disgust.

Bringing Aisha here had been a way to introduce her to his world, to let her see it wasn't all that bad. But it was just as bad as she'd assumed. He had to figure out how to disentangle himself from his parents. For real this time. Not just removing his clothes from their house, but everything.

He glanced over at Aisha, and his heart stuttered to see how bright and cheery she was tonight. After all that worry walking in, she was doing fine, just like he knew she would.

It might not be a world she wanted to be a part of, but she was fitting in.

The question was, would she still want Bram if he was no longer a part of it? His heart told him yes, but who was he if he wasn't a Lowther?

THIRTY-NINE
AISHA

Making small talk was usually Aisha's favorite thing in the world, but as she let herself be led around by Darcey to talk to what seemed like every single person at the party, she quickly realized this was not her typical small talk.

"Aisha, this is Wolfie. We went to school together, and now she's the lacrosse coach there."

Yet another of Darcey's friends introduced by their nickname instead of their name. As they'd walk away to the next person, Darcey would whisper their real name and the story about how they got the nickname. Sometimes they were funny like Bram's Wellington story, sometimes it was just because of a favorite food or song.

"Nice to meet you." Aisha gave Wolfie her typical wide, friendly smile. All she got back was a flick of the woman's dark-green eyes up and down her body and a slight upward tilt of her blood-red lips that might have been a smile but was closer to a smirk.

"Aisha works at the aquarium with Bram," Darcey said just like she had to everyone else. Next would come the little tidbit of information to give Aisha a jumping-off point for a conversation. "Wolfie just got back from Spain."

"Wow, that must have been amazing." This was the third person she'd met who'd been to Europe this summer. No one had been to France, however, leaving Aisha without a solid connection point. She tried something more basic. "I've always wanted to go. Was the food incredible?"

When Wolfie wrinkled her nose, it made her look a little bit canine. Perhaps a hint to the origin of her nickname? "I didn't go to eat. I went to Ibiza. Like we do every summer." Her suntanned skin was testament to the hours she must have spent on the beach.

"Ibiza? Who'd you go with this year?" There was a flash of sleek blond hair and a pearly white smile as someone Aisha had already met joined them. Racking her brain, she tried to remember if it was Bunny who was actually Barbara, or Katherine who went by Bun because she danced ballet and that's how she wore her hair for years.

"Mark," Wolfie said, flicking her long, auburn ponytail over her shoulder.

"Mark Jefferson or Mark Stirling?"

"Brooks."

Bun-or-maybe-Bunny gasped and Wolfie launched into a very detailed description of the house they'd stayed in. Darcey asked her own enthusiastic questions, while Aisha just stood there, smiling widely and pretending to be listening.

Tonight was all about pretending. Pretending she didn't see the stares, pretending she was interested in whatever people would be talking about, and pretending she didn't wish she was anywhere else.

She'd been pretending for weeks at work. What was one more night?

Besides Wolfie's smirk, people had actually been decent enough. Just not that interested in her, or that interesting to Aisha. Nobody asked her where she was from or returned any of the compliments she gave for people's clothes. This just confirmed her fear that she'd made the wrong choice. At least the jumpsuit would have gotten some comments, even if they were snide remarks. Nothing at all was worse somehow.

It was everything she'd been worried about. Being with Bram would mean this was her life. Pretending not just for a day but forever. It was one thing to curb her more chaotic tendencies at work. That was something that could only benefit her long-term.

There was no benefit in learning to fake smile and pretending to care about tennis. Beyond the cute skirts some of the women wore, it held next to no interest for Aisha.

Was Bram the sweetest, hottest guy she'd ever dated? Yes.

Did his adopting Brownie and becoming totally obsessed with the dog make her heart melt? Absolutely.

But could she live the kind of life at his side that his family and social circle required?

A voice in her head that sounded suspiciously like Krista was telling her that she could do anything she put her mind to. Meanwhile, a softer voice that sounded a lot like Brooke was asking her if that's what she really wanted.

The loudest voice, however, was her own, reminding her that this world rejected her once and would do it again, no matter how much pretending she did.

Once the Mark Brooks story had been fully told, Darcey flashed a grin at them all.

"Looks like we need more ice." With a wink, she left Aisha alone with Wolfie and Bun—someone had thankfully said her name during the conversation.

The two women turned slightly toward each other, not completely turning their backs on her, but making it clear she was no longer part of the conversation. Looking around the room, she caught Bram's eye, and relief flooded through her. They wove their way between the small groups of people toward each other, maneuvering around the sleek modern furniture that decorated Darcey's living room. If it had just been her and Bram, Aisha would have stopped to examine every piece and ask about where it came from. In a room full of eyes on her, she let the magnetic pull of him keep her focused, and they met in the middle of the room.

"You doing okay?" He put a hand on her hip, and it was like the world stopped. Everything felt better with him close to her. "I didn't mean to leave you on your own, but Darcey kind of took over."

"Yeah, she was playing hostess." Just like Aisha was playing girlfriend. It didn't feel like a real thing yet, still just a role she was inhabiting for one night. If all the eyes on the two of them were any indication, she was doing a pretty good job of it. "I should go see if she needs any help."

"I'll come with you."

"No, no." She shook her head. "These are your friends too. You should be able to spend time with them. I've been hogging all your nights and weekends for the past few weeks."

He leaned in close, and the hand on her hip tightened its grip. "I do not mind in the least."

With just that burning look in his eyes, all the unchecked, wild emotions running rampant in her chest telling her she was failing tonight were tamed. He'd wanted her here, she reminded herself. Even if nobody else here did, Bram wanted her next to him. As his girlfriend.

Hopefully he'd still want that when the night was over.

In the kitchen, Aisha discovered Darcey's easy hostess smile had vanished as she bustled around in high gear pulling things out of the shiny fridge and surrounding pristine cabinets. It reminded Aisha a little bit of Krista.

"I'm glad you came." Darcey smiled at her, and for the first time all night, Aisha relaxed. Nobody who called Bram "Wellington" for almost thirty years just to remind him of crashing a party dressed only in rain boots could be all that bad. "He's been really stressed lately. It's good to see him smile."

"Stressed about the gala?" Aisha frowned and watched as Darcey dumped an ice tray into the bucket. There were at least two dozen in the giant freezer, all in different fun shapes. Aisha was ashamed to admit she'd been assuming there'd be staff working the party, but Darcey's kitchen was as chaotic as Aisha's was whenever she had people over to her place. Open bags lay scattered on the black marble countertops, and the double farmhouse sink was overflowing with dishes.

"The gala and everything with his parents." Dumping a bag of chips onto a serving dish, Darcey cursed when a few fell to the floor. A peek at the label let Aisha know it was store-brand. So was the salsa she scooped out of the jar and into the little bowl attached to the serving dish. "I'm not directly involved in the case, but my firm is handling it. I'm sure he's told you all about it."

"Oh, yeah, of course." Unease roiled in her stomach, but she kept her tone neutral, like it was a topic she'd discussed so much with Bram it wasn't even that interesting anymore. "Do you need any help?"

Darcey's eyes lit up. "Thank you. You're the first person who's asked all night. Could you go into the cabinets above the sink and grab more wine glasses?"

While she followed Darcey's instructions, Aisha's mind went into overdrive. Was this the legal thing Krista and Darcey had been talking about at lunch the other day? Did Krista know something about Bram's family and hadn't told her? This stung more than she thought it would, even if she knew, logically, that Krista couldn't discuss certain things about her work.

Aisha had never been a fan of being logical.

Triumphantly brandishing the wine glasses, Aisha nodded to the doorway. "I'll take these out to the living room."

"Thanks, you're such a sweetheart." Darcey winked at her. "I know everyone out there can be a lot, but you're holding it together so well. I can see why Bram likes you so much."

Heat crept up her cheeks as she left the kitchen with her hands clutching a half-dozen wine glasses upside down by the stems.

He liked her enough to bring her here as his girlfriend, but not enough to share his worries about his parents with his girlfriend. Because how could Aisha possibly understand something dealing with yachts or money or whatever the case was about? Not the way the other women out there would. He was already excluding her, even when he invited her in.

The moment when she'd be kicked to the curb suddenly felt a lot closer.

Once the glasses were on the drinks table, Aisha looked around to find Bram. He was nowhere that she could see in the spacious living room, and the possibility of walking up to one of the tight clusters of people seemed very unappealing at the moment. There was a limit to how much pretending she could manage in a single night.

Turning on her heels, she decided to go in search of the bathroom. There was only one long hallway in the apartment, with the kitchen at the end, so she figured it had to be one of the doors. The walls were decorated with framed photographs, and she slowed her steps to glance at some of them.

There was Darcey with a group of people Aisha assumed was her family, standing in front of an Egyptian pyramid. There was an absolutely gorgeous beach with tiny figures jumping in a cerulean sea. There was even one with Bram, standing under a palm tree with his arm slung over Darcey's shoulder, her sleeve rolled up to show a fresh tattoo. When she stopped to look more closely at that one, she heard voices floating out of the kitchen door just a few feet to her right.

"You'll need to make a clean break soon if you don't want

things to get messy." Darcey's voice was hushed, so it was easy to hear Bram's frustrated huff.

"You say it like it'll be easy."

Everything inside Aisha stilled. She barely took a breath, and she kept her eyes focused on the photo in front of her, the swirls of colors blurring together as she strained to hear more but didn't dare move closer.

"Of course it won't be easy, but you need to be on your own. Not making all your decisions based on what someone else wants and needs."

"But Aisha—"

"This will be best for her, too, you know it is."

Aisha held her breath, waiting to hear what Bram would say. Waiting to hear him defend her, defend them being together.

There was only silence.

The urge to throw up battled with the need to throw something. And yet, Aisha wasn't really that surprised by how his oldest friend reacted to her. Nice to her face but trying to get Bram to break up with her behind her back.

Nothing about tonight had been a surprise, other than how messy Darcey's kitchen was. Even that had probably been just a ruse, a show for social media, look at how normal I am, look at how relatable. These people weren't any different from her mother. Rich and heartless.

Tears filled her eyes as she turned away from the photo of Bram's smiling face and hurried toward the front door. Nobody spoke to her as she rushed by the living room. Nobody asked where she was going. Why would they? They didn't know her. She wasn't really a part of this world. Nobody wanted her to be, not even Bram, despite how he'd been acting, despite everything he'd told her. He hadn't said a word to support her, just accepted Darcey's instructions to get rid of Aisha.

Out in the warm early September evening, Aisha's temper rose even more. She looked around the parking lot, not sure where she wanted to go, only knowing she couldn't stay here. The heels she was wearing would start hurting her feet in approximately five minutes, but that would get her far enough away to call for a ride. There was no question of asking Brooke or Krista, not when she'd made such a big deal about knowing what to expect tonight.

"Aisha!"

Her heart trembled to hear Bram's voice. She didn't quite trust her ears and kept walking through the parking lot past cars that probably cost more than her apartment.

"Hey." A hand on her arm stopped her, and she turned to find him looking at her with more concern on his face than could be real. "What happened? Why'd you leave without me?"

"I just had to get out of there."

"Was someone rude?" His expression darkened, and her traitorous heart fluttered with hope. "Tell me who and I'll take care of it."

She shook her head. "Nobody was rude. Nobody was even talking to me."

His arms wrapped around her, and even though she knew she shouldn't, she let herself melt into them. It might be the last time she ever felt his arms around her.

"I'm sorry," Bram said into her neck, sending shivers along her skin. "I shouldn't have left you on your own. It looked like you were getting along with people so well."

"I'm good at pretending."

He sighed and let his hand trace along her spine. The motion was both soothing and sent tingles up and down her back. She snuggled closer, enjoying the feeling of having him close, knowing that it wouldn't last. Not after tonight.

"I wish you didn't have to." He pulled away slightly and brought a hand up to her cheek. "I wish I didn't have to."

This was it. Her heart beat in her throat. "What are you pretending about?"

"You mean other than acting at work like I'm not falling more and more in love with you every day?"

Oh. That . . . wasn't what she'd expected.

Heat spread through her body. Words, usually so easy for Aisha to blurt out, escaped her.

When she didn't say anything, an anxious look tugged down Bram's lips. "I've been pretending all night I'm not worried."

"About the gala?" Everything was on track according to Bram's detailed checklists. This was the most prepared Aisha had ever felt for anything. For Brooke's events, she just did what she was told, and while she knew generally how things should go, she wasn't the one people asked, so she didn't keep it all in her head.

This time, she knew every detail. From the time the caterers would arrive to the number of napkins they'd ordered, she knew it all. Instead of feeling overwhelmed the way she thought she would to be so involved in something, to be responsible for it, she felt calm.

Maybe Bram didn't. Maybe in the past weeks she hadn't been a help to him the way he'd been telling her almost every day, but a hindrance.

"No, not the gala." He smoothed a hand over her bare shoulder, and goosebumps prickled along her arms.

With a hand on her lower back, he led her to a bench by the front door of the apartment building. They sat in silence for a moment before he ran a hand through his hair and leaned back with a sigh. His expression was pulled tight, the worry etched into every line of his perfect face. "There's something happening with my parents. A lawsuit."

"Oh?" This was what Darcey had mentioned, thinking Aisha already knew all about it. The shame she'd felt earlier that Bram hadn't told her yet melted away when he nodded.

"Darcey's firm is involved, and it's been hard for her not to be able to share details with me. Someone else tonight told me what it is and—" He shook his head. "It's going to be really messy."

Messy. Was this what Darcey had been talking about in the kitchen? Maybe she hadn't been telling Bram to break up with Aisha.

Hope fluttered again in her aching heart.

"Is that why you don't want me to come to dinner with your family?"

Scooting closer on the bench so their legs were touching, he wrapped his arm around her shoulder. "I can't even handle my family. I won't subject you to all their drama. Especially not now that I know just how bad this case is going to be."

This was a very logical explanation for what she'd overhead. "So you're not worried about . . . me?" It was hard to speak around the thickness in her throat, but she pushed through it.

"I'm worried that you ran out of there without telling me." He leaned his head against hers and dropped a kiss in her hair, still tight in a bun. "Are you sure someone wasn't rude? I know Wolfie can be a lot, but she's still annoyed that I passed more AP exams than she did back in high school. They're not bad people once you get to know them. Not all of them, at least."

There it was again, the reminder that he was so entrenched in this world, there was so much history, being with Bram meant being a part of it.

"It's not any one thing. It's all of it." She sighed and gestured around her at the apartment building with a doorman, the cars, her dress that she thought would be so perfect tonight. Where did she even start?

"Tell me. Please." His voice cracked on the last word, and something inside her broke to hear just how nervous he was. He really thought that he was the one who'd messed up tonight.

"My mother's family never—" She shook her head, then took a deep, shuddering breath and tried again. "They didn't want me in their life. She picked them over me, and she hasn't contacted me since I turned eighteen. All night I've been trying to fit in, knowing I never will, but also not wanting to embarrass you. I know these people are your friends, so I was trying to find ways to connect, pretending to have fun with that big, fake smile, but I've just been waiting for them to reject me. The way she did."

A tear slipped down her cheek, and Bram's thumb was there instantly to wipe it away.

"I don't care what they think," he said softly.

She scoffed. "They're your friends, of course you care."

"Not as much as I care about you."

The warmth of this spread through her along with the kiss he planted firmly on her lips, and she let it wash away some of her fears. When he pulled away, the look in his eyes was as serious as she'd ever seen.

"I meant what I said before. I'm falling for you. Hard." The hand on her cheek brushed away another tear. "I know I come with a lot of baggage, and you may not feel the same, but—"

"I'm falling for you too." The words that had been so hard to find earlier now burst out of her in a rush. "That's why this was so hard tonight. I want to be with you, but this—" She gestured around them again. "I don't think this will ever feel comfortable for me."

"Why don't you let me worry about that. It's my family that's the problem, not you. I wish you could have just been your usual sunny self tonight. There's no reason to change for anyone. Especially not Darcey and this crowd."

He still didn't get it, did he? "Changing is working out pretty well at the aquarium."

"That's who you always were, though." His lips ticked up. "I told you, it's possible to be more than one thing at once. You were always smart and creative and organized and responsible and enthusiastic. I wish it hadn't taken wearing those terrible suits to let you see it for yourself."

Or maybe he did get it. Maybe he did see her, the parts of her that had always been there, and her friends had never really seen.

When he told her to be herself tonight, he meant one of those parts he'd always known were there and she was only just discovering.

She'd kicked herself out of the party, not Darcey, not anyone else. And Bram had come running after her. He hadn't stayed behind and let her go. He'd come looking for her.

There was no way to describe the emotion that filled her veins, her heart pumping it from the tips of her fingers to the soles of her feet squished into the most stylish yet uncomfortable shoes she owned. All she could do to show him how she felt was to kiss him, and let her lips and hands and arms tell him what her words couldn't.

FORTY-ONE
BRAM

Despite what he'd told Aisha, Bram wished she was with him as he drove the familiar road up his parents' house for dinner the day after Darcey's party. Facing everyone without her by his side felt like part of him was missing.

I'm falling for you too.

The rest of last night was a bit of a love-drunk haze, but those words were flashing clear in his mind like she'd spray painted them in giant block letters.

He parked his car and looked up at the gray house that, after thirty-two years, finally no longer held any of his possessions. This desire to pull away had been there long before Aisha, but she was the push that would get him over the edge.

It was still better she wasn't here, he reasoned. If bubbly, friendly Aisha had felt like she needed to be someone else with the crowd at the party, then dinner with the Lowthers would be unbearable. Even if the gala went well, he knew she'd never feel comfortable in his world, not after what her mother had done.

Walking up the brick path to the door, rage still burned inside of him. It had taken everything in him to stay calm when listening to her last night. What kind of mother just left her daughter because her family disapproved? Aisha had only been eight when she'd moved from France. There was nothing a little kid could have possibly done to be abandoned like that.

As he was ushered into the house by a maid, uncertainty over what he had to do snaked through him, biting him open from the inside. He still hadn't figured out a way to make a clean break from his family, but were they really that bad?

Well, besides the extremely sketchy environmental protections that had landed them in court.

Were they terrible people? Every family had their issues. Nothing about the criticisms, pressure, or sibling rivalry he experienced was any different from what it was like for Darcey or anyone else at her party last night. It was nothing compared to what Aisha had gone through. Everyone in his family still talked to him.

They were all here tonight, sitting around the dinner table. His brother Stephen worked for their parents along with his wife, Caroline. Both were somehow involved in sales, though Bram had never fully understood their roles. It involved lots of travel, which was how he'd gotten so many madeleines for Aisha over the past few months.

His youngest sister, Josephine, had brought her boyfriend Carl, who also worked for Lowther Yachts in accounting. Despite having seen him almost every week for family dinners for close to a year, Bram didn't know much about him.

Or any of his family, really. They weren't terrible people, but they weren't terribly interesting. They were all chatting about things at work, or people they knew, upcoming trips they were taking. Sometimes it felt like Bram was a guest, invited to observe but not participate. Or maybe he was like an anthropologist, someone who understood them but wasn't really a part of their group.

Why was it so important for Aisha to meet them, when they wouldn't even recognize how amazing she was?

"I got a dog." The words burst out of him without thinking. It was a very Aisha move. Six sets of eyes swiveled his way, with expressions ranging from his father's irritation at the interruption to Carl's complete nonchalance.

"That's . . . fascinating." The corner of his mother's mouth lifted. "I suppose we should all be happy it wasn't a fish."

Everyone tittered, and embarrassment spread through him. What had he been expecting? For them to gush the way Darcey had? Even Anderson had been excited to see photos, and he was a total egotistical prig.

"I hear that's not the only thing you've gotten recently." Josephine smirked. "Were you going to tell us about your new girl-friend you took to Darcey's party yesterday?"

Dread pooled in his belly. He should have been expecting it. Of course someone at the party had mentioned it to someone in his family. It had been too much to hope that they wouldn't hear about it at all.

As much as he wanted to wax poetic about his beautiful, talented, intelligent girlfriend, it wasn't the right time yet. When he'd dropped Aisha off the night before, they'd talked about when she might start coming to these dinners. Now that he knew how important it was to her, he would have brought her today if she wanted. After how she'd felt at Darcey's party, however, Aisha said she wanted to wait until after the gala, worried it would add even more pressure on them for such a busy day.

Since Bram was physically incapable of denying her anything she wanted, meeting his family would happen one day. Just not yet. So there was only one way to answer his sister's question.

"She's just a friend." Bram shrugged and speared a mushroom on his fork. "We work together at the aquarium. One of her best friends knows Darcey, so she heard about the party and asked for a ride. That's the only reason we arrived and left together."

The lie felt sour in his mouth, but other than Josephine raising her eyebrows at him, everyone seemed to accept this.

Except, of course, his mother.

"Friend isn't the word I heard." The look in her eyes was dangerous. "Apparently, everyone is saying she's your fiancée."

All six pairs of eyes around the table were on him again, scrutinizing his reaction.

It wasn't true, but if he protested too much, they might realize something was going on.

Or realize how much he wished it were true.

He had to protect Aisha from them. After everything that had happened with her mother, any kind of rejection from his family would crush her. It was up to her when she wanted to meet them, whenever she felt ready to be put under the same microscope that he was under now. If there was some way to avoid it entirely, to run away from his family so she'd never have to meet them, he'd do it.

That wasn't possible. All he could do was keep the two parts of his life separate for as long as possible. Until after the gala and the funding for the aquarium was secured. Maybe even until after the legal mess Lowther Yachts was dealing with was over.

Maybe forever, if he could just figure out how.

"Didn't they say that about Bun Armstrong just because I happened to stand next to her at Sterling's Christmas party last year?" Bram shook his head and scoffed. "She went with me to some vendors for the gala to help out. It's not my fault they all assumed it was for a wedding."

"If you work with her, I presume we'll see her at the gala next week." Piercing blue eyes, so similar in color to Bram's but shrewder than he'd ever be, were fixed on him. "You're not involved with this girl at all?"

"Of course not."

It was the biggest lie he'd ever told his mother. Not even assuring her that the trip to Mexico with Darcey in high school had been for medical reasons and waving around a forged doctor's note had felt as dangerous as this. Pretending he wasn't involved with Aisha at work was one thing, but pretending he wasn't in love with her was something else.

It felt like a betrayal. One Aisha had asked for, and he would never be able to stop himself from giving her what she wanted.

His mother considered him with her eagle eyes for another moment, then bent to sip from her spoon.

"Stephen, how did that meeting in London go? I saw your email, but I want to hear the details."

Relief flooded into Bram, along with disbelief. It had worked. For now. He wasn't sure he could get away with it at the gala next week, but hopefully they'd stay busy enough organizing everything that they'd just never be close enough to raise suspicion.

Bram left dinner no closer to cutting ties, and with the feeling that the gala was now important for an entirely different reason.

After a week that passed in seconds, it was finally the night of the gala. Everything was going so well, Aisha felt like she was floating. A sense of pride that she wasn't entirely used to kept bubbling up at unexpected moments.

Someone asked her where the extra tablecloths were, and she knew.

Someone wanted confirmation of the number of guests, and Aisha was the first one they asked.

The coat check was full, was there a second space available? Yes, they'd planned for that, she could show them the way.

Could you please direct me to the art auction? Of course, ma'am, right this way . . .

There it was. Her painting. On the temporary walls they'd erected, next to other paintings, like this was real art. Like she was a real artist.

Movie night last week had been, for reasons understood only to Krista and her Wes Anderson obsession, *The French Dispatch,* and a line from it had been going through Aisha's mind all night.

All artists sell all their work. It's what makes you an artist. Selling it. If you don't want to sell it, don't paint it.

It was a ridiculous line from a ridiculous movie. Aisha had never fully understood Wes Anderson. The France he liked to portray was as far from the France Aisha had known as you could get. There was no room in his pastel, picture-perfect scenes for the dirty, gritty reality of life in Paris when your father didn't speak the language and barely had enough for rent.

And yet, here it was, the first painting she'd ever parted with for money. The money wouldn't go to her, but it would be sold. And she would be a professional artist. Like her dad.

In more ways than one, she thought, looking around at the transformed aquarium. Small, high tables were positioned next to the tanks, with a bouquet on every third table. The glittering guests had started to file in, the women's jewelry glinting in the spotlights they'd set up to show off the tanks and the art—with Stella in the place of honor, of course.

Just like her dad, she'd surrounded herself with the wealthy, and was now holding her breath, waiting to see how much her art could fetch.

The waves of conversation flowed around her as she moved from person to person, chatting with everyone and reassuring herself that they were in fact having a good time. Thanks to Darcey's party, Aisha actually knew quite a few of the people who were there, and they greeted her warmly. It was fake warmth, but at least they weren't acting like they didn't even know her the way she'd expected them to.

Obviously, she avoided Bram's parents, too anxious to even approach the imposing couple. Diamonds sparkled at his mom's ears and at her throat, while the cut of his dad's suit was so perfectly tailored to him it looked like it was a part of him. The deep-purple jumpsuit Aisha was wearing was one of her best colors, and she knew she looked incredible, but she still felt shabby just looking at them.

"This is going so well." Brooke suddenly appeared at her side and took her arm in hers. "You did such a great job. Everything is beautiful."

Legs buckling from the praise she didn't realize she'd been wishing for, Aisha let herself sag into her friend. Every day this week the only wish she'd made to Stella had been to *just let everything go as planned at the gala.* "Thanks. It's been a lot of work. Especially this week."

All the last-minute details had been a lot to remember, but with Bram's trusty checklists, everything had gone smoothly.

"The music is kind of a yawn though." Now Krista was at Aisha's other side, wrinkling her nose. The bored-looking DJ was cycling through a mix of classical and jazz at a low enough volume that people could talk. "When's the dancing start?"

"Not going to happen." Aisha shook her head. "First of all, there's not really space to dance."

"What are you talking about?" Krista waved a hand at the open area directly in front of Stella.

"Second of all," Aisha continued, ignoring her. "Drunk people plus giant glass tanks full of water aren't a good combination."

These were the reasons Bram had given her when she'd asked, but he'd avoided her eyes and used a tone she'd only heard a few times. Which meant it had something to do with his parents. Anxiety gnawed at her stomach to think that even after everything he'd said, he would still do whatever they asked of him.

He came to find you when you ran away.

The reminder calmed her enough to keep her attention on her friends.

"Well, I think it's nice." Brooke looped her arm in Aisha's as they navigated around the tuxedo and bejeweled crowd toward the food table. "Almost like we're underwater listening to whales singing."

Aisha laughed. "Oh you don't want to listen to that. It's fine at first, but after a few hours—"

Music suddenly blared over the speakers.

"SOMEBODY CALL 911 . . . SHORTY FIRE BURNING ON THE DANCE FLOOR . . ."

Heart pounding in her throat, Aisha froze.

"What on earth?" Brooke turned, taking Aisha along with her. The beat picked up and there was a flurry of activity in the area Krista had gestured to just moments before.

"He didn't," Krista growled from behind them.

Both Aisha and Brooke swung their heads to stare at her. Eyes narrowed and hands in fists at her side, Krista had never looked more murderous.

"Who didn't do what?" Brooke asked, but she might as well have been talking to one of the fish for all the answer she got. Instead, Krista stalked off toward what was now apparently a dance floor.

Brooke tugged Aisha along, and she was grateful her friend was taking charge, because for the first time all evening, she had no idea what to do. Even if whatever was happening wasn't her fault, she was the one who would be taking the blame, she could feel it in her bones. With trembling legs, she let Brooke lead her toward the scene unfolding at the front of the aquarium.

Five impossibly tall and handsome guys were dancing in perfect coordination to the Sean Kingston song playing. They moved with a surprising amount of grace considering the muscles barely contained by the suits they were wearing. The crowd that surrounded them was entranced by their synchronized swaying bodies, stunned into silence. Krista was standing with arms folded tightly across her chest, an expression that promised murder on her face. It made Aisha shiver to think about the retribution these guys would be dealing with when this was over.

Beside her, Brooke's muttering wasn't quite as dangerous, but it was close. "If I find out Ethan knew about this . . . "

A glance at her friend's boyfriend standing in the corner, his mouth hidden behind a glass of champagne, didn't give them any hints. But something clicked for Aisha, and she realized these were all firefighters from Adamsville, Ethan's former colleagues. They looked somewhat familiar, from the auction they held last year for the animal shelter and their help every month at the adoption events.

Recognizing them did little to reassure her. It actually made her feel worse. Aisha's chest felt frozen, her heart unable to beat and her lungs unable to take in air. If it had been anywhere else, any other event, she would be loving this. It was fun, and silly, and surprising. It was exactly the kind of thing she would have even been a part of planning in another job, even if it would have gotten her fired.

Unfortunately, this was the worst thing that could happen to her in this job, the first one she didn't want to lose.

Her eyes roamed the crowd, trying to determine their reaction. Or, more specifically, three people's reactions.

On the other side of the dance floor not far from Ethan, Bram looked mildly amused, his lips twitching in a familiar way that let her know he was trying to keep from laughing. Like during staff meetings when the director went on one of her long-winded mono-logues about the importance of washing your own dishes in the staff kitchen.

Mrs. Rhodes, however, looked confused, her eyebrows drawn together and her mouth turned down in a frown as she stood in front of Stella's tank with her arms crossed. It was like she felt she had to protect it from the shenanigans unfolding in front of her narrowed eyes.

Cody was standing next to his mother, whispering in her ear, with Sandra from accounting behind him. Maybe they were discussing liability and insurance?

None of these reactions did anything to settle Aisha's nerves or spur her into action. She remained frozen next to Brooke, unable to do anything to stop the dancing. No one did. In fact, people were now starting to dance as well, the firefighters' infectious moves and the catchy song making their way through the crowd.

Once the first couple was brave enough to join in at the fringes of the makeshift dancefloor, more followed, and the DJ put on an upbeat techno song. What had been a calm, quiet, dignified party was quickly devolving into a club-like atmosphere.

While Aisha watched Krista's face slowly turn the same shade purple as her jumpsuit, Ethan wandered over. "I told Jake not to do anything stupid tonight."

"Did you now?" Brooke turned and raised an eyebrow at her boyfriend.

Ethan shrugged sheepishly. "I don't think we have the same definition of stupid."

A smothered snort was Brooke's answer to that. It took all of Aisha's energy not to grab him and shake him until he told her everything he knew.

"So you thought this might happen?" Her voice was calm as her eyes tracked the crowd. Overall, people seemed entertained, clapping and cheering. It was probably the only reason Bram hadn't put a stop to this.

Ethan shook his head. "No, but I did tell some of the guys at the station about tonight."

"And they came here to give us all a show?"

"More like Jake came to get Krista's attention."

His words hit Aisha hard, knocking the wind out of her. This wasn't jealousy. It wasn't worth the energy being jealous of Krista. She hadn't asked to look the way she did, and she'd learned to use it to her advantage, the same way anyone would use whatever they could to get ahead, especially for someone as ambitious as her.

No, it wasn't jealousy that settled like a heavy rock in Aisha's belly. It was rage.

With her arms still crossed and smoke coming out of her ears, Krista looked even more irritated than Mrs. Rhodes. One firefighter in particular seemed to be locked in Krista's steely gaze. The tallest one, the one who'd been dancing in the middle of the others. Aisha watched him approach her friend, a smile on his face, and bend his head to whisper something in her ear. Whatever it was, it made Krista turn on her heels and stalk off.

Fire burned hot in Aisha's chest, one part embarrassment, one part fury. Krista always had guys doing ridiculous things for her attention. Even when it was an important night for Aisha, they couldn't help themselves.

In some back part of her brain, Aisha knew it wasn't Krista's fault, that she hadn't asked for this. But Krista was very good at letting guys down easy, letting them know it wasn't worth their time to try again. If this guy was here, it meant she hadn't done that to him. And it had ruined everything for Aisha.

FORTY-THREE
AISHA

Leaving Brooke and Ethan without a word, Aisha stalked off in search of Krista, the pounding dance music echoing off the tanks around them. Stella had disappeared, no doubt scared by the vibrations.

Before she'd even gone two steps, Mrs. Rhodes cornered her in the quiet corner by the educational panels about eels nobody ever seemed to visit. They hadn't even bothered putting a table back here. Bram was hurrying right behind their boss, with a determined slant to his eyebrows Aisha had never seen before.

Twitching lips were the only sign that the director's typical placid demeanor was disrupted. "I didn't realize part of your help for the gala involved booking entertainment."

"I didn't." She glanced at Bram, who nodded his support. "We didn't. No one informed us of this."

"But these are friends of yours?" Mrs. Rhodes raised an eyebrow and pursed her lips. With her hair pulled back so tightly it tugged at her skin, the overall effect was one of tight irritation.

Panic laced Aisha's veins, and heat crept up her neck. "Not really, no. I've never met them." Not entirely true, but she'd never talked to any of them directly. It wasn't worth it to describe the small-town dynamics that meant she'd seen all of the firefighters at one event or another.

"Your friends seem to know who they are." Mrs. Rhodes gestured to where Ethan and Brooke were talking to the tallest of the dancers, and Aisha's stomach dropped. This must be Jake, who'd been so determined to get Krista's attention he'd staged a flash mob at a gala thirty miles away from his town. Men had driven much further and done wilder things for Krista, but Aisha's brain was too anxious and angry to think of any right now.

"They didn't know anything about this either." The second the words were out of her mouth, she knew they were the wrong ones. From the way they were chatting easily, Brooke and Ethan clearly knew the firefighter, and now the director would think Aisha was lying.

Mrs. Rhodes sniffed, and Aisha's attention zipped back to her, heart pounding. "Be that as it may, this wasn't at all how we'd agreed to the evening going. Surprises like this aren't appreciated."

"Not even if they get people bidding more?" Bram jumped in, and Aisha couldn't tell if she was grateful or irritated. This was his event, not hers, so he should be the one getting a grilling from their boss. "I just took a peek at the silent auction app, and things just shot up in the past ten minutes."

That was incredibly lucky if it were true, and Aisha cast a glance at Stella's empty tank, sending a silent wish her way. Until the music had started blasting, the starfish hadn't moved from her spot directly in the middle of the glass all evening, like she knew full well she was the star and everyone was here to see her. Hopefully her disappearing act wouldn't slow down the donations.

"Have they now?" Mrs. Rhodes's lips stopped twitching. "That's good news, whatever the reason. Bram, please go talk to the DJ about going back to the approved music."

"Of course," he said, with only the briefest of glances in her direction.

"Aisha, I'd like to see you first thing Monday in my office."

With that final ominous directive, Mrs. Rhodes turned and walked away.

Defeat whipped through Aisha like waves crashing to shore in a storm. Whatever meager progress she'd made in the past few weeks had been totally shattered. There was no way Monday would bring good things.

"Hey, it'll all be okay." Bram's voice was soft in her ear, his hand warm on her back. "I'll go remind the DJ who's paying him tonight, and you find Krista and tell her to get those guys to leave."

Aisha nodded weakly, her stomach somersaulting like she'd just gotten off a roller coaster. It had been her decision to keep things quiet at work, but all she wanted to do was have Bram wrap her in his arms and tell her he'd fix this. Instead all he could do was brush her arm gently before he left her alone with the eels.

Typical Aisha. Even after everything she'd accomplished in the past few weeks, the confidence boost she'd been riding high on, nothing had really changed, had it? Someone else would be cleaning up this mess. For once she hadn't caused it, and yet she was suffering the consequences.

Taking a deep breath, Aisha hurried back toward Stella's tank and the main area of the aquarium to go salvage whatever she could of the evening.

After all these weeks of her wishes coming true, tonight it had failed. Everything had not gone as planned. Unless the starfish had intended for the firefighter's plan to ruin everything.

Or maybe the wishes weren't actually real, and Aisha only had herself to blame.

It took all of five minutes to find Krista, fuming at one of the tables with flowers, slowly picking apart the coral reef design between shaking fingers.

"What the hell, Krista?" Stomach still unsteady, Aisha's cheeks were burning to see yet more destruction. It had taken hours to get those flowers right, and now Krista was wrecking them just like she'd ruined everything else. "This is the last thing I needed tonight."

"I had nothing to do with it." Holding up her hands, Krista tossed a scathing glance in the direction of Jake, who was talking to Brooke and Ethan. "It's all Jake Stevens. I told him not to—"

In the space where the rest of her sentence should have been, Krista just sucked in a breath, realizing she'd put her foot in it.

"Told him not to what?" Aisha whisper-yelled, her fist balled so tightly at her side she could feel her nails digging into her palm. "Is he 'J'? The one you never talk about?"

In a very un-Krista like move, she pulled her bottom lip under her teeth and nodded. The vulnerability in her eyes should have made Aisha melt, but all she could think about was what the fallout would mean for her job. Not Bram's. The director hadn't asked to see him on Monday. Just her.

"So instead of dealing with this like an adult, you let him come and ruin something I've worked weeks on." Tears were prickling in the corner of her eyes, but she blinked them away. "I might lose my job."

"What? Why?" She shook her head, blond curls bouncing and catching the light. "That's not fair, I'll look at your employee handbook and see what I can—"

"No. I'll handle it." Aisha wanted to scream. Even now, Krista couldn't help herself. "You don't always know what's best. You're not so impossibly smart that you know everything and nothing that happens ever surprises you. Otherwise you would have seen this coming and stopped it before it started."

Krista stared, open-mouthed, blinking with hurt and confusion.

They'd fought over the years, of course they had. All best friends did. But nothing Aisha had said in those moments of irritation had ever come close to this. For the first time, Aisha was looking to hurt her. Whether it was totally fair or not didn't seem to matter at the moment.

"Or maybe you did see it coming and you just can't help your-self from batting your eyes and getting the adoration of everyone you meet. If you're not the smartest and the prettiest, who even are you?"

Now anger spread across Krista's perfect features. Her eyes narrowed. "That's not what I do, it's not my—"

"Not your fault, yeah, yeah." Aisha waved that away, her chest so tight with anger it felt like she was on fire. She let out a harsh chuckle. At least there were plenty of firefighters around to take care of it. "But there are consequences for what you do. This constant adoration you're always seeking impacts others."

"At least I don't act like I don't do the same thing."

The words were like a punch in the chest. Aisha took a step back.

"What?"

"You think it's easy having everyone's expectations for me be sky-high? Meanwhile, you get to be the fun one, the one who can make all the mistakes she wants, knowing someone else will be cleaning it up."

Voice shaking, Aisha lifted her chin. "That's not who I am anymore. I'm trying—I'm trying to change. If you'd let me."

Of course that's still how Krista saw her. Whatever strength inside Aisha that was so easy for Bram to see was invisible to the person who'd known her and loved her since she was a child.

So maybe it wasn't actually there at all.

"Planning one fancy dinner isn't quite the same as giving up everything for the people you love."

What was she talking about? What had Krista ever given up? Was she talking about moving back to Adamsville to take care of her father? Or did this have something to do with Jake?

Too angry and hurt and tired and a thousand other things to be able to worry about her friend, Aisha took another step back from the table.

"Just tell Jake and his friends to leave, and go with them. The longer you're here, the worse it'll be for me."

After a long, seething beat of silence that seemed to stretch for hours, Krista turned and walked away. There was still too much damage control to tackle to worry if things had only cracked between them or completely shattered. For now she'd just focus on keeping her job and worry about the rest tomorrow.

After reminding the DJ he was being paid to play jazz and classical, not the Ibiza club music that the gyrating crowd was clamoring for, Bram looked around for Aisha amid the boos echoing in his ears. It had been almost impossible to walk away from her all tense and anxious, but Bram had dealt with worse crises at galas before. Though it had been a while, and never when his parents had been in attendance.

It was unfortunately his mother he found first, before he could lay eyes on Aisha.

"Bramwell, come look at the paintings with me." His mother turned and walked away without waiting for him to reply.

Frustration mounting, he followed her to the back of the aquarium where they'd set up the art auction. Getting people to walk through all the tanks, past all the informational posters about what they did with their funding had been Aisha's idea. She'd done so much to make tonight a success, it was completely unfair Mrs. Rhodes was blaming her. Hopefully if Bram could ensure donations blew past their target, all would be forgiven. And to do that, he had to keep his mom happy.

"There now, it's much quieter back here." She flashed him a

closed-mouth smile that still managed to be sharp and shark-like. Ironically, the painting they were standing in front of was of a hammerhead. "There's a reason I requested quiet music. How am I supposed to appreciate the art with that noise?"

"It was a prank, Mother, one I had no control over."

"And what about the tables? I thought this would be a sit-down dinner, not a cocktail party." Shaking her head, she walked past a few more paintings, all of different sea creatures. "This evening has been very disappointing."

He started to explain that there wasn't the space for large tables but then stopped.

There were other large donors besides his mother. Some of them had been on that dance floor, having a good time. The Lowthers might be the largest, but they weren't the only ones.

If Bram had been less worried about sticking to what his mother wanted, then maybe there would have been different music tonight, and Aisha wouldn't be in trouble. She hadn't even met his family, and they were already ruining her life.

The tide of change he'd been avoiding for months—for years, really—was coming in fast, rising in Bram's chest and filling him up with courage to finally do things differently.

"I'm sorry to hear that."

At his curt tone, his mother pursed her lips and narrowed her eyes. Clearly she'd been expecting the deference he'd always given her.

"This piece is very interesting." The eagle eyes that were usually focused on finding fault in everyone around her were now gazing intently at Aisha's painting. "Do you know the artist?"

"I do."

Her eyes snapped to him, and his stomach sank to the depths of the ocean. How could she tell, from just two words, who Aisha was? She'd probably looked up her name online, trying to see if she was an artist her friends would know.

"So, your non-fiancée is an artist." Her eyes roamed around the room. "I assume she's here? Was she responsible for that display earlier?"

"That wasn't her fault, and she's not my fiancée." He tried to keep the irritation out of his voice but knew he was failing. This wasn't where he was needed, not now. Not when Aisha was off somewhere panicking or yelling at Krista. He wanted to yell at the blond lawyer as well, and he didn't even know her that well. Though she'd looked just as surprised as everyone else, the guys had been here for her, that much was clear. And they'd made Aisha doubt herself, on a night that otherwise was going so well.

"The artist is here tonight, but she's very busy. We can arrange a meeting later, if you end up winning the painting."

"What makes you think I'm bidding on it?" His mother lifted her chin slightly.

Now it was Bram's turn to raise his eyebrows. "Really, Mother? 'This piece is very interesting?' The last time I heard you say that, it was for a gold statue of a croissant that you forked over half a million for."

She sniffed. "Well, I hope you don't expect me to bid that high tonight."

"Bid what you think it's worth." He was losing his patience. He could be with Aisha right now, instead of dealing with his mother's nonsense.

The longer she stared at the painting, the wearier Bram got. They'd been through the same song and dance so many other times. This wasn't a career, this was living in terror of stepping out of line.

As hard as he'd been trying to live his life the way he wanted, he always would have to toe that line as long as he was beholden to his family's money and patronage. Even if he didn't see how right now, he had to trust that he'd be able to figure it all out without their support.

It was for Aisha, but also for him. If she could finally recognize what had always been inside her, then it was time he did too. Otherwise, how could he think himself worthy to be with her?

"You know, that's fine. We don't need your money." He shook his head. That's not what he really meant. "*I* don't need it. I haven't needed it for years. I come to dinner because I want to see my family, but I haven't touched my trust fund since I got it."

"I figured as much, based on how you've been dressing lately."

He ignored that jab, brushed it aside in a way he wouldn't have been able to just a few weeks ago. "I like the way I dress, and the way I live. I like the life I have."

His mother narrowed her eyes. "Your life with *her*, you mean?"

The anger that had been simmering away started to rise. "No, I don't mean that. I was happy with my life before her, and I'll be happy whether she's in it or not."

This wasn't the full truth, but it was what his mother needed to hear. If she thought for a second that the only reason he wanted to give up this life was because of Aisha, then the beautiful woman he had fallen for would never have a moment's peace.

In reality, the thought of a life without Aisha seemed as dull as colorless as the one his mother had been keeping him on the edges of, forever begging for scraps.

"So you don't plan on having a life with her?"

"No." It was a lie to protect Aisha, to protect that life he wanted so badly. "She doesn't factor into any of my decisions."

A raised eyebrow and a head tilt. "Does she know that?"

A wave of dread crashed over him. There was only one reason his mother would look that smug in the middle of such a public confrontation. He turned, heart ripping in two inside of his chest, to see Aisha standing just a few feet away, her face crumpled in pain. Before he could say a word, she rushed past them both and back into the main area of the aquarium.

"Even for you, that was disgusting." Body trembling with rage, he kept his voice low, but the edge of danger was there. "What on earth has she ever done to you to deserve that?"

"If she's so important, then why didn't you bring her to dinner?"

"Because you all are monsters!" The word seemed to shock his mother to hear it as much as it did him to have said it. He lowered his voice, frustrated with himself he'd picked such a public place to finally say what he'd been holding in for years. "I love you, but whatever is going on with the lawsuit is terrible."

She actually had the nerve to look annoyed at that. "What some people in our employment choose to do regarding ignoring safety measures is not my responsibility."

"Whether you knew about it or not, it's your company. Even if you bid a million dollars on a painting tonight, it couldn't erase what you've done."

His mother sneered. "Would she even know what to do with a million dollars?"

That's it.

He'd been wondering where the line would be. The one that once she crossed they'd never be able to come back from. The next words he said were forced out of his tightly clenched teeth, while his brain turned red with rage.

"Goodbye, Mother. I won't be coming to dinner next week. Or ever again. "

"Bramwell." Her mouth dropped open. "I don't—I never—"

"Save it. It's too late."

As he turned away from her, heart pounding, he could only hope it wasn't too late to find Aisha.

The good thing about the secondary coatroom was that it was in the staff area and away from the main part of the aquarium where the gala was.

The bad thing was that hiding here meant Aisha would have to walk back through the crowd if she wanted to leave.

No, she couldn't leave. This was her event. That her friend had ruined. Ex-friend, probably. They'd never fought like that before.

No, it was Bram's event. Bram who'd told his mother Aisha wasn't a part of his life. Which might have been what they'd been acting like was true at work, and what she'd asked him to pretend with his family until the gala was over, but this felt like something else. Something more than pretending.

When she'd seen him standing by her painting with his mother, she couldn't help herself. She'd wanted to hear what she had to say.

Eavesdroppers never hear anything good about themselves, do they?

Everything Bram said about himself had been amazing. He was finally telling his mother how he felt. It had given Aisha such a rush to hear him take a stand, to defend the life he'd chosen without their money.

Then he'd told his mother Aisha was nothing to him. That he hadn't chosen her.

Given everything he'd said right before that, what else could it be but the truth?

Tucked behind a bunch of coats that smelled like the childhood memory of her mother's closet, Aisha let the tears fall and checked her phone. The aquarium's thick concrete walls made it hard to get a signal even when it wasn't filled to the brim with people, so while she wasn't surprised to see no messages or texts, it still stung.

At Darcey's party, Bram had run after her. Sure she was hiding in a closet right now, but if he'd really wanted to find her, he would. Making sure his mother was happy might not be top of his priority list anymore, but Aisha clearly hadn't taken her place.

There'd been almost zero chance of Krista trying to contact her, but some small part of Aisha had still been hoping. The fights they'd had over the years had been about things like not returning borrowed clothes, or finally letting Krista have it when she'd picked what they watched for movie night too many times in a row.

This was different. This felt like a fight with a parent. Like pushing away the person who'd always been there for you, who you knew would always be there loving you when you calmed down.

Except Krista wasn't her mom, and neither was Brooke. They were friends, as close as sisters, but it wasn't their responsibility to parent each other, even if over the years they'd fallen into that role more than once.

Dropping her head into her hands, Aisha groaned. Nothing she was mulling over would be solved by staying in this closet. She'd give herself another ten minutes, then head back out there. If there was even a chance that Monday's meeting with the director wasn't going to involve HR, hiding here wasn't helping show how professional she was.

The countdown was cut short, however, when the door opened just a minute later. Probably the coat check guy coming to do his job. Aisha stood up and brushed at some of the inevitable wrinkles on her jumpsuit before emerging from behind the coats.

"I'm sorry, I know I shouldn't be in here—"

Stopping short, her mouth dropped open. Cody and Sandra were standing hand in hand, looking very much like they'd been planning to do something other than cry in the coatroom.

"Um, hi, Aisha." Cody pushed up his glasses on his nose, looking guiltier than she'd ever seen another human in her entire life. Until now, she hadn't suspected his face could even hold such an exaggerated expression. "We were just, um, looking for our coats."

"Were you really?" Despite everything else going on tonight, Aisha felt her lips turn up in a smile. Then it grew wider, and she started to giggle, which turned into a laugh. What else could she do? All those months of pining over Cody, trying to turn herself into someone he'd like, when Sandra had been there the whole time. Sandra was perfect for him, and didn't need to change a thing about herself.

Aisha's mirth echoed in the small room, growing more unhinged by the second, while Cody and Sandra exchanged a concerned look.

"I'm sorry, it's just been a long night." Aisha shook her head and scooted past them to the door. "I'll leave you two alone."

"I'd appreciate it if you . . . " Cody's cheeks turned pink, something she'd also never seen before. "Didn't mention this to my mother?"

"I won't." A thought struck her. Nothing she would have tried before, but there was no more generosity left tonight. Sneaky and self-serving was all that she could find inside of her. "As long as you remind her how well the gala was going before the flash mob showed up?"

"Of course." Nodding enthusiastically, he glanced at Sandra, who did the same thing. "It's really been an incredible night. You and Bram should be really proud of yourselves."

The smile froze on Aisha's face, brittle and hard. "Thanks."

Then before she could do or say anything else that might make things even more awkward, she walked into the hallway and closed the door behind her.

Somehow, the gala continued on like nothing had happened. Like Bram hadn't just messed up everything, like his heart wasn't breaking.

In between requests for his input on something, or a question from a vendor, he looked everywhere for Aisha and asked everyone if they'd seen her. Nobody had. It was possible she'd gone home, but when he looked in the parking lot, her car was still there.

His parents' Bentley was no longer there, he'd been relieved to notice.

Standing by Stella's tank, he kept scanning the space, still hoping he might spot her. A few people stopped by to ask about the starfish, but she'd been hiding for the past hour. With all the noise and chaos, she wasn't in the mood to be seen, even if she was the star of the show.

It might be bad luck to wish on an empty tank, but Bram did it anyway, turning to put a hand where Stella should have been.

Please don't let this be the end of us.

"Well that was . . . interesting." Darcey's voice floated over him, and he balled his fist on the glass, not bothering to turn around. "Definitely different from your other events."

"It's not the time, Darce." He leaned his head on the cool tank, just for a moment, and took a few deep breaths before facing her. With everything else going on, this was the first time he'd seen her all night. She was dressed in a simple, fitted black dress and the thinnest of stilettos, wearing an expression he couldn't quite read.

"I heard what you told your mother." Her lips ticked up and she tilted her head. "Well, I heard what your mother told my parents. Something about ungrateful children?"

With a groan, Bram pulled her away from Stella and toward the staff area. He wasn't going to have this conversation out in the open.

"Is that what she said? Well, this is what she really said . . . " As he led Darcey through the crowd, he kept his voice low until they were finally into the staff area, her eyes growing wider with each step. Once the door closed behind them, she let out a string of curses.

"You were being nice to her. I would have said something way worse." Darcey wrapped her arms around him. "I'm sorry, Wellington. I know what it's like to be on the outs with your family. I wish I could tell you things will somehow magically resolve themselves without a lot of uncomfortable conversations, but they won't. If you never want those to happen, that's okay too. You still have me, no matter what."

"Thanks," he mumbled into her shoulder. Was that what he'd been afraid of? That he'd lose his best friend as well if he cut ties with the Lowthers? The reminder that he wasn't alone in this was what he needed right now.

Well, that and to find Aisha. It felt like he hadn't been able to take a full breath since she ran away from him earlier.

Pulling out of the hug, his stomach growled, and he realized he hadn't eaten anything all night, he'd been so busy. "Do you want a snack before we go back out?" The staff kitchen's tiny fridge was filled with extras of dessert that he'd snuck in there earlier.

"Sure." Darcey looped her arm in his and he led the way down the hallway. "Then we can figure out what to do about Aisha."

"There's nothing we can do. I can't find her and—" He stopped so suddenly, Darcey nearly toppled over in her heels.

Aisha was standing on a chair, reaching into the topmost cabinet for the madeleines.

In an instant, Bram's lungs filled with air, and the vise that had been tight around his heart unclamped. The sudden influx of oxygen and blood in his system made him lightheaded. Luckily Darcey was still holding on to his arm, or he would have dropped to the floor.

"You're here," he managed in a strangled voice. "I thought you'd left."

By the time Aisha had gotten down off the chair and put it back under the table, Bram was feeling a little steadier. With a squeeze of his hand and a whisper that she'd let him know if anyone at the gala needed them, Darcey scooted out of the kitchen. Finally just the two of them, Bram watched Aisha lean against the counter and wrap her arms around herself.

She looked as distraught as Bram felt. Her hair was disheveled, like she'd been running her hands through it. Her eyes were red and puffy. Her jumpsuit, such an amazing color on her, was wrinkled.

"I've—I've been looking everywhere for you." Stuttering, Bram took a step toward her. "You weren't anywhere in the aquarium, nobody had seen you, I thought maybe—"

"I was hiding in the coatroom." She bit her lip. "At least until Cody and Sandra walked in."

"I don't care about them, I care about you." He saw what she was trying to do, gossip like they were just colleagues, or make him jealous. Though some corner of his brain was of course curious about what she'd seen, that wasn't what was important right now.

It was hard not to run to her and wrap himself around her, but he could tell she was still upset about what she'd overheard. "I hope you didn't think I meant what I said to my mother."

"About not needing her money?"

"No, that was true. What I said about you wasn't though. "

Her lower lip grew pinker as she nibbled away at it, her eyes not quite meeting his. He took a cautious step toward her, hoping this was just a misunderstanding and not the end of everything.

Come on, Stella, don't fail me now.

"All I can think about is a life with you. You factor into every single one of my decisions, including telling my mother tonight I don't want to see her anymore."

At this, her head whipped up and her mouth dropped open. "You can't do that just for me. They're your family."

"They're boring jerks who care more about money than me." He shrugged, but the pain was there. Maybe it always would be. "And it's something I've wanted to do for a long time. I just didn't have a good enough reason until you."

"But we'll lose their donations to LCRA and then Mrs. Rhodes will be mad at both of us and then—"

"There will be other donors." Bram closed the distance between them and put his hands on her shoulders. Slowly, her arms unfolded and she let out a breath, like she'd been holding it in for days. He took her hands in his. "There have always been other donors, but I just didn't trust myself enough to be able to do it without them. You helped me see the world differently."

"I never wanted you to lose your family." She blinked away tears and then finally, finally, leaned her head against his chest and buried herself in him. "I know how hard that is."

"You have a family." With slow, steady hands he rubbed her back, reveling in the feel of her that he'd been so sure he'd lost forever. "Not just your dad. You have so many people who care about you. I don't have quite as many, but I do have some. I won't be alone. And if my mom ever wants to reach out and apologize to both of us, she knows where to find me."

"Do you think she will?" Aisha looked up at him, her eyes sparkling with unshed tears.

"I doubt it. I'm not going to waste any breath wishing for it." He let his forehead fall to hers and breathed her in deep. "I did wish for something tonight."

"Yeah?" The word was a quiet puff of air on his lips.

He closed his eyes and dropped his voice to a whisper. "I wished this isn't the end of us. It's not, is it?"

He could feel the shake of her head against his, the hitch in her breath when she spoke. "I think it's just the beginning."

The kiss they fell into felt like a beginning. A new beginning. As sweet as that first one weeks ago, but with a deeper edge to it, full of a promise that there'd be no more pretending after tonight, no more doubts or misunderstandings.

It could easily have gone on all night, but a ping from Bram's phone interrupted them. When he looked down, his heart almost stopped.

"Someone just made a bid for ten thousand dollars on a painting." The app was alerting him since it was the maximum amount allowed, two hundred times the fair market rate. "That pushes us way above our goal."

"What?" Aisha leaned closer to see his screen. "Who? Which painting?"

Before he even opened the app, the rumbling in Bram's chest told him he knew the answer. He could hear Aisha suck in a breath when he tapped the icon, but he said it out loud anyway.

"Yours."

FORTY-SEVEN
AISHA

Walking back out into the gala holding Bram's hand should have felt amazing, but all Aisha could focus on was the churning in her stomach.

Well, the warmth of him next to her did feel pretty good. As did the tingling she still felt on her lips from their kiss, and the words they'd said to each other still tumbling around inside her brain.

"I can't believe you said my painting was worth five thousand dollars." She'd let him handle the details of the auction, so she'd had no idea until now what any of the bids were, or what they'd been based on.

"That's a perfectly reasonable fair market value for an oil canvas of that size." His lips twitched up. "And maybe a little extra on top for how good the artist is at kissing."

Of course that would be the moment they ran into Mrs. Rhodes. She glanced down at their joined hands and when Bram tried to pull away, Aisha held fast. Her job was already in jeopardy, this couldn't make things any worse.

"I'm so glad I found you," Bram said, smiling at the director. "I wanted to let you know we've reached our goal. Exceeded it, in fact."

"Really?" She looked at her watch. "There's still an hour to go."

"We had a very generous bid on Aisha's painting."

If that was supposed to do anything to calm Aisha's nerves, it did the opposite.

"Well that's . . . good to hear." Despite her words, Mrs. Rhodes frowned. "I just spoke with Cody and, well, I want to thank you Aisha for everything you've done tonight. I don't think it would have been a success without you."

The emotional rollercoaster Aisha had been on all night just hit its highest peak. This was incredible to hear, but there was one thing that could still have her crashing right back down to earth. "Do you still need to see me Monday?"

"Yes, there's a project I've been meaning to get to, and I think you might be the person to help me with it." She nodded at Stella's tank. The starfish had made her way back into the middle of the glass and was waving her arms happily. "I think it might be time for a new logo. Maybe something involving sea stars?"

Happiness flooded into Aisha's chest, and it was all she could do not to jump up and down and hug the director. She settled for squeezing Bram's hand so hard he let out a little choked sound next to her.

"That sounds great. We'll talk Monday."

Aisha's smile was so wide as Mrs. Rhodes walked away, her cheeks were hurting. Beside her, Bram's phone pinged again, and Aisha finally released his hand so he could grab it. "It looks like every single painting's maximum bid was reached. We sold everything and doubled our goal for the night."

"What?" Excitement swept through her, but was quickly squashed when she saw his frown. "Do you think it's your mother?"

Bram shook his head. "No, but it's odd. It's not a person's name on the account, it looks like a trust or something."

Before he could say more, the caterer came by with a question and they fell right back into the swing of things. The rest of the night passed in a blur streaked with a heightened sense of celebration. When Mrs. Rhodes announced to the crowd that the paintings had all been sold, it seemed to act as a catalyst for even more donations. The flooded in as people left for the night, chattering about what an eventful evening it had been.

It was all going to plan, just like Aisha had wished for.

Well, everything except her fight with Krista. In between stacking chairs and finding a missing chafing dish someone had misplaced, Aisha was able to find Brooke to give her the summary of what had happened.

"Do you want me to talk to her?" Brooke's worried eyes shone with concern. "Or not talk to her out of solidarity?"

"That's a good question." Too much had happened in a single night. Before, Aisha would have blurted out the first thing that came to mind, but now she needed time to think things through. "Can you ask me that again tomorrow?"

"Sure." Brooke leaned in to give her a hug. "I hope you're still proud of yourself for tonight. I am."

It meant so much to hear that, and yet it still didn't feel like enough.

Before Bram and Aisha left for the night, they both stopped in front of Stella's tank and put a hand to it.

"I can't think of anything else to wish for." Bram grinned at her, then bent down to kiss her cheek. "Tonight went so well."

Aisha opened her mouth to say the same thing, but then stopped herself. "I want to wish for something about Krista, but I'm not sure what."

"Why? What happened?"

With everything else going on, Aisha realized she hadn't filled in Bram on the fight she'd had with her friend. Once she'd laid out every single terrible thing they'd said to each other, Bram wrapped his arm around her, keeping his other hand on the tank.

"I don't think you need any of Stella's magic to fix anything." He dropped a kiss on the top of her head. "It wasn't as bad as you think. I also have a lawyer as a best friend, remember? You both just need a few days to cool off."

They both dropped their hands and turned away from the tank. As they walked away, however, Aisha couldn't help looking over her shoulder at Stella's waving arms.

Maybe that very first wish Aisha had made hadn't been about Cody, or Bram.

I wish someone would love me for who I really am . . . I wish Krista would love me for who I really am.

Stella had granted every other wish, but in her own way. It was like the starfish knew what you needed better than you did. Only time would tell how and when this one would come true too.

EPILOGUE

The mystery of who had bought the paintings lingered for an entire week. It was still a busy week, with social media posts to create around the success of the gala, brainstorming the next event, and a conversation with both the director and human resources to officially let them know about Aisha and Bram's relationship. It all went much better than expected, and the weekend arrived with only one big unanswered question.

Whenever Aisha asked Bram if he had an update on the buyer, he said he didn't have any news. The trust that had made the winning bids sent someone to pick things up, without revealing who they were working for.

"But that's so weird," Aisha said for the hundredth time since the gala, as she dumped a bag of microwave popcorn into a bowl. Once again, she was hosting movie night, this time actually at night. Saturday evenings were the only time both Brooke and Ethan weren't at the shelter. "Why won't they say who hired them?"

"Maybe they can't say." Grabbing a handful of popcorn, Brooke shrugged and stuffed it gracelessly into her mouth. That was the only proper way to eat it. Unless you preferred tossing in a single kernel at a time like you were trying to impress a talent show judge. "It could be a legal thing."

At the L-word, they both froze. In a normal week, it wasn't as if Aisha and Krista spoke daily. The group text between them and Brooke was mostly logistics about meeting times and places, with the occasional Hayden Carmichael meme or outfit photo to get approval.

The chat had been entirely quiet since the gala.

This movie night was technically a double date. Bram and Ethan were taking up the entire couch between the two of them in Aisha's living room, deciding what they would all be watching. A double date was exactly the kind of grown-up, serious kind of thing that Aisha had been hoping for.

So why did it feel like there was a Krista-shaped hole in the air of her apartment?

"Have you talked to her at all?" Aisha asked. Brooke shook her head.

Now it was Aisha's turn to stuff a handful of popcorn in her mouth. This was not a single-kernel-at-a-time kind of conversation. "I'm not even mad anymore, I just don't know how to say I'm sorry without it feeling like I'm giving in and she won. She said some stuff too."

Brooke gave a little hum of understanding. Apologizing wasn't something Brooke did easily either, but Krista could take it to a whole new level. When someone was that smart, it was rare for them to be wrong, and Krista did not have a lot of practice with it.

The doorbell buzzed. "That must be the pizza the boys ordered." Aisha grabbed her wallet and made her way to the door.

When she opened it, however, it wasn't the pizza.

It was Krista.

"I'm sorry." The words were out of Krista's mouth so quickly, they were jammed together into a single syllable.

All Aisha could do was blink at her. "You are?"

Nodding, Krista shifted on her feet, looking more uncomfortable than Aisha had ever seen her. And shabbier. Her blond curls were up in a very uncharacteristic bun on the top of her head, and the sweats she was wearing looked like they'd been slept in.

"I've been practicing all week." She gave a weak smile, so unlike her usual brilliant grin that could make men organize flash mobs for her. "How'd I do?"

"Krista, are you okay?" Aisha stepped out of her apartment and into the vestibule, closing the door behind her.

"I'm fine, just a lot going on." She shrugged. "Work and stuff."

Uh oh. That could only mean one thing.

"Your dad?"

Tears shimmered in Krista's eyes, and in an instant, Aisha's arms were around her. She knew her friend wouldn't want to talk about whatever health crisis her dad had been going through, but at least she was letting Aisha hug her.

"I'm sorry I wasn't there for you this week," Aisha said. "I'm sorry about what I said."

"You were right though," Krista mumbled into Aisha's shoulder as she hugged her back. "I do need constant adoration. I do need to be the smartest and the prettiest."

"I don't usually mind, you know." Pulling back, Aisha gave her a rueful smile. "It was just a big night for me and stressful and I'd been trying so hard to make sure everything went well."

"It was a great event." Krista wiped the corner of her eye. "I realized on my way home I hadn't even told you that."

"Thank you. We ended up doubling our target."

"You sold all the paintings, right? At the maximum bid?"

Something prickled on the back of Aisha's neck. How did she know? Neither she nor Brooke had talked to her since the gala.

With a groan, Aisha let her head fall into her hands. "Please don't tell me Jake bought them all just to make it up to you."

"No, my boss did." Now there was some of the Krista-confidence back in her voice. "I got an offer from a firm in Charleston, so I told him if they wanted to keep me, they'd have to buy all of the paintings."

"Were you really going to go to Charleston?"

"Of course not. I'm needed here." Krista tucked a loose curl behind her ear. "By my dad. Not you and Brooke."

"We still need you, you big nerd." Aisha reached down and squeezed her hand. "Just not the way you think we do."

With a pitiful sniff, Krista nodded.

"Your boss really bought all of them?" Aisha asked.

That got a sheepishly smug smile out of her friend. "Our offices need a refresh. They do it through a trust so all the partners can get a tax deduction."

"You're incredible." Aisha shook her head.

"Well, they did also offer me a lot more money." Her smile widened into a more familiar dazzling grin. "I'm thinking it's time for a girls trip? My treat?"

"Where to?"

"Las Vegas." She rocked back on her heels. "I have a conference there next month and I could take a few days when it's over to hang out with you and Brooke." She narrowed her eyes. "No boys allowed. I don't want one of my friends coming home accidentally married. Getting out of a Vegas wedding is not an easy thing to do while living in South Carolina."

Heat spread up Aisha's neck and she pressed her lips together to stop from smiling. The image of her and Bram standing in front of an Elvis impersonator flashed through her mind. One day that would be her future, when the time was right. For now, things were perfect just the way they were.

Even better than she could have ever wished for.

The end

AUTHOR'S NOTE

Whenever I read a romance novel, I always wonder what's real and what's not.

Yes, I realize the entire point of fiction is that it's made up. But there are always hints of real places, people, and events tucked in between the imaginary dialogue uttered by inexplicably buff and beautiful characters.

Here's a short and incomplete list of what's real and what's not in this book:

- Lowcountry Research Aquarium: Not real! I based it loosely on some smaller aquariums both in South Carolina and in New England.
- Sunflower sea stars: Real! And they really are critically endangered, though research has helped figure out what was making them sick, and there have been sightings in areas where they'd disappeared. This does not, however, include the east coast. Their native habitat is the Pacific northeast. My apologies to any marine biologists for the creative license I took with these (and so many other aquarium-related) details!

- The song *Aïcha*: Real! It's by the Algerian singer Khaled and I put it on the very chaotic A Touch Of Magic series playlist on Spotify.
- Madeleines: Real! They are delicious.
- *Escape To New York*: Not real! I made this movie up, along with its heartthrob star, Hayden Carmichael, for my book Man Of My Dreams. If you read my other books, you may see both the movie and Hayden pop up from time to time.

Sweet Adult Contemporary Romance:

Houseplants and Hardcovers

Man Of My Dreams

A Touch Of Magic:

Love Potion Number 99

Wish Upon A Starfish

Miller Family Medical:

A Shot At Love

Wrapped Up In You

Braced For Heartache

Wedding Games:

The Bridesmaid and the Reality Show

The Bridesmaid and the Ex

The Bridesmaid and Her Surprise Love

ABOUT THE AUTHOR

Daphne James Huff has been writing romance for adult and YA audiences since she was a young adult herself. Her favorite kind of story has a main character who thinks they've got it all figured out until someone barges into their life and messes everything up. She never says no to free cake or cheese, and can usually be found eating both to stay awake after reading all night.

Follow her on Instagram **@daphnejameshuff**